THE HONORED SOCIETY

MICHAEL GAMBINO

THE HONORED SOCIETY

POCKET BOOKS
New York London Toronto Sydney Singapore

This book is a work of fiction. Names, characters, places and incidents are products of the author's imagination or are used fictitiously. Any resemblance to actual events or locales or persons, living or dead, is entirely coincidental.

POCKET BOOKS, a division of Simon & Schuster, Inc.
1230 Avenue of the Americas, New York, NY 10020

ISBN: 0-7434-4279-2

First Pocket Books hardcover printing November 2001

10 9 8 7 6 5 4 3 2 1

Designed by Jaime Putorti

Printed in the U.S.A.

This book is dedicated to my mom.

You have given me life, and from that day, you have always been there for me through all of my ups and my downs, and at the darkest point of my life. Instead of judging me, you stood by my side and gave me support, and helped me find the strength to survive. Without you, I would never have found my way. Thank you with all my heart.

Love,
Your son, Michael

PREFACE

From my mother's heart

I'm sitting here, staring out the window, thinking about my life. It has been like a wild roller coaster ride, up and down with twists and turns, but the ride never ends. Not until death.

I was married to Vito Gambino, an important member of the most violent crime family. If you think it was difficult, you're right. But having a son, Michael, also a member, was much harder. And it hurt even more. Think about how it feels to watch your baby boy grow up to lead a life that could destroy him. Why did I think things would change? How could I believe he would grow up any differently?

I'm Carmella Rose, born in New York, daughter of Frank Natalli and Angelina Rose Pellegrino. My father was also a member of the New York crime family, and he was known as one of the top ten hitmen in the country. I know how difficult it was for my mother. I watched her suffer. You would think, being brought up in this life, I would have married a different kind of man. Well, that's never the case. It's like, sometimes no matter how much you try to change your life, it just doesn't work. You might be able to change how you live your life, but you can never change who you are.

When I was younger, I tried dating some men who were not in the Family business. I thought I was going to make big changes in my life. It didn't happen. First of all, no one outside the Family wants to get too close to us because when they know the truth, exactly who our Family is and its reputation, they are uncomfortable. I had to face it. The average person is afraid of this crime family life; they don't understand it. I can't blame them. They didn't fit into my circle, and I didn't fit into theirs. So what could I do? I stayed within my family and life continued in the only family I ever knew.

I knew what to expect when I married Vito. I knew I would have to handle anything that came with that. We had our son, Michael. He is the greatest joy in my life but has, because of the life into which he was born, sometimes brought me the deepest sorrow and pain.

One morning in the early eighties, there was a knock on the door. I opened it, and two FBI agents stood there. I gave them a cold stare and asked them what they wanted this time. I was used to this kind of harassment because of Vito's work. But this time it was about Michael. They asked me all kinds of questions and said all kinds of stuff about my son. In anger, one of the men finally blurted out, "Carmella, can't you see it? Michael is just like his father." I told him he didn't know what he was talking about and threw him out. But I knew.

Michael always loved and admired his father very much, and yes, I could see Michael was going to be just like Vito. Nothing I could say or do would stop him. Vito was a very strong, aggressive man, one of the most powerful men in the Family. Growing up around Vito and his friends and business had a big influence on Michael's life. As his mother, I could see Michael liked the power, money and respect that his father had. In reality, it was more fear than respect that people had for him. Vito saw where his son was headed, too. One day Vito said to me, "Carmella, I don't want Michael to be like me. This is my life but it's not the life I want for him." I knew it was already too late. There was no way to stop him.

By the age of seventeen, Michael was far more like his father than ever and I knew where his life was heading.

Very late one Sunday evening in 1984, I got a call. Michael had been arrested for extortion, counterfeiting, prostitution, bookmaking . . . you name it. The FBI had him. This was the most difficult time in my life. They held Michael for seven days before we could get him out on a bond of a half-million dollars. We had no problem getting the money, but Vito couldn't go with me to post the bond because he himself had a case pending and couldn't be seen in the courtroom. Vito sent one of his friends, Louie, with me. But we couldn't bring Michael home because he had to go through so many red-tape procedures. We went back to the house and just waited for another call. It finally came from Michael's lawyer who had Michael in his car and was taking him to his office where we could pick him up.

You cannot imagine how happy I was to see Michael. My son was too young to be going through all this. When I looked at him, my heart beat so fast. I held back my tears and just kept hugging him. I didn't ever want to let him go. But I never questioned him about anything. The lawyer told us the charges and my main concern was to help him get out of this mess. Asking questions, pressuring, wouldn't do any good anyway. Michael was so much like his father. He would avoid any conversation about business except to say, "I'm sorry I caused you to worry, Mom."

As we were driving home, I was thinking about how much Michael was like his father. I could also see Michael was also a lot like his grandfather, my father, Frank Natalli. I was praying that everything would be okay, that Michael would realize this is not the life he had to live. But deep in my heart, I knew this was just the beginning.

As for myself, the daughter of Frank Natalli, wife of Vito Gambino, and mother of Michael Anthony Gambino, you might say it's been a life sentence. You can't just walk away. You stay to the end. And like I said, this was just the beginning.

A year and a half went by. Michael was scheduled for his sentencing hearing, and I could feel the tension in Vito and Michael as they were getting ready to go to court that morning. Neither said anything until they were leaving. I gave Michael a big hug and told him I would be praying for him. All Michael said was, "It will be okay, Mom. Don't worry."

I walked the floors waiting for the news. It was like a nightmare, but worse. There was no waking up. I felt empty inside, frightened, helpless. There was nothing I could do to help my son. Finally, I heard a car pull up. As I started to walk toward the door, Vito walked in. He stood there with Michael's coat and hat in his hand, just looked at me, and said, "They took him."

I felt the life wash out of me. I started screaming, crying, "They took my son. Oh my God, please don't let this be true!" I was hysterical; I couldn't stop crying. My son was gone.

I screamed at Vito that this was all his fault, he was the one who caused this to happen. I told him I hated him so much. He never said one word. He just looked at me. In the living room, Vito sat on the couch and I just broke down, kneeling on the floor by him. He grabbed me in his arms and held me tight. I cried my heart out.

Michael was sentenced to two years in prison, the longest two years of my life. I would travel to see him almost every weekend, even though it was an eight-hour drive and I had to go alone because Vito still had his case pending and everyone else we knew was under investigation. I learned to handle things myself. I didn't have a choice. You cry alone and you walk alone. That's exactly what I did. I went into the prison, they searched me, and then I'd wait until they brought Michael down. I'll never forget walking through those gates, then hearing those big doors close with a loud, heavy metal *Bam!* behind me. It was horrible.

But I found the inner strength to keep on going for my son. We were eventually seated at a table and Michael wasn't allowed to move from it. My heart broke every time, but I never showed him a tear. I kept him laughing, kept his faith and strength going. Each time I had to leave, I could see the sadness and pain on Michael's face. I hid my emotions because it was already too hard on him. I'd go back to my hotel room, and that's when I would cry my heart out. For two years I felt like I was doing time, too. It felt like a lifetime for me. When Michael came home, I prayed so hard that things would be different.

But, as I said earlier, it was only the beginning. Things would be different all right. But not for the better.

—Carmella Gambino

INTRODUCTION

Family tradition is a way of life. My dad, Vito Gambino, was a career gangster whose father before him was also a gangster. My mother, Carmella Natalli, was born into a crime family, too. From the start, my life was laid out before me. At eighteen, it was fate that brought me into the Honored Society, a Family where members are supposed to respect and trust each other as brothers. Now, after spending a third of my life in prison, I've learned that the Honored Society is based on the betrayal of everyone, including, maybe especially, its own members.

I have been arrested for murder, kidnapping, extortion, gambling, money laundering, robbery, running a house of prostitution, bribery, impersonating a federal agent, counterfeiting, burglary, bid-rigging, bookmaking, interstate wire fraud, possession of guns, running a chop shop, tax evasion, and drug trafficking. Sometimes I was convicted, sometimes not. Still, like everyone else in the life, I treasured being a part of a secret society that played by its own rules. It was powerful. It brought in lots of money. I felt important.

Most people on the outside, whether they fear or respect the crime lifestyle, are in awe of the power, or at least the audacity, of what organized crime can do. Organized crime is involved in everyone's everyday life. Wherever there is money to be made, there is Family influence. Farmers need trucks to haul their product; the syndicate is heavily involved in transportation and commerce.

There are politicians from local level to federal who have been, and are, on the take for doing Family favors. Today's syndicate has become corporate. It has plenty of control in construction, transportation, garbage, the garment industry, the produce business, toxic waste removal, casinos, entertainment, and local neighborhood businesses. The syndicate has learned to manipulate millions of dollars through the stock market. These days, syndicate guys love high-tech scams and use online trading for their pump-and-dumps to make money and launder money. Even though the mob doesn't deal directly in drugs, it gets a share of the drug trade, too.

It's been called the mob, Mafia, Syndicate, Cosa Nostra, Family, and other things. The Honored Society. Bullshit. There is no honor. No loyalty. Members lie to each other, betray and kill each other. Everyone in the organization is clawing and climbing over each other to get to the next plateau. Every level of the pyramid offers nothing but a temporary resting spot. The crime life takes a toll in every way. I slept with a gun by my bed. When the phone or the doorbell rang, I was immediately on guard. I was *always* on guard. I never knew when law enforcement was going to arrest me, my best friend would try to kill me, or I might have to kill him. When I go out now, I still sit with my back to the wall. Many gangsters are in and out of prison; few die of old age. It's a dark, lonely, and empty life. I've sacrificed many valuable years. For what? I did whatever I wanted. I had everything I wanted. But what I did to get those things I wanted so damn much just brought me more time in jail. Enough is enough. I've decided that I'm going to make my own destiny.

Now I'm committed to making a different life for myself. Not that things are easy. They're not. I'm on my own. The Family guys aren't coming around, knocking on my door. When you are involved with the business, you get money when you get out of prison. Your Family friends, your crew members and associates each give you an envelope with cash in it to get you started again, to get you fresh. They help you get on your feet so you can get your action going. Coming out of the joint, if you're still in the business, you are good for two hundred thousand dollars or more. Not me. Not anymore. I put the word out that I'm moving away from the Family. I'm doing it nice, calm. I'm laying down. I got no envelopes.

I gave up a lot of money and power, but I feel so much better. I sleep at night. I'm clear. My parole officer came to my door the other day, and I wasn't worried, I wasn't nervous. I wasn't in trouble. I hadn't beefed on somebody. So I'm at ease. It's a new feeling, and I like it.

When I was sitting in prison, in solitary confinement, I wrote a poem. I started hearing God differently. While I was writing, suddenly, so many memories and emotions started going through me. I thought about my life. What had I accomplished? I made all this money and lost it, made it again, and lost it again. The power I was supposed to have was doing me no good. The people that were supposed to be behind me turned their backs on me. What kind of life was this? How did I get here? What was going to become of me?

I thought about how I used to be a guy who got manicures and wore nice clothes, hung around with senators. In the joint, I was around bums and degenerates. I showered with other guys, ate slop, and lost my dignity and my freedom. I knew I couldn't live in a way that would land me back in there ever again. I wanted more in my life. I wanted positive things, like a normal existence and money earned honestly. I finally understood God saying, "You're a smart guy. Make your life worth something."

When I began to really focus on all the horrible things I had done, I started having terrible nightmares. For the first time in my life, my conscience was bothering me. But that's when I became human again. Facing my feelings, my conscience, saved my life. While I was working in the crime world, I could never let anything bother me. It would have destroyed me. Like anyone else in that life, I had to be cold and had to protect myself. It was survival. Now I see things differently. I feel alive in a way I never have before.

And now I am going to show you what my life was like. I am going to make you feel the things I felt. You will know my mind, my heart, my soul. You will find out, as I did, what the Honored Society is all about.

—MICHAEL GAMBINO

AUTHOR'S NOTE

I was born into a loving, and a treacherous Family. I've spent almost all of my adult life involved in organized crime. This much is fact. The persons, places, situations, and crimes in this work are true to their background and circumstance. They are not, however, real. Characters are based upon composites of many of the people I have known. The experiences of these characters are based upon reality, barroom boasting, and my overactive imagination. Many of the names, crimes, places, and circumstances have been changed to protect the guilty and innocent alike.

THE HONORED SOCIETY

1

HOW I EARNED MY NICKNAME

CHICAGO, 1984

My guts told me something was wrong. Outside of Dreamway, one of the many strip clubs I managed for my dad, I paced up and down the sidewalk, in and out the club. Where the hell was my cousin Marcello? He had called earlier and said one of the guys was celebrating his birthday. I told him I'd fix him and his friends up with some girls. That was two hours ago, and they should have arrived within a half hour of the call. My guts were churning. They felt trouble.

Just as I started to go back inside, Marcello's white van nearly capsized, turning from Roosevelt Road. It came speeding and swerving down Cicero Avenue, and before it screeched to a stop I knew something really awful was going on. When the side door slid open, all I saw was blood. It was everywhere. The guys, the ones who could, were yelling for help. I ran into the club and got some of my men to help pull them out. I yelled to my cousin Paulie to bring his car around from the back.

When my cousin Marcello was laid on the sidewalk, it broke my heart to look at him. He was beaten the worst I'd ever seen. His face was smashed. His head, face, clothes—right down to the shoes—were covered in blood. What shocked me most was his left eye. It was hanging out of its socket.

Meanwhile, Tommy kept shouting, over and over, "It was a trap! They tricked us! I'm sorry, Michael. I'm sorry!" After I helped everyone into Paulie's car and off to the hospital, I got Tommy, who wasn't nearly as badly beaten as the others, calm enough to tell me more about what came down. It was typical of the things that happen in this part of Cicero with guys who don't know better.

Tommy told me the whole story as we got into the van. It all started less than ten blocks away from the club. Marcello had turned off the highway to Cicero. Tommy hung out of the passenger window, whistling at the strolling whores. He was excited about going to Dreamway, but he was hot and thinking only with his dick. He wanted some action right away. Marcello didn't want to stop, but Tommy jumped out of the van and started hustling two hookers.

Joey and Charlie wanted some action, too, so Marcello gave in and got the whores to agree on a cheap price for some blow jobs. A black hooker in leather hot pants and a stoned Asian streetwalker told them to pull into an empty lot behind a warehouse across the street. Marcello got in the back, and Tommy stayed in the front. All four were unbuckling their belts and arguing who would get serviced first when the hookers knocked on the panel door. None of the guys saw the two black pimps make their way along the warehouse wall and hide behind the van.

When Charlie yanked the sliding door open, the girls stepped aside and their pimps burst into the van, swinging as they came.

Charlie, with his jeans around his ankles, was shoved out the door and kicked in the head so hard he didn't feel a thing when his face was shoved into the broken glass and metal shards on the ground.

Marcello lunged but got his teeth knocked out by a brass-knuckle punch. Still he kept coming at the guy, but got knifed through the ribs and cracked across the face for his trouble. Joey broke one pimp's nose before being put out of commission.

Tommy had been stuck in the front seat because the hookers leaned against the passenger door. He tried to stop the pimp who tore out the stereo and tape deck, but he couldn't do much. He got smacked in the mouth. When he could, Tommy got to the driver's seat and started the engine. The pimps had ripped off the guys' watches and wallets, too. They also took the boxed TV, a birthday present, that was in the back.

Charlie crawled into the van, and Tommy floored the accelerator; the van raised dirt and burned rubber as it careened out of the lot and bounced painfully through potholes along Cermak Road.

I was furious with those pimps who fucked with my family. I could hardly see straight. These kids were just looking for some fun. They just wanted to get laid. There's no way they deserved what happened to them. Marcello was nearly killed. I knew something had to be done, and done fast, to teach those pimps a lesson.

I told Tommy to get in the van. He looked at me, like he was scared to go back, but then he must have seen the look in my eyes, and got in. I told him to drive. As we passed a gas station, I had Tommy stop. There was a bucket of water with a squeegy in it. I tossed the water and filled the bucket with gasoline.

We found the lot, then drove up and down the streets looking for the two whores who made the setup. It took us about an hour, but Lady Leather and her Asian cohort finally showed. We drove slowly up the street like we were cruising for a good time, then stopped at the corner where they were standing, waiting for a couple of guys just like us.

I told the pair we wanted to have a good time and showed them a hundred-dollar bill. We made the deal and agreed to pull into that same empty lot just down the street, but I insisted they walk alongside us as we drove. They were too stoned to recognize the van, or Tommy.

Once we were in place in the lot, I pulled open the van's side door and surprised the hookers. I robbed them of their money, only about forty dollars, and a man's watch that turned out to belong to Charlie.

"Now you fuckin' nigger, take your goddamned slant-eyed bitch back to the gutter where you both came from. Go. Get the fuck outta here." I added insults to injury just to piss off their pimps even more. And then I shut the door, and waited.

Tommy wanted to get the hell out of there and started to panic when I grabbed the keys out of the ignition. He saw I had a gun and was scared about what I was going to do. He yelled and cursed and nearly ruined everything until I threatened to shoot him. He shut up real quick, then his eyes opened wide as we saw the two pimps. He could never have guessed what I would do next.

When the two black men got close enough to the van, I opened the side door.

They stood there. One had a knife in his hand and the other held a crowbar. "I'm gonna cut yo' dick off, honkey, and shove it up yo' ass!" said one.

I only laughed as they both moved a little closer.

The one with the crowbar said, "I'll whoop yo' ass first. Like I did those other white boys tonight."

I laughed even louder, and as they moved still closer, I threw the bucket of gasoline across them both. From then, everything happened real fast. They didn't even recognize that it was gasoline all over their fancy-pimp duds. They kept yelling: "You's gonna pay for this, muthafucka! You's gonna pay."

Before they could figure out what I'd thrown and try to run, I made sure they saw I had Tommy holding my gun on them, and I lit one of the matches I had in my hands. The pimps were still confused.

"So what do you two smell?" I asked, playing with the matches.

Realization showed in their widening eyes. They couldn't run for fear they'd get shot, so they begged and pleaded, "Oh man, please. Don't do this! Please don't!"

I just stared at them and lit the next match, and the next, while I listened to their high-pitched pleas. Finally, I asked, "Do you know who the hell I am?"

They shook their heads, "Uh-uh."

As I lit up two entire matchbooks, I told them, "I'm the man who did this to you," then flung the fiery matches, hitting them both squarely in their chests. They burst into fire and danced like flaming scarecrows, screaming, until they fell and tried to roll out the flames.

I grabbed the gun from Tommy's shaking hands, slammed the van door before the smell of burning flesh could make us sick, and shoved Tommy out of my way. He smelled bad, too; he had shit his pants. I gave him a look of disgust and got into the driver's seat, started the engine, and tore out of there.

Back at Dreamway, one of my dad's soldiers, Marco, was waiting to take me to the Roman Cafe, a hole-in-the-wall social club in Berwyn where my dad was with some of his guys. Everyone had heard what happened to Marcello and his friends and wanted to know how I had evened the score, and if I was all right. I told my dad and the others what happened. Dad listened, then picked up the phone and called a police captain, asked him for a favor, and gave him the location of the two fried pimps. The problem was cleaned up. In the next day's newspaper there was a report of drug-related deaths. There were no witnesses. Case closed. Protection is a great arrangement.

Before I left my dad's company, he did one more thing.

In my world everyone has a nickname. Like my friend Joey "Diamonds." One of his first jobs was a $5-million diamond heist in London. Joe "Batter" Figorelli used a baseball bat to teach his victims a lesson. I didn't know what was on my dad's mind when he stared at me for a few seconds, then kind of nodded as he made what turned out to be a proclamation.

"The Match," he said. "Mike the Match."

That's been my nickname ever since.

2

LESSONS MY FATHER TAUGHT ME

My dad, Dominic D'Angelo, taught me a lot. I watched him and how he was in the world. Among other things, he taught me never to underestimate anyone. Clothes, be they rags or cashmere, do not always make the man. Be smart, perceptive, and weigh what a person does, not what he says or how he looks. Be more cautious of a calm man than one who rages because they are usually the smarter ones and can kill you before you know what hit you. Feed a man, but don't let him get too fat; he won't need you anymore. Always protect the weak. In any fight, go for the biggest, toughest guy first and the others will back off. That usually works.

My dad was a powerful man in status and stature but he kept a real low profile. He was maybe five-foot-five-inches and was husky, with a big neck; no way anyone could choke him. He had black, wavy hair even when he died of cancer in 1992. He had these eyes, a little droopy and very mean.

He was never fancy, but he would dress very nice, with pullover shirts and custom-made pants. Carwise, he never drove anything brand new. Usually, he just borrowed whatever was around. If you had a car in the garage, he would borrow it. He knew who he was. No flash. One thing, though, he always had about ten thousand dollars in cash in his pocket at all times. If my mother or I saw something we liked and we wanted it, he'd buy it for us. That was him. There was never any doubt how much he loved us. I loved and idolized him.

My dad learned from the best. My grandfathers on both my father's and mother's sides were very active in organized crime. It's a multigeneration family tradition that goes back to Italy. I remember my grandfather Vince, my mother's father. He was a good man and treated me well but he wasn't a warm person. Grandpa Vince was a notorious contract killer, a button man, the one who pulled the trigger. Obviously, he was very dangerous. I didn't see very much of him but I remember him as quiet and laid-back. He had a bulldog look about him. He had a very stocky build and outrageously big hands. He could easily choke a person to death. But he would do that slowly, because he was a vicious and cruel person who made his targets suffer. They would beg for death. I had heard stories of toes and fingers that were broken with pliers, and private parts screwed in a vise. He would visit us for parties and sometimes come to baseball games with us. He expressed his love in his own reserved way but was not the kind of man to babysit the kids.

To tell you the truth, both of my grandfathers were very cold when it came to the family. They were loving only to a certain extent; they were old school.

I was just a kid when Grandpa Carmine died. I didn't see him as often as Grandpa Vince. He didn't come to many family gatherings because it was awkward. My dad was Carmine's eldest son and had been born in Italy, "the other side," where Carmine had been previously married. Carmine was a Mustache Pete—a member of the original Family organization in Sicily who often wore flamboyant mustaches. After my father's mother died, Carmine came to the U.S., married again, and started a second family. He was quiet and gentle and never dressed fancy. He liked being in the shadows, unseen in a cloak of silence. He didn't enjoy having lots of people around him; he was always better one-on-one. When Carmine came to this country, he had nothing but his brains and a lot of guts. He was cunning and decided he was going to make a mark for himself and for his family. Along with several others, he really organized the mob in America with the biggest and best crime family ever—the D'Angelo family. Yet, to Carmine, the Cosa Nostra was about money and power, not about status and celebrity. The less people knew, the better. Grandpa Carmine was physically small, very meek looking, but, I was to learn later, dangerous. He made his bones, his share of hits, but was very cautious and never got caught. Carmine planned things out. He didn't make a move until he knew what the outcome was going to be. He set the standards for the organization of thousands of made men, about three dozen bosses and thousands more associates. Grandpa Carmine led the D'Angelo family for two decades, the longest time any boss had control over any family.

Carmine wanted a more low-key approach to business. It wasn't like the organization wasn't already busy. It was making plenty of money through loan sharking, gambling, hijackings, selling stolen goods and racketeering. The D'Angelo family also had a ruling hand in construction, food distribution, trucking, sanitation, the garment business, seafood industries, health maintenance companies, and lots more. He made money without doing things that would make headlines at the same time.

During Prohibition, Grandpa Carmine made his money by bootlegging, gambling, and later, dealing in black market food ration stamps and gasoline. After Prohibition, Carmine made money making legitimate booze. He also had legit companies in the meat market, linen-supply, bakeries, night clubs, restaurants, real estate, union consulting, and marine insurance.

When it came to drugs, he drew the line. Much later he was one of the last bosses to allow the Family to make income from drugs being brought into New York City. Rather than be directly involved, his people taxed the drug dealers and taxed the other families for selling. It kept the D'Angelo family at least one step removed.

Under my grandpa Carmine, the D'Angelo crime family became the richest and most powerful criminal organization in America, worth hundreds of millions of dollars. He ruled all of New York, Atlantic City, and Las Vegas, with operations in Chicago and Philadelphia. He made the Family wealthier and stronger than anything Al Capone could put together in Chicago.

BACK THEN, MY AUNTS, UNCLES, and cousins were all more like brothers and sisters, very close and living in Chicago. We had great times together. Kids in the family were never left out when adults were having a good time. Me and my cousins were never left with babysitters. House parties were the way my parents entertained. In the warmer months we had lots of barbeques with sixty to seventy people, lots of kids, dogs running around, everybody having fun playing ball or jumping in the pool. There was enough food for a small army: homemade Italian sausages, steaks, chickens, ribs, and the usual hamburgers and hot dogs, too.

My dad never did a lot of talking around people, but he loved having people around him. Lots of people. After my mom's parents divorced and my grandmother remarried, my mom practically raised her sisters, all younger than she was. I was an only child, but it was like I had five older sisters. My mom was only fifteen years old when I was born; her youngest sister is six years older than I am. I also had plenty of cousins from my dad's side because he had thirteen brothers and sisters. On our city block, every house had ten or more children inside. Relatives lived no more than four blocks from each other. Everyone had their own bed in other homes, but our house was filled with relatives and friends for breakfast, lunch, and dinner. Dad just loved feeding everyone.

After we moved to the Chicago suburb of Oak Brook in the early seventies, he missed having a crowd around the table and so he would call my old girlfriends, even ones I didn't really like, and have them bring their friends over for dinner. I'd come home and there were three, four girls with us at the table. He was like a big kid. He'd do business all day but when we came home, he'd just relax, be with family and friends.

My mom liked having people around too, and she enjoyed making the holidays special; she would go all out.

After our move, it was very important to me to still go to the school in the city so my mother would drive me thirty miles a day back and forth to school. She always had time for me. During our rides to and from school, we talked about a lot of things. She was smart and instilled in me a great fear of using drugs. She actually said to me, "If you take any drugs, you make sure you go ahead and overdose because otherwise I'll kill you myself!"

She was loving, but tough. When I was very young, she always invited all my friends over rather than have me go out on the streets or to other people's houses. Everybody was at my house all the time. She always knew, until much later, who I was hanging out with, who were my friends.

And Mom had an infatuation with dogs. I would always have the same dog, but she would bring home any stray she found, then find its owner or get it adopted. Sometimes we'd have three or four dogs around at a time. Mom was hilarious. She's a tiny woman, not even five feet tall. One day, she brought home a Great Dane that looked ten feet tall next to her. For whatever period of time, I've had every kind of dog. I had a collie, a German shepherd, a Doberman, a rottweiller, a Labrador, a golden retriever, a cocker spaniel. There was one, Major, a German shepherd police dog that was retired from the department after he got shot. He was so protective. He once took a bite outta Nick's arm when we were fooling around, wrestling. Nick Napolitano, an accomplished assassin, who would later play a leading role in my life, could've killed Major with his bare hands, but he didn't get even a little bit mad. He just shrugged, "The dog's doin' his job." I had a yellow and green parakeet, Sam, that I taught to ride on top of Major's head. It was hysterical.

My mom and dad were married almost thirty years, until Dad died in the early nineties. They were very devoted, very affectionate with each other. He was always obviously very proud to be with her, just as she was always proud of him. They walked arm in arm, held hands, and were very physical, very much in love. He would call her Baby. When they walked in anywhere, no matter how many people were there, everybody knew they were together. Mom wasn't a jealous person because Dad made sure she was the only one. His heart never strayed. They really were a great couple.

Not that they never had arguments. They did. Boy, they had some doozies. Never any violence, but there were words. Mom was very verbal, but when she got good and mad she would take her ring off and throw it. She must have thrown that ring ten thousand times until she finally lost it. Of course, Dad replaced it for her. He really didn't like to argue with my mother. He would say one or two sharp nasty words and then refuse to talk to her. My mom would go on, but eventually lose steam, and then he would make her laugh. He just had that way with her. She couldn't stay mad at him for long.

With me, my mom would chase me with a big wooden spoon. Not the cooking kind, but those really big spoons and forks that you can hang on the wall in the kitchen for decoration. She'd grab one and chase me all over until she could give me a little spanking or give me one good shot to the head.

I did plenty of just regular kid stuff when I was younger. My dad loved sports because it was fun, and let's face it, important to his bookmaking business. So it was a way of life. I grew up loving basketball and baseball. We went to basketball games a lot. Usually some of the guys would come with us. And we had a box at Soldier Field for the football season.

I'll never forget the first time my dad took me to a baseball game. I was about eleven and wore my Cubs' jersey, hat and carried my baseball glove. We started out the day by going out to breakfast together. Then we went to the stadium for a daytime game. (I don't think they had lights in the stadium in those days.) The Cubs were playing at home in Chicago's Wrigley Field against Cincinnati, and the first one hundred people into the park got a baseball bat. We had great box seats right behind the dugout, behind home base. But first, we went up to the press box, high in the stadium. My dad knew the announcer, Jasper Tuft, and he brought us down to the field where I met everyone. Dave Kingman, Bruce Sutter, Ernie Banks, Johnny Bench were there. We even went into the dugout and I got to shake Johnny Bench's hand. Dave Kingman signed my bat. They gave us autographed baseballs. I had my picture taken with all of them on the mound. Pete Rose was always my favorite. Funny how he and I ended up doing time, at different times, at the same prison years later. But that day, no thoughts like that were in my head. Back at our seats, we had hot dogs, pretzels, Cracker Jacks—I loved Cracker Jacks—and lots of soda. It was a scorching day. We both drank gallons of soda, and I ate so much I got sick; but we had a blast. The Cubs won after fourteen innings.

Afterward, Pop and I went to the social club and I showed everybody my bat and balls and autographs. We played a little foosball and then went to a nice restaurant for dinner. Just the two of us. A real father-and-son thing. It was the best day, the first time we ever did that.

My mom went to a couple of baseball games, but never basketball or football. It wasn't her thing. But she and my dad took me to the circus. From the time I was a baby, they took me every year until I was fifteen. I loved the circus. Ringling Bros. and Barnum & Bailey. We would bring kids from the neighborhood with us, and we all had a great time buying cotton candy, popcorn, souvenirs, those spinning lights. Before the show, we would feed the elephants peanuts and watch the guys on the big stilts walking around.

My favorites were a guy on a motorcycle who rode it on the outside of a metal wheel structure that spun high off the ground, and the high wire acts. Oh, I loved those! I always thought they were going to fall. Clowns were great, too. I loved it when some twenty clowns all came out of a tiny car. I tried to figure out how they got in there.

Dad was a kid at heart himself, and it would come out when we least expected it. For example, he loved ice cream. I remember one night, when Dad, my cousin Marcello, and I had been sitting around watching television. About three o'clock in the morning, Dad got up from the couch and went to the kitchen. He came back annoyed and said, in his deep, gravelly voice (because he had throat polyps), "There's no ice cream. There's no fucking ice cream!"

So me, Dad and Marcello went to Mimmo's grocery store, where Dad took a shopping cart and filled it with at least one of every kind of ice cream in the store. He even started eating ice cream as he walked up and down the aisles. At home we filled all the refrigerators and freezers. He could be the biggest kid in the world or as tough as he had to be.

He loved to cook, too, but not always carefully. One Sunday afternoon, he made spaghetti sauce and spilled a whole pot as he carried it from the stove to the table in the dining room. It poured all over the gorgeous white carpet. He was such a character. Dad immediately ran to the sofa, threw himself across it like he had been napping, and yelled out, "Oh Michael! My God, look what you've done! Your mother is going to be so mad at you!" Mom was upstairs and when she came down, I took the rap. Dad knew I wouldn't rat on him, and Mom never got very upset with me. I never told Mom the truth, but I think she knew.

I WAS ABOUT NINE when my father bought a bigger family house with a big backyard on Mason Street. My mom and dad brought me with them when they first looked at this house that belonged to a mortician, Tony Morrizzo. In the attic there were all these weird-looking things, tables with drains, hoses, aluminum pans and trays. It looked very strange, but intriguing to me. I was a curious kid.

Downstairs, on the back porch, we saw three big black bags. They were bodies that had been embalmed upstairs and were waiting to be taken to Salerno's funeral parlor. We wanted to take a look at them, so he unzipped a bag. We took a look and a touch; the bodies felt waxy and cold. My mom took me to funeral homes for wakes of friends and family members from the time when I was a baby. But this was different. A few days later, my mom took me with her when she went to talk to Tony about the house again. I stayed with Tony for a few hours while she did other errands. It was fascinating for me to watch Tony embalm a body, see how he sewed the mouth closed.

Another day, I asked him if I could go with him when he picked up bodies from the hospital. When we got there, a doctor was doing an autopsy. Tony tried to get me to leave, or at least not look, while he was getting the bodies to his van. But I refused to move. I watched the doctor make that Y cut through the dead man's chest, pull out different organs. I saw him open the skull and weigh the brain. The doc saw I wasn't squeamish so he explained everything he was doing. It was even more fascinating than the embalming, in spite of the awful smell. For a while, I thought I wanted to become a coroner, or a mortician. Dead bodies, blood and gore never bothered me. Even at age nine, this was not the first dead body I had seen.

That had been in my dad's store, a shoe store he had bought on

North Avenue at Austin Boulevard, just on the Oak Park border, about two miles from our house. I was maybe seven years old at the time.

Over the course of several months, there had been a series of rapes in our neighborhood. This was very unusual for our area. In Oak Park, where the population was predominantly Italian and Greek, we kids would be out until well after dark catching lightning bugs in a jar. Our mothers and their friends would sit on tall, fifteen-step cement stoops. We played in tree houses. There were block parties. Crime against each other or among us was rare and petty. So the rapes had everyone in an uproar.

Then the sicko rapist attacked a little boy who was able to identify the man to his father, who had connections. A few days later, that rapist was found in my father's store. When I got there I saw the yellow police crime-scene tape around the front entrance, police all over, and then I saw the body. The dead man was a bloody mess. He had his eyelids cut off and a broomstick down his throat. I learned later that his cock had been cut off and shoved up his ass. I remember overhearing the police tell my father that the man's death looked "accidental." The cops had been getting ready to arrest this man and were glad someone saved the taxpayers the expense of a trial and jail time.

While the cops were talking to my dad, people from the other stores and the neighborhood were crowding around. I remember that I felt very scared inside. I was a little kid who saw what looked like a horror movie monster, all mutilated, but I knew it was real. My cousin Paulie showed up. When he spotted me, he came over to me and said, "Michael, let's go get a Danish and a glass of milk." He was protective of me, the only adult who really noticed me in the middle of all the commotion. I was glad he was there. I think he knew that actually I was very scared about what I had seen. But because I was around adults who made me feel okay, like it was no big thing, eventually, I believed it.

3

GROOMED FOR CRIMINAL SUCCESS

The Chicago mob in the early seventies was strong and in control of just about everything, including most of the legal system from the beat cop to high-ranking judges. It would be more than a decade before hotshot prosecutor Scott James, a self-styled Elliott Ness, would be part of the shakeup that would bring the FBI into the city in full force.

My dad bought the mortician's house and we always had lots of my dad's friends hanging out with us. Some were local like Joey Antonetti and Jackie Cicero, and others, like Paul Farentino and Neil Delrosa, from out of town. There were a lot of important, well-connected guys. Cicero was Chicago boss Anthony Capelli's protégé. Antonetti was the boss-in-title from 1969 to 1987, but although others like Sam Gialoti, Sam Rizzo, and Joe Figorelli were also given that title, Capelli actually ruled the Chicago family until he died in 1992. Farentino took over as D'Angelo family boss in New York after his brother-in-law, my grandfather, Carmine D'Angelo, died in 1976. Delrosa became his underboss, and I remember old-timers talking about how he was allegedly involved, along with the Gallo brothers, in the death of Albert Anastasia. These men loved being with my dad, and they really liked my mother, who would cook for us all. The house was full of food, people talking and laughing, and playing pinochle. They didn't like to be interrupted while playing.

All kinds of guys were always at the house, like Louie Velman and Lenny North, who were among the last surviving members of the famous Purple Gang out of Detroit. They were, actually, rich, rebellious men who had been cut off by their families. They were just naturally very tough guys. They taught me a lot. Louie was born with a silver spoon in his mouth. When I asked him why he did what he did, he said, "I was born a criminal, and I'll die a criminal. That's all there is to it." He simply loved the high of getting away with bank robberies and a counterfeit check scam that cost a major Hollywood studio a cool ten million dollars.

These men were like uncles to me. They loved the way I was, a smart kid with a little bit of mischievousness, and a lot of attitude. I was a sharp little dresser. I was never the kid in the baggy pants and gym shoes. I'd go to school wearing nice slacks, shirts, and suspenders. Before I ever started to shave, I'd get up in the morning, shower, and splash on my cologne. I was dapper; I was the best-looking kid in the world.

My cousin Paulie was an impeccable dresser, too. He was older, by almost twenty years, but we bonded early. Like me, he was an only child. He was more like a big brother, a pal, who never talked down to me. He never judged me, or anything I would tell him. I could share more emotional things with him than I could most of the other men in my life. I liked the way he dressed, too. Vests were a big thing. Everybody wore them then, including Paulie and me. Jewelry was always a big thing, too. Paulie wore nice jewelry. Not a lot, but really classy pinky rings and a Rolex watch. Italian horns were really popular. When I was eight, Paulie gave me a big, two-inch, solid gold one for Christmas. Of course, at the time I had no clue that most of the gifts he gave, he didn't buy. They were usually hot items that he paid maybe twenty-five bucks for, or got for free as a payment for a favor, or stole for himself. By the time I was a teenager, I had a fortune in jewelry.

Paulie showed me that if you want to be somebody, you have to dress like somebody. Louie and Lenny taught me that, too. The guys loved that I followed their example. I saw how these guys lived. I saw the big Lincolns they drove, and how they were always impeccably dressed, and had nice rings. I liked what I saw. I wanted to be like them, especially like Lenny.

From the time I was maybe ten, I drove around in their cars while they were doing business. They'd be over my parents' house and say, "We're going to play foosball down at the club. Com'on, Michael." On the way down to any one of the clubs—the Italian-American Club, Sons of Italy, or the Sicilian Club—where, eventually, we played foosball, we would make maybe ten stops. If we stopped at a hot dog stand, I ate a hot dog, and the guys talked with the guy behind the counter, collected money, ran numbers, and did other business. As time went on, I'd see people get smacked around, would hear threats. I never questioned anything. I was starting to learn more on the streets than in school.

With my parents, aunts, uncles, and older friends I could do no wrong. And if I did, I usually got away with it. But not always. The nuns and a priest who I almost killed at St. Angela's elementary school saw to that.

One time, my friend Danny and I found a bowling ball behind St. Angela's Church. I wanted to see if it would bounce, so we carried it up a metal fire escape. The highest level had a solid metal floor, so we couldn't see below when I took the bowling ball and rolled it over the edge.

The bowling ball was already out of my hands, over the edge and falling when we saw Father Lou had just parked his new Cadillac and was getting out. There was nothing I could do. It went right through the windshield. We waited. Those were the longest minutes of my life.

Finally, I heard Father Lou swear, and I knew he was okay. He looked up and saw me. Danny hugged the floor and hid. Not knowing what else to do, I came down. Father Lou took me by the ear and pulled me by it all three blocks to my house, all the while yelling about what a bad apple I was.

We burst through the door. My father sat there, playing pinochle with his pals. They looked up.

Father Lou told my dad I had just dropped a bowling ball through his car. My dad turned to me.

"I didn't do nothing," I said. Father Lou turned to me and yelled that I had better tell the truth.

"I didn't do nothing, Pop," I repeated.

Father Lou said things were getting out of hand. Dad told him he would take care of the damage and would see him on Sunday, meaning he'd put some extra cash in the collection box.

After the priest left, Dad took me aside and asked me again; by now he figured I was lying. He told me again to tell the truth, and I finally did. It was an accident after all.

"Why didn't you tell me the truth to begin with?"

"You told me never to rat on nobody, so I didn't want to get my friend in trouble, too."

The tension in the room started to evaporate. My dad was trying not to laugh, because his friends Rocco, Sal, and Joey were taking my side and saying that he taught me well.

I added, "You told me always not to confess to nothing."

The guys at the table laughed some more. Dad gave them the eye to quiet them down.

"You told me not to confess to nothing," I repeated. "I gave it a shot."

Dad said that was right, that's what he taught me. But when he asked me for the truth he should get it. By this time, everybody was laughing and having a good time and he couldn't help himself and started laughing, too.

"Keep up the good work, kid," Sal called to me as the guys turned back to their game. "Someday you'll be as smart as me."

There was something in Sal's voice that made me stop and look at him. I noticed then that the others were exchanging glances. At that moment, pieces of gossip I had heard about Sal throughout the week came flooding back to me. I suddenly knew that Sal had done something terribly wrong.

I didn't say a word. I just went into the kitchen to watch my mom as she cooked. Later, I pretended not to notice when Sal didn't come around the house anymore.

BY THE TIME I WAS IN FIFTH GRADE, I always had something to say, and I used swear words. Once while I was talking in class, the nun in charge heard me swear. Sister Mary Gestapo of the Holy Rod came over to me. I had my hand flat on the desk, and *bam!* She hit me with her pointer. It was as big as a pool cue.

I reacted with one word, "Shit!"

She hit my hand again, harder, and I let out, "Son of a bitch!"

That did it. Sister Gestapo took me to the principal's office and called my mother. We lived only a few blocks away, so she and my great-grandmother, a real spitfire, showed up right away. I was crying; I was pissed off, but my hand really hurt. My mom was really angry to see my hand bruised and swollen. Her attitude was that if her son needed to be reprimanded, she would do it. Then the principal said maybe I wasn't being raised right, that something was going on at home. That's when my mom said, "I pay for my son to come to this school. I don't pay for you to beat him." After that, she put me in public school.

In public school, I was better, free from all the rules they had at Catholic school. And being around older kids usually kept me in my place. The school had grades from kindergarten all the way to twelfth grade. The older kids in eighth and ninth grades wanted to be close to a gangster's son, a kid whose father's pals used to work with Al Capone. They were curious, so I was sort of popular.

And I was a smart kid, and very industrious. I always knew how to make money, and money got me a lot of things, including respect. Even when I was in the lower grades, my parents gave me an allowance. Twenty bucks a week. I did little odd jobs around the house for it; I cleaned out the garage, washed the car, mowed the lawn. With cash in my pocket, I made more. I'd talk to neighbors and arrange to have their lawns mowed. Then I hired kids to do the work. Three bucks would go into my pocket, and two into theirs. They also washed windows after I got them to drum up business by going around adjacent neighborhoods and throwing mud balls at houses.

I never let an opportunity go past me. My dad had a friend who worked for the Mars Candy Company. He would bring us gross-sized cartons of Mars Bars, Snickers, Milky Ways, and Three Musketeers. I'd set up a little stand in front of the house and sell the candy. Above retail. When a kid got wise and challenged me with, "I can get it cheaper at the supermarket!" I reminded him I was there, at the moment, in front of him with the goods. He didn't have to ride his bike or walk the two miles or more to the store. It was a convenience charge. Take it or leave it. They always took it.

Every now and then I would get into a fight at school. The principal of my junior high school was an Italian guy who also owned a trophy shop. He knew most of the guys because most of the bowling teams bought awards through him at the end of a season. When I would get into trouble, he would let me call my cousin Paulie, instead of one of my parents. Paulie would come down and kind of bribe the principal not to suspend me or make a big deal out of things. He wouldn't say it straight out, but Paulie and the principal would talk about the bowling tournament coming up, and Paulie would mention he could send the order for trophies to him. The principal understood.

I'd leave with Paulie and as soon as we got outside, he'd ask, "So did you get the best of the other kid? Did you punch his teeth out for him?" There was no lecture, no punishment. He didn't care about those things. He just wanted to be sure I was all right. Paulie helped me out like that a number of times. I always had that sense of security, that backup. I loved the guy.

When dad had business in another town, Paulie often drove. Every now and then I would go along, too. Once, Dad finished his business in Dixmoor and we got back on the highway but there was some construction, and somehow Paulie went the wrong way through the detour and in a short time we were in what was then still an undeveloped area outside East Moline.

We were driving along a country road when the car sputtered and slowly rolled to a stop. My dad didn't like this.

"Where the hell are we?" he grumbled loudly.

"I don't know, Uncle Dominic," Paulie said and started to squirm.

"What the hell is wrong with the car?"

"I don't know," Paulie said again.

"You don't know nothing!" Dad shouted, and stared at Paulie, who was afraid to take his hands off the steering wheel, shift his eyes off the road, or move even an inch.

"I don't understand how this car can be breaking down on us," my dad said, quieting down a bit. "It's almost new."

Meanwhile, I was in the back seat with a huge bag of jellybeans. I knew there was nothing to be gained by opening my mouth so I just kept eating my candy, careful to leave the black ones that I didn't like.

Finally, Paulie looked down at the panel.

"Oh geez," he moaned. "We're outta gas."

"Outta gas?" Dad yelled. "I can't understand how you let this happen! How could you forget to put gas in this car?"

"I'm sorry, Uncle Dominic," Paulie started.

"I'll tell you what. Michael and me are gonna sit right here and wait while you get your ass outta the car, walk to the next service station, and bring back some gas."

That might've sounded reasonable except that we were in the middle of nowhere and hadn't seen a gas station or even a house in the last ten miles and there didn't seem like there were any lights of a town ahead either. Still, my dad nudged Paulie out of the car.

"I don't know where I'm going!" Paulie protested. "There's nothing out here and it's getting dark. Who knows who or what I'll run into?"

"Yeah, it's getting dark, so you better walk fast and get back here in a hurry," Dad ordered. "Bring back some gas. This will teach you to remember to fill the tank next time."

"Can't we all go?" Paulie tried.

"No, this is too new a car," he answered. "It wouldn't be a good idea to leave it here."

Paulie, wearing a suit and dress shoes, had no choice but to start walking down the road in the direction we had been heading.

Within a half hour, it was pitch black. I kept eating my jelly-beans, thinking about how Paulie was still walking down that road, dreading ghosts, hatchet killers, and packs of wild dogs. Dad picked out some jellybeans, avoiding the black ones, too. He didn't like them. Even Paulie didn't like them.

After a few mouthfuls of candy, Dad shook his head. "That

Paulie. I love that boy, but he isn't the smartest guy around," and then he fell asleep in the front seat. I loved Paulie, too.

Two hours later, a pickup truck drove up. Paulie got out, hauled a gas can from the truck bed and went to the back of the car without saying a word. The truck pulled off. Dad was awake but didn't say anything.

When Paulie got back into the car, he looked really worn out. He had walked almost ten miles.

"Boy, am I hungry!" he said after getting back behind the wheel. "Hey, Michael, hand me some of those jelly beans."

I took a handful from the bag and handed them to him.

"These are all black!"

"We ate all the others," I said, "but we saved these for you."

He ate them grudgingly, then asked for more. That's when I gave him the handful of assorted flavors, with lots of his favorite green ones that I had saved for him. He kept driving but gave me a wink in the rearview mirror.

I started to see a different side of Paulie when I was in my early teens. Cousin Marcello and I were making some money working in a liquor store stocking the refrigerator cases with beer and soda. Bruno, a big man who was like six-feet, six-inches and weighed nearly three hundred pounds, was my cousin and Dad's ultimate button man. A shooter. And vicious. Heaven help anyone who tried to hurt my father in any way. Bruno went nuts. That was his way. He enjoyed any opportunity to go wild.

Bruno was doing some money business with the owner of the liquor store, who was one of our guys, when a man came in and tried to rob the place. He didn't stand a chance. Before he could turn around and run, Bruno whipped out his gun, opened up, and nearly emptied his entire clip into the guy's head. As if that hadn't been enough, Bruno came around from the counter and shot him one more time with his last bullet. I watched and it didn't bother me at all.

Paulie walked in and saw the robber lying on the floor full of holes. His first words to Bruno were, "I can't believe you whacked the guy!" He said it with sympathy or like it must've been some kind of a mistake.

That was wrong. The guy had tried to steal from us, and Paulie was feeling sorry for him. You gotta be tough, but Paulie wasn't. I didn't lose affection for the man, but I was starting to come into my own identity. To make it big, to get ahead, I knew I had to be tougher than Paulie.

Not long after that Bruno popped a cop. He was in a bar, having a few drinks and flirting with a woman when an off-duty Chicago cop came in and hit on the same woman. Bruno told him to back off, but the cop took a bottle of beer and cracked it upside Bruno's head. The blow knocked him to the floor. He got up, saw he was bleeding, went home. When he came back, he shot the cop nine times and got arrested.

The next morning my dad and I went to the police department to talk to him. My dad sat down and asked, "What's wrong with you? You must be fucking nuts. Why would you shoot him?"

"He pissed me off when he hit me in the head," Bruno said.

"But why the fuck did you have to shoot him nine times?"

"Uncle Dominic," Bruno said, "every time I pulled the trigger, I just felt like I was coming. I just had to keep shooting."

Bruno got a twenty-year state sentence. He served only two because Dad bought off a judge who reversed the court's decision.

Back then, you could do that and get away with it. My dad knew how to take care of his family in every way. He took care of me and Mom, his brothers, sisters, nieces and nephews, sisters-in-law, everybody. Even strangers.

He had a real soft spot for children, and was very protective of them—and also of people with disabilities. If you parked in a handicapped parking space but didn't have the handicap license plate or a placard, he'd bust all the windows of your car. That's how he was.

One night, Dad and I and some of the other guys were at a Denny's restaurant. Sitting across from us, there was a big blue-collar kind of guy with five kids around him at the table. When one of the kids asked for dessert, his father told him he couldn't have any because there wasn't enough money. Dad overheard this and had the waitress bring that table desserts. He paid the whole dinner bill for them. But the guy wasn't sure how to take what Dad had done and tried to insist on paying the bill himself. Dad got him into a conversation. It turned out that the guy's wife passed away six months before, he had just moved to the area, and he didn't have a job. He had been an iron worker all his life but couldn't get into the union. My father gave him the name of someone he should go see the next day, and told him everything was going to be okay. The guy looked up my dad's friend and got a job on the spot.

A few days later, the iron worker came looking for Dad and found him at one of the social clubs. It was a funny scene to see this big guy so humble, towering over my dad as he thanked him. My dad told him that the next time he found himself in a position where he could do the same thing for someone else, he should do a favor like he did. To this day this father of five is a union member and a foreman. When my father passed away, he sent flowers to my mom and asked what he could do. There really wasn't anything, so he told her he would send a thousand dollar donation to the Cancer Society every year from then on.

My father's business might have been mean and vicious, but he was often very kind and generous. He would do anything he could for some people. He was a good man. He just did business a different way. He had the money and the power to do things like he did for that stranger with the kids. That's what made me want to be like my dad.

LOOKING DEATH IN THE EYE

Around that time I was feeling pretty full of myself. I was becoming more independent, acting more like a man. I was doing little errands for the Family. A crew member, one of the nearly forty men who was assigned to jobs by my dad and reported to him, would give me a bag with a bunch of numbers on rice paper to drop off somewhere. I'd run numbers up and down Harlem Avenue, in and out of bars and liquor stores. When I finished the job, they would hand me a bill and say, "Here's a hundred dollars." I knew what it was all about, bookmaking. What did I care? I was making big money. I was a tough guy. I felt important.

"Running numbers" is a lottery, similar to those run by most states. Let's say a crew boss had ten guys that were going to be spending the day on bookmaking. They took some rice paper, because it's easy to dissolve in case they had to destroy it fast, and sat at their local restaurant, hot dog stand, social club, anywhere people would know to find them. To make a bet, all a person had to do was pick three numbers from one to ten and write them down with their name on the paper, like six-one-three, and put some money on it, maybe five bucks. On humongous blackboards, who bet what, when, where, and how much was written up. At six o'clock, three random numbers were drawn, and they checked the board to see who matched. If you play state lottery, the payout is four to one; the street lottery was six to one, which was much better.

As a kid, I'd go pick up bags of numbers and money from the bookies at restaurants and stores. I'd take it back to one of the social clubs where the guys would process the bet. A lot of people play, but few actually win. On an average day, with ten guys out on the street and the right clients, you could book ten thousand dollars because some people played only a couple of dollars but others played thousands. When nobody had a winning number, the pot rolled over and more people wanted to play for a bigger prize, just like with the state.

For a kid like me, picking up the daily numbers was exciting, and a responsibility that I welcomed. I visited a lot of people who knew I was working for important guys.

I carried a simple brown paper bag. At every stop, I picked up a small bundle of rice paper notes, each with numbers and a name on it. On top, there was a note with the name of the store. Each bundle had a rubber band around it. I collected one bundle from every place that was in the numbers game.

One day, I noticed a new patrolman, a young guy, in the neighborhood walking his beat. No big deal. I continued doing my job going in and out of stores up and down North Avenue.

When I stopped at Carlo's Deli, the patrolman was in there.

"I'll have a salami and cheese on a roll," he ordered, "and a cup of coffee, black." He took his lunch to a table outside when it came.

Meanwhile, I walked in, went behind the counter and into the back room. Carlo gave me his bundle, and I left. My next stop was across the street at Georgio's Produce. Same thing. I walked in, went to the back, Georgio dropped his bundle in my bag and I left. A few doors down, I was in and out of Johnny's Shoe Repair in less than a minute. I didn't think about the patrolman who ate his lunch and watched me from across the street. The cops in our neighborhood knew what was going on and didn't care because the guys in charge took care of them.

So I was surprised when, on the next block, the same cop showed up at Funicello's Bakery. He walked in just as I was leaving and blocked the door.

"Hey, kid," he said to me with a phony smile. "What do you got in that bag?"

"Ah, bread," I said.

"Doing some shopping for your mom?" he kind of chuckled, but his eyes narrowed.

"Yeah," I said, trying to get past him and outside. He moved side to side a bit, blocking me.

"Funny, you do a lot of shopping, but I don't see a whole lot of groceries. No fruits or vegetables, no deli goods, nothing," he said, cocking his head to one side. "Lemme see that bread."

As I stepped back a little, I started to open the top of the bag like I was going to show him something. When he stepped forward and reached for it, I darted around him, out the door and ran down the street.

He ran after me, but I was faster and got to Joey's bar, another joint where I picked up numbers. I burst through the front door and yelled to Joey behind the bar, "There's a cop chasing me!" And I ran to the back door.

As I was going through it I heard the out-of-breath cop try to bellow, "Where's the kid?" The son of a bitch was still after me.

I couldn't see Joey, but I knew he must have shrugged and said, "What kid?"

I ran through the alley and came out the side street. As I turned around the building, I saw the cop charging down the alley. He was not giving up.

I was back on North Avenue and there was a sewer grate at the corner. Before the cop came around the building, I dumped the numbers out of the bag and into the sewer. Then I tossed the bag, too. It had been raining the night before, so the rice paper would dissolve fast. The water rushed along fast down in the darkness. No more evidence.

Before the cop turned the corner, I was halfway down the block, empty-handed. I slowed down, and then stopped. The cop was on me in a second.

He grabbed me by the collar of my shirt and glared as he caught his breath. Then he asked, "What are you up to?"

"Nothing," was all I said.

"Where's that bag you were carrying?" he asked.

"What bag?" I asked back, with wide eyes and a shrug.

He let go of my shirt and stared at me, not sure what he could do, then said, "You're a smart-assed little bastard, aren't you?"

I said nothing. He turned around and glanced up the street, as if to see if I had dropped the bag in the gutter or on the sidewalk. I saw his eyes fall on the sewer grate. Then he looked back at me.

"You got lucky this time, kid," he muttered.

I lost all those numbers, but the older guys liked that I didn't get caught with them. I showed them I was smart, that I could think quick. What did they do? They found that cop and put him on the payroll. Whenever I saw him again, he would wave, nothing else. And the guys rewarded me. They took me out to Brooks Brothers in downtown Chicago where Lenny and Louie bought me my first double-breasted, black cashmere overcoat. Paulie bought me a beautiful white silk scarf to go with it. These men sometimes bought me a hundred-fifty-dollar cashmere sweaters, a dozen at a time. I started to like it.

I knew there were risks in what I was doing: getting popped by a cop; being robbed by some punk. But I always felt protected. Besides, danger was part of the fun. The bigger the risk, the harder the adrenaline pumped. The rush. That made it exciting.

Picking up the money was part of the numbers game, too. One late afternoon I picked up a bagful of cash from a bar. As I went out the back door, I was blindsided. A punk, a guy of about thirty, was waiting for me. He hid behind the opening door, then rammed me. He slammed me so hard against the building, I thought my head had cracked open; my teeth cut my tongue and I bled from my mouth. He thought taking money from a kid would be easy. But I kept a tight grip on the cash bag.

"Gimme the bag!" he shouted, as he tried to yank it from me.

When I refused, he bashed my head against the wall again and again, and yelled, "You stupid fuck! I'll blow your pissant head wide open!"

Still, I held tight. I was on the ground, dazed and couldn't get at him.

Furious, he shoved the gun into my mouth, chipping my teeth and nearly choking me.

"I mean it, asshole. Gimme the bag!"

Even half unconscious, I was mad. He was not going to win, no matter what. I looked him in the eyes. He fired his gun. It jammed. Not once, but twice; then a third and fourth time. It's strange, but I remember counting: click, click-click, click. As he backed away, I tripped him and was on him, punching his face with my fist still holding the money bag tight. Other guys came into the alley from the bar, some with pool sticks they used like bats. That punk learned a lesson he would never forget. He ended up in the hospital for almost a week.

I LEARNED A LOT ABOUT how to handle myself from Louie and Lenny. They were both fancy guys but very tough. One time I went to the grocery store with Louie in his brand-new Lincoln Continental. In the parking lot, a punk kid was leaning against his new Camaro and mouthed off to Louie that he was parked too close to his car. Louie told him to get lost. The kid spat on Louie's car, but Louie did nothing. When we came out of the market, we found the mirror on Louie's car busted.

Louie, in his sixties, said nothing. He went into the glove box of his car and pulled out a screwdriver. It was filed sharp like an icepick, and he poked the sidewall of the Camaro's tire. The kid went crazy swearing at Louie, who threatened to stick him in the eye if he made one more move. Still, the kid raised his hand, but before he could do anything more, Louie shoved the pick into the side of the kid's thigh. Louie went calmly to the trunk of his car, took out a rag and wiped the blood off the pick before putting it back in the glove box.

I told Louie that I thought he should have whacked the guy, but as we drove away, he told me, "You never whack nobody unless they deserve it. Now he's gonna remember and never fuck with an old man again. But don't ever let nobody ever get away with nothing."

These things shaped me into the person I would become. Certain actions require certain reactions. If someone commits a crime against you, the punishment has to fit the act and then some. Death is punishable only by other death. If someone works over someone really bad, or whacks someone, they have to be whacked. Punishment is equal, plus one up. You don't bring a knife to a gun-fight. You bring a knife, I bring a gun. You bring a gun, I shoot you. Simple.

MY DAD WAS ALWAYS VERY GOOD about teaching by example, too. For maybe a year, my cousin Marcello lived with me and my parents in Chicago. His father was in the joint, and his mom was having trouble coping with being a single mom.

One day, while I was home just hanging out, Marcello walked in the door. He had a shiny stud earring in his earlobe. I was stunned.

"Like it, Michael?" he asked, all pumped up. "Cool, isn't it?"

"You better get that out of your ear before my dad comes home," I told him. "He's going to hit the roof."

"Oh, I am not worried about Uncle Dominic," he said with a smile as he checked himself out in a mirror.

"Yeah, sure," I shrugged.

A few hours later, when Dad came home, Marcello was in the kitchen, making himself yet another huge sandwich. This one was salami with who-knows-what else on it. The kid, tall and beefy, ate six times a day. Dad walked over to him.

"Mmm, looks good," he said close at Marcello's elbow, about eye level with the earring. "Make me one with an extra slice of provolone and tomato, on a roll."

"Sure, Uncle Dominic," Marcello answered without looking up from the counter. He made the sandwich and the three of us sat at the kitchen table together. There wasn't much talk.

What's with this? I wondered. I was surprised that my dad didn't say anything about the earring, but I sure wasn't going to bring it up. He must have seen it. Marcello seemed relieved, even a little smug.

Then, all of a sudden, my dad says, "Let's go. Take your sandwiches with you and eat them in the car. The three of us gotta go somewhere."

We learned long ago that when my dad said "go," we went, no questions asked.

Dad drove in silence. That usually meant this was going to be strictly business, so Marcello and I didn't understand why Dad brought us to the local shopping mall.

I finally had to ask, "So what are we doing, Dad?"

"We gotta take care of something," he said without expression. "It won't take long."

He led us through the indoor mall and into Victoria's Secret, a store devoted to sexy women's underwear and nighties and things. I was thinking, what the fuck is this all about? There must be somebody here we got to collect money from.

We walked all the way into the place and were surrounded by silk and lace lingerie in all colors, half-naked mannequins, women picking out thongs and bustiers and asking about bras to make their breasts look bigger. Dad just stood there. Marcello was getting fidgety, and I was taking in the sexy sights, waiting for Dad to make some move. We must have looked like fish out of water. The saleswomen looked at us and finally, one came up to us.

"Can I help you gentlemen?" she asked in a sultry tone while the others continued to size us up.

"Yeah, you can," my dad started. "I would like you to find me the most gorgeous, most beautiful, sexy outfit you got. Something maybe in pretty pink."

"What size?" the saleswoman asked.

"Extra-large," my dad said, and Marcello and I looked at each other. My mom is less than five feet tall and tiny.

"Can you be more specific?" she asked. "Something for the bedroom or day wear?"

"Oh, something short, cute, and lacy for the bedroom," he said, then gestured to Marcello, "something special to go with my nephew's beautiful new earring. Doesn't he look pretty? Yeah, I think pink is his color, or maybe light violet."

Well, this six-foot-two-inch guy turned blood red. The wind was knocked out of him faster than a ramrod to the gut could've done. Marcello almost died of embarrassment as heads turned, women elbowed their shopping pals, and several ladies giggled.

As Marcello stood frozen, Dad went on, "And maybe some nice panties and a bra, something to make him look real sexy, very feminine."

When Marcello looked like he was on the verge of tears, Dad let up.

"Gee, maybe today's not a good day," he said slowly to the saleswoman, who looked like she'd now seen and heard about everything. "You look kind of busy, and the fitting rooms are filling up. We'll come back another day."

Dad turned around and walked out of the store with me and Marcello, wound tight and ready to bolt, right behind him. We walked halfway back to the car before my dad turned around to Marcello, got in his face, and said, "Don't you embarrass me by doing something so stupid ever again. An earring! What's the matter with you?!"

Dad didn't wait for an answer, he just turned and we got back into the car. We drove home in silence. Marcello disappeared for a few hours that evening and when he came back, the earring was gone. He never wore it again.

Whether by words or actions, when my dad wanted to get a point across, he made a lasting impression. I loved his way of getting things done and I learned a lot from him. But there was so much I had to learn by trial and error on my own.

5

A CLASS OF HIS OWN

It's not surprising that things changed for me in high school. As the other kids heard about what I was doing, more of them distanced themselves. They started to understand what "gangster" really meant. So did I.

By the time I reached sixteen, I remember thinking, "What am I doing here? Everyone else is out dancing, partying, drinking, having a good time while I've got responsibilities. I'm supposed to be a kid, a teenager." I wasn't. I didn't even know how to be a teenager. I hung with the greasers, the supposedly tough kids. They weren't tough. They dressed in leather jackets and threw around a lot of attitude, that's all. When I did go to a party, I felt out of place.

"Have a beer," they'd say.

"Beer? If I'm gonna drink, I'll have Absolut," I'd say. I thought I was too sophisticated for beer with these kids. Besides, what's the point of sitting around and getting drunk? After getting business done, that's when I would drink a little hard stuff with the old guys at the clubs.

I tried to go to parties, but I hated it. Nothing good came out of them. One time I stopped by the tail end of a party on the way home from playing foosball at one of the Italian-American clubs. A couple of gangster kids were with me. I walked into the house where one of the high school jocks lived. His football friends were all hanging around. They had this one gorgeous cheerleader, Mandy Lewis, sprawled out on the couch, totally drunk out of her gourd.

"Let's have a little fun," one jock, Stanley, said, getting the other guys all worked up. He started to unbutton her blouse. Another took off her shoes.

This was nuts.

"What do you think you're doing?" I demanded. "She's drunk. Almost unconscious."

"Mind your own goddamn business," Stanley shot back, as his football buddies laughed.

"This is rape!" I yelled. I was bold. "What's the matter with you? You fucking pervert!"

The two guys that had come with me were scrawny little greaser guys, Pete and Larry, all talk, no action. But I still went on, "If any of you goons touch her, I'll knock you upside the head."

"Who the fuck are you to tell us what to do?!" Stanley barked back at me.

By now they had Mandy half undressed. I decided to show him just who the hell he was messing with. I went back out to my car and got a tire iron. When I came back in, I saw they were taking Mandy's pants off.

I went ballistic, swinging the tire iron, breaking things in the house. Brian, another, older guy, who was already in college, got in front of me and we squared off. I looked him in the eyes, and for the first time ever, I said: "Do you know who I am? I'll have you killed! Do you know who I am?"

I said it like I was already somebody. I wasn't, but he didn't know for sure. But I was the gangster's son. When it clicked in this guy's head that I was Dominic's boy, he changed his tune.

"We don't want no problems with you," Brian said, suddenly humble.

He motioned to the other guys to back off, then told them to make Mandy presentable again. Pete, Larry, and I took her home. As she sobered up and realized what could have happened, Mandy was mortified, then very grateful. She and I became good friends. It made me feel good to help that girl. What they were doing was wrong.

Like it was wrong when the jocks picked on Jake Werner, the smartest kid in the school but also the ugliest, nerdiest guy around. And he wore a retainer. An old-fashioned kind that came out of his mouth and connected with wires around his head. The bullies would give him no peace. They'd pull down his pants to embarrass him, things like that. I'd tell them to leave him alone, but I also tried to tell him to like, maybe, get some nice clothes, ditch that wire thing until he was at home. I was the defender. My dad was like that.

Being someone who defended the weak made me popular with the girls. I'd get lucky most of the time, but I didn't really date. Once I picked a girl up at home and took her out for a real date. I even met her parents. But they knew about my family, and that was the end of the romance.

So I always went out with older girls. When I was a sophomore, senior girls and some in college liked to be with me. I was with lots of girls, but that year I saw Angela Sorrento in a whole new light. We had grown up together, same neighborhood, parties, family friends; her father worked closely with my father. Angela was older by a few years, a real looker who developed pretty early and was well put together. You know, the hair, the nails, the clothes just right, a great body, but I didn't think of her as anything other than one of the neighborhood girls until she was a senior in high school. Then we clicked.

What happened was, Angela's car broke down and it was inside the school shop. I was in there that afternoon and we started to chat. I could feel something going on between us. For the first time, I saw her as a very desirable female. I asked her about the guy I heard she was dating. Will, a tall, skinny, blond guy, was just starting trade school to become a mechanic. I never understood how Angela and Will could be together. I told her they didn't seem right for each other. Anyway, she didn't say much about him, but I told her I was getting into working out, doing a lot of weight lifting. I was going to the gym every day and every night, getting into shape. I suggested that she should come to the gym sometime. Right away, she invited herself to come with me the next night.

Angela picked me up at my house, looking hot even in a sweat suit. That girl had some great body. Even before we got to the community center gym, Angela was flirting like crazy. I loved it. The gym was a little crowded, so we went into an adjacent room used for wrestling. It had mats on the floor, it was empty and kinda dark, compared to the other parts of the gym. We tried doing a few situps. I held her ankles and she did a few, and then she grabbed me. She was an aggressive girl. She didn't want to work out, she wanted to make out. So we made out. We wrestled on the mats in the dark until it was time for the building to close. Out in her car, we talked some more and we made love. It just happened.

We started seeing each other every day for two or three months straight, even though Will was still in the picture. He would come home from trade school on the weekends. He'd see Angela during the day, and I'd date her at night. I don't think he knew about me. Since I wasn't being exclusive to Angela, she didn't feel she had to be exclusive to me. She wasn't crazy about that arrangement, but she couldn't stop me and didn't try. Angela let me be who I was. And she had to do what she had to do.

I was jumping every girl I could. There were several girls I'd go out with regularly. There was Corinne, who always gave it to me at the drive-in on Friday nights, and Roxanne, who only had sex on her brain. If I picked her up before school, she'd give it to me. We would do it on lunch breaks in a car or van. After school, we'd do it in her parents' basement. We'd be around my house together and she'd ask me to take her to the grocery store for something. It was just an excuse to get in the car and get some. Roxanne could have a box of three dozen condoms, and within a week they would be gone. I got pissed off with her after she fucked my cousin Marcello. She hung around for a while, but she got into the business and decided not to give it away for free anymore.

On and off at the same time, I dated a Swedish bombshell, Erica. When we got out of high school, she really developed into a gorgeous girl, and my father loved her. She loved to eat and he loved to eat. Whenever she was around, the two of them enjoyed big meals. She was an easygoing, fun girl but got too attached to me. My dad instigated that, and that made my mother mad. She liked Angela the best. So did I, but having a good time with the girls was the only thing I had in common with other guys my age. It was the most fun I had in high school.

Most other times I didn't feel like I fit in. One time, a couple of juniors were arguing, getting really loud at a diner. One guy was pissed off with the other because he was hitting on his girlfriend. They kept bickering like old ladies. So I finally got up and walked over to their table. I punched one guy in the face and told the other, "Be a man! Knock him upside the head and get it over with." That's what the old guys would do. They react right away, don't take crap from anybody.

The kids at the diner were stunned. "It was just an argument!"

they told me. I had to think about that. I was wrong, but I didn't know how to be all right around those kids.

I WAS HAPPY TO HAVE my own action with my dad's business. It was always more interesting than hanging with kids my own age, and full of its own surprises. There was a situation with a kid who accidentally shot another seventeen-year-old boy when they were playing Russian roulette. His father wasn't a connected guy, but he had connections. He called Sam DiNapoli all upset because he figured his kid could be in real big trouble. He needed help. Sam took me along when he went to fix things. I felt privileged to go along with him because Sam was like a second father to me. We had a tight bond from the time I was a kid and it grew tighter over the years.

He borrowed someone's van and picked me up at one of the social clubs and we went to Sam's friend's place, where the kid's body was. We knew nobody would be home because Sam told his friend to take his son out for a while. Sam rolled the kid up in a carpet that he had been bleeding on and the two of us carried him out of the apartment and put him in the back of a waiting van. Sam dropped me back at the club and that was the end of it. I don't know what happened to that body. It was the first time I ever helped move a dead one. I just did what I was told and never said a word. The thing was, I felt good that Sam trusted me. His approval was always the most important thing to me.

I was feeling a lot of other things, too, but I learned a while back to keep my feelings in check. When I saw that first dead person in my father's shoe store, I was taught it was no big deal. So, when I helped Sam move the body, even though the kid was only a year or two older than I was, and looked much younger, I told myself it was nothing to think about. Just a dead body. Not a person. A dead body, period. Any other person, who hadn't been around the kind of things I had already seen by high school, would have freaked out.

In my circles, if someone had to deal with a dead body, the first thoughts were about what could be done to get rid of it: chop it, bury it, burn it, whatever was fastest and brought the least attention. Even if you had nothing to do with the death, it was never good to have a dead body show up in your business, unless you were making a careful public statement so others would take notice, like my dad did with the rapist's body in his shoe store. I was trained by example to think logically about it, not to feel anything, and solve the problem. After a while, I didn't spend much time having to convince myself everything was okay. It was okay.

ABOUT THIS SAME TIME, my dad had an adult bookstore in Dixmoor, Illinois. There was a browsing fee of fifty cents to look around and use the peep show in the back. Couples weren't allowed to go back there together so no one could accuse the store of being used for prostitution. But one married couple, who knew Arnie, the manager, asked if they could go in the back and watch a dirty movie together. Arnie asked my dad if it would be okay.

Since they were married, Dad gave in and told Arnie, "Wait until we're gone and when the store is empty, go ahead, let 'em. But nothing kinky."

The couple laughed and agreed to be reasonable. Dad and I left to do some other business on the way home.

About fifteen minutes later, my dad and I were driving, and his car phone rang (he was one of the first guys in the neighborhood to have one of those big car phones).

"Michael, I gotta talk to your dad," said Arnie, sounding upset.

"He's driving," I told him. "What's the matter? You don't sound good."

"I'm sorry, but the guy and his wife had a problem," he said.

"What kind of problem?" I asked.

"The guy is dead," Arnie said.

"The guy is dead," I repeated to my dad.

"What guy?" Dad asked.

"The guy who was with his wife," I explained.

Meanwhile, Arnie jabbered in my ear, "He's dead, and his wife is hysterical, crying. He had a heart attack while he was doing her in the booth. Should we call somebody?"

I repeated this to my dad who said, "Fuck! No. Don't call nobody. Let me think."

"Arnie, where's the body right now?" I asked.

"Still in the booth," Arnie said. "His wife is in there, too, crying loud."

"They're your friends, Arnie," I quietly reminded him.

"Yeah, I know, but . . ."

"Get that body outta there!" my dad shouted, loud enough for Arnie to hear over the phone. "Take the body and put it across the street, make it look nice, leave it and call an ambulance."

Arnie heard him shout that, too. I didn't have to repeat it.

"Okay. Across the street." Arnie understood, and hung up.

We drove about another two blocks before Dad and I looked at each other and had the same thought.

"He's gonna fuck this up," Dad fumed. "I don't need any questions from the cops. I don't need the heat."

Dad made a U-turn and we headed back to the store. Sure enough, things weren't going very smoothly. As we pulled up to the store, we saw our two clerks carrying the dead guy across the street. He still had his dick hanging out of his pants while his wife ran alongside yelling, "What are you doing? What are you doing?"

From the car, my dad was yelling, "Put his dick back in his pants! What's the matter with you? Put his dick back in!"

It was as if the guy's wife finally saw her husband's indecent exposure. With a horrified look on her face, she ran up and stuffed her husband's privates back through his fly while the clerks were still trying to hustle the body across the street.

They no sooner put the body down and propped it against a building when, all of a sudden, we heard the *whoop-whoop* of a cop's car siren.

"What's goin' on here?" the officer demanded as he swaggered out of the car and over to ours.

My dad didn't let him say another word. He immediately said, "Sean, I'm glad you came along! I think this man needs medical attention."

The cop looked over at the guy, and turned back to my dad. "Dominic, that guy is dead."

"He don't look too good," Dad agreed.

"No, he don't," said the cop. "He's dead."

"Son of a bitch!" my dad said, looking down and shaking his head. "That's really too bad."

Sean looked at Dad and said, "I want to make sure he's got no holes in him."

"I'm insulted that you would suggest such a thing!" my dad shot back.

"Dominic, does he have any holes in him? Tell me the truth," the cop asked again.

"You're insulting me!" Dad repeated. "No. He ain't got no holes in him." And then my dad told Sean that the guy had been in the bookstore, had a very good time, and he expired. Just like that, nothing more.

By then, Sean had gotten a closer look at the guy, came back to our car, and was trying not to laugh in front of the guy's wife.

"Go home, Dominic," said Sean. "I'll take care of the wife and the body. Don't worry about anything. Go on home."

When we got home, my mom was cooking dinner, and as we came in, she asked how the day was.

"Some guy had a heart attack in the store and died," Dad said.

I added, "We put him across the street and propped him up."

Mom just kept cooking, never asked anything more, and commented, "Oh, that's good."

NOT EVERYTHING WAS LIFE AND DEATH. There was another time I was going to meet someone so we could collect some bookmaking money from a shopkeeper in a local mall outside New York City. I was waiting for him behind a strip mall that had some upscale shops. I was sitting in my car just minding my own business when I saw a van pull up near the garbage dumpsters. I watched. Two teenagers started rushing around, acting fidgety and jumpy. Then they loaded up their van with tons of heavy-looking garment bags. I knew they were up to something. It didn't look good. Then I saw that they were taking those bags out the back door of a furrier shop. And it was still daylight, summer, about eight o'clock in the evening. The mall shops closed at six.

My guy hadn't arrived by the time they finished loading the van, so I decided, "Well, fuck 'em." They were in my neighborhood and were robbing the joint. They were supposed to pay tax for that stuff and should have come to get permission. So I followed those two numb nuts to their house. As they pulled up the driveway, I pulled straight in, blocked their van, got out with a gun in my hand and put it to one of their heads and said, "You know what? You fucking robbed my neighborhood. I watched the whole fucking thing go down and now you gotta pay tax."

They were two scared-shitless punks, so I made them unload all those coats and put them in my car. I left them with two coats because, as I told them, they had some initiative, but fucked up. I told them that before their next score they should do the right thing: come get permission and give me a little bit of tribute. They nodded and I drove home with more than two dozen furs in my car. The next morning was like Christmas. I gave blue fox coats and jackets to my mother, some girls I knew, my aunts, to Paulie for his latest girlfriend, and I sold the rest.

THIS IS THE FUCKING STUFF that used to happen to me all the time. My dad loved to hear things like that fur story. "Genius. Innovative," he'd say, as he patted me on the back. But that deal was small stuff compared to the jobs he did, and jobs he turned away. The thing my father, like his father before him, hated most was drugs, but the thing he loved most, just like me, was the money. The hundreds of thousands of dollars in small bills coming through every week was a lot of money to move. Just to get that kind of cash from one state to another, you had to do more than a bank wire transfer. We had to physically move the money and because drug dealing was on the rise, things were hot. We were never drug dealers, but we were damn good at money laundering. Dad bought a produce company as a way to move the money. We used to take hundreds of thousands of dollars and put it in fruit boxes. We would put fifty thousand dollars in a crate of apples, peaches, plums, or bananas and cover it with more fruit and seal it. Those crates would get shipped to another state. There was always someone set up at the other end to handle it and take it somewhere else. "There is always a way," my father taught me.

Through high school I kept learning lessons of all kinds. There was something new all the time. I suppose I had sacrificed one thing for another; fun as a teenager for career training with the mob. I don't remember it being a conscious choice, but I finally came to terms with that, accepted it. I'll always be the gangster's son.

My mother, my father, they wanted me to be somebody. They wanted me to be a lawyer. My mother always told me, you should be a lawyer, you are such a good person, so smart, you know how to talk to people. My dad, he wanted me to be a doctor, because the cutting up and the blood never bothered me. The reality was that I didn't find any of that interesting. It was okay, but I wanted to be like my dad. I wanted to be a man that you feared and respected. I wanted to be a powerful individual.

My dad had no choice when I got older but to show me how to do things the right way. Because if he didn't show me, somebody else would. When someone's got his mind made up and is becoming a man, nobody can tell him what to do. My dad was a smart man, he saw that I was a smart kid. He figured well, if the kid is going to go that way, I am going to show him how to be the best he can be.

I got more satisfaction hanging out with guys three times my age. We talked about politics, which I loved; the stock market, economics, street business; we listened to classical music. I had an awesome collection of seventy-eight-speed records. I treasured them. Even alone, I listened to a lot of Mozart, Bach, and Beethoven. With the older guys, I was accepted. I was understood. I was where I belonged. Trying to fit in with teenagers only left me feeling frustrated and angry, tired of trying to be someone I wasn't. By the time I was sixteen, I felt like forty, and I knew what track my life would take. It would be, like my father's life and both grandfathers' lives, filled with danger, ambition, wealth, power, and brutality. There could be no other way.

SURVIVING AL'S HEART ATTACK

Lenny was always like a second father to me; Louie was like an uncle; and Paulie, my best friend. Two other guys who took me under their wings were Tony and Al. They were both my father's friends, in their sixties, and they controlled a major vending operation. They were like the odd couple, always bickering. No matter what the circumstances were, they were fun to be around.

Tony and Al had jukeboxes, cigarette machines, but of course, their big money came from poker machines, Cherry Masters in the back rooms of corner bars. They had controlling interest in plenty of bars and had millions of dollars in loans out on the streets. They were old gangsters who still did their own collecting.

"I'll go get my own fuckin' money," they'd say.

I had plenty of things going for myself by then, but I'd sometimes go out collecting money from the bars with them just to be around them. If we went into a bar and a guy tried to put us off, they'd rough him up a little. That's the way things were done.

We always came and went through back doors, through alleyways. One time, as we left, Al had the money in an envelope in his hand. Some guy in his twenties, who obviously didn't know who he was dealing with, tried to hold us up with a knife.

I told the guy, "Go fuck yourself."

The guy became belligerent, so Tony picked up a garbage can and tried to hit the kid with it. At the same time, I tried to tackle him. Al picked up another can and crashed it down on the guy, then picked up the lid and kept hitting him with it.

I wrestled with the guy, backed off to get out of the way of the flying cans, and came in for another tackle. That's when I fell and broke my arm.

Al and Tony never stopped smashing the punk, but Tony noticed I was holding my arm and in pain.

"Hey, Al, Michael's hurt!" he yelled as he kicked the punk.

"Let's take him to the hospital," Al answered. Still, as they were talking, neither of them missed a beat smashing the punk.

Finally, they dropped him cold and the three of us got into the front seat of the car. But Al couldn't find the keys.

"Tony," he asked, while he squirmed this way and that, "Where the hell are my keys?" He turned his pockets inside out.

"How the hell do I know where your keys are?" Tony answered.

"You had them last, didn't ya?" Al tried.

"Why the fuck would I have your keys?" snapped Tony.

"Just check your pockets," I yelled, getting into the act that began to feel like a Three Stooges episode.

I sat in the middle of those two guys, looking back and forth while they bickered over who lost the keys and where. Meanwhile, I was in quite a bit of pain.

Tony turned his pockets out and, lo and behold, there were Al's car keys. So we started off for the hospital. But none of us remembered how to get there. Al was driving and making turns in every direction until I realized we were just going round in circles.

"We gotta ask somebody for directions," Tony said more than once. But Al ignored him.

"I swear, he never stops for directions," Tony went on.

"Oh shut up already!" Al spat back. "If you know where the goddamn hospital is, you drive!"

"I don't know where it is and you don't either, and neither does the kid. So stop and ask somebody who knows!"

"How the hell do I know who knows?" Al yelled back, still refusing to stop.

"Fuck you, Al!"

"Fuck *you!*"

And then there was cold silence for a few minutes before they started arguing again. My arm was hurting more by the minute.

"For crissake, stop the car and ask this guy right here!" I jabbed Al with my good elbow. "Just ask him!"

Finally, Al slowed down enough for Tony to yell out the window and get directions from the pedestrian.

At the hospital, I sat down with the admitting clerk, but she no sooner started asking me questions than Al grabbed his chest and gasped that he was having pain. He held his hands to his chest and looked like he was going to pass out. So they ignored me and started taking his information.

"Hey, fuck the paperwork, get my buddies fixed up!" Tony bellowed and people came scurrying with wheelchairs. They took Al down the hall first. While one doctor was checking my arm and ordering X rays, another team of people took care of Al. They had him stripped down to his boxer shorts and tank tee, but he insisted on keeping his tweed beanie cap on his head and his shoes on as he lay there in bed with EKG wires attached to his chest, arms, and legs.

After the film of my arm came back, they saw the fracture, set it, and put the plaster cast on it. I was glad they gave me something for the pain.

From down the hall I could hear Al yelling, "Bring me back my pants! All my money is in there."

Tony had gone to the men's room as soon as the wheelchair came for us, so he didn't know where they had taken Al. But he heard him and tried to follow the voice, while he was also yelling, "Al, where the hell are you?"

"I'm in here," Al shouted. "I can't move with all these fucking wires on me. Where are my pants? Tony, find my money."

"Okay Al, but where are you?"

Tony was upsetting everyone as he moved through the emergency room corridors, peeking into rooms and behind drapes as he went.

"Where's Michael?" Al yelled out. "Wha' they do to him? Is he okay?"

"Just relax, Al," Tony yelled, loud enough for the whole place to hear. "I'll find you. I'll find the kid, too."

"I'm okay," I yelled from my cubicle around the next corner.

"Michael? Where are you?" Tony shouted.

By now, Al was totally out of patience and no longer in any pain. He pulled off the EKG wires, found all his clothes on a chair outside his drapes, picked them up and started walking around looking for me. He was dragging his shirt behind him when Tony ran into him.

"I got to know how Michael is," Al insisted. They found me, just sitting on a bed, listening to the commotion. The shot the nurse had given me had made me very, very mellow.

I took one look at Al standing there with only his hat on and not much else, holding his shirt and pants, and I had to fight real hard not to laugh.

Al threw his arms up and asked, "Well?"

"I'm already done and ready to go," I told him. "They just want me to sign some papers."

"To hell with that," Al huffed. "Let's go."

We walked out the door with Al still in his underwear and a nurse running after us.

"You both have to sign some papers," she insisted, as she trotted along.

"And you, sir," she addressed Al, "We have to make sure you're okay."

"Fuck the paperwork, honey," Al blustered. "I'm not signing out. I never signed in."

"But, sir . . ." she tried again. She wouldn't let go.

Al turned in front of her and stopped her in her tracks, as a doctor also ran up to us. "Hey, listen up. Nobody did much of anything for me. Just hooked me up to some wires."

The doc and nurse didn't know what to say for a moment, then looked at me.

"Okay," Al gave an exasperated sigh, "Here's some cash. It should cover everything."

"No, give me your address, we'll send you a bill," the doctor tried, but Al shoved the cash in the doctor's pocket.

"Fuck the bill," Al said, while me and Tony edged to the nearby car and opened the doors.

The doctor finally just rolled his eyes, put his arms up in surrender and waved us off. He and the nurse turned around and walked away.

Al started toward the car and stopped, looked down and asked, "Where are my pants?"

"In your hand," Tony said, shaking his head.

"Oh," was all Al said as he began to put them on. He bent over and put a foot in one leg and tried to pull them on but hopped around on one leg. He struggled and finally noticed he had his shoes on.

"Give him a hand," I said quietly to Tony.

"No way," he said. "When he gets like this, it's better to stay ten feet away until he gets himself straight."

Al leaned on a car, took off his shoes and got dressed before getting into the driver's seat.

Back at my house, we walked in and my mom saw my cast and wanted to know what had happened.

Immediately, Al and Tony started talking at the same time.

"We went out to get something to eat," said Al. "The restaurant floor was wet, and Michael slipped."

Tony opened his mouth with, "We stopped by the rink, and Michael wanted to skate and fell."

My mom never believed anything that came out of their mouths anyway, so she just looked at me. And, not to embarrass them further, I just said, "I fell."

Of course, later, I told her the whole story, except about the actual business we had been doing, because we never discussed those things with the women in the family. But getting jumped in the alley and, especially the drive to the hospital and what went on when we got there, was enough without giving her information she didn't need. She had a good laugh.

Did Al actually have a heart attack? Who knows? It was more likely indigestion.

7

SMOKEY AND SOUTHERN DISCOMFORT

Cousin Paulie was sent to take care of some business in Kentucky. Back in the late seventies, there was a time when we could buy up old coal mine land real cheap. We also brought video poker machines to the country taverns. Paulie was a great salesman, a terrific opener. He really did have some smarts, even if he didn't have the muscle. When negotiating came down to the wire, he'd go soft, so somebody had to take up his slack, and make sure the deal didn't go sour. So a couple of us were sent to visit him in redneck country for a week. It was really just a show of strength in numbers. I went with some other cousins, Marcello, Anthony, and Ricky. We were just kids, all sixteen and seventeen, but we looked older.

It was summer and we had been in New York. My dad got me

a good deal on a car. I bought a brand new Lincoln Towncar, Signature Series. It was a sharp-looking four-door; silver, with plush gray velour inside, with power everything in it. I really wanted to take it out of the city and hit the road. So we planned to visit Paulie, first in Nashville to see some friends and talk about some poker machine business, and then go back to Kentucky.

We made good time out of New York, but we got lost in Princeton, Kentucky. I got off the parkway for gas. The sign said there'd be gas at the next exit, so we took it. And drove for what seemed like twenty minutes of twists and turns on back roads before we finally came to the gas station. We got our gas, used the john, got back into the car and headed back to the parkway. But we got lost. Couldn't find the friggin' parkway. It was almost eleven in the morning. We kept driving but we didn't see anything but fields.

Then Ricky called out, "Hey, Michael, there's a guy on a tractor. Go ask him."

I looked, and sure enough, there was a guy about a half mile off the road working his field. So I pulled over, got out and started waving to him. When he finally saw us, he drove that tractor on over to the fence, got down and strolled over to me. He was a tall man and wore denim overalls and a cap with John Deere lettered on it, to match the words on his tractor. He said nothing, just walked over to me.

So I started. "Excuse me. Can you tell me how to get back to the parkway?"

He took his hat off, scratched his head, and pondered a moment before he asked, "Well, where you going?"

"Nashville."

"Oh. Who's you going to see out there?"

"I don't think you know him," I said. "A friend of ours."

"Oh. Where are you boys from?"

"We are from New York," I said slowly and clearly, beginning to wonder if the noise of the tractor had affected his hearing. "We are just traveling. Can you tell me how to get back on the parkway?"

"Oh. Well," he said, looking back down the road, "if you go out this way," he continued, pointing, "go down yonder, oh, about five or six oak trees which takes you over two hills. Then you turn left at the third hill; go down a spell, go a little farther yonder and you will see it."

I looked at him. "Are you serious?"

"Oh. Yeah. That's the way."

I walked away. I could see I was getting nowhere. I was talking to Forrest Gump. He turned and headed back to his tractor, and I got back into the car.

My three cousins saw me talking to the guy, but didn't hear. The air conditioning was on, and the windows were rolled up.

"So, where are we at?" Ricky asked.

"Just a fucking spell away. Don't worry about it."

"But where are we and how do we get back on the parkway?"

"Don't fucking ask. I have no fucking clue, a couple hills or something," I said and repeated what Farmer Forrest told me, as well as I could remember.

So we started driving again, now yelling at each other.

I asked, "How many oak trees was that?" I mean there's twenty thousand trees around us.

"How the fuck do I know one tree from another?" barked Anthony.

I don't know. I was fucking lost. Then we came up on a tomato stand. There was a nice middle-aged lady selling her tomatoes. We bought a couple and stood there eating them.

Finally, after a little bit of chit-chat, I told her, "We are so lost. Could you please explain to me how to get back on the parkway?"

"Oh. Where are you boys going?"

"We're going to Nashville," I said.

"Oh. Who you going to see?"

At this point I had to say, "I think you have a brother somewhere down the road."

"I do?" she said, looking at me a little surprised. "Well, I do have relations down there. . ."

I interrupted her. "That's great. Can you tell me how to get to the parkway?"

"Oh. You are just a spell away."

"Could you be more accurate?" I knew I had to push. "Like, is it two or three miles or more?"

She calmly said, "It's just down yonder, and if you go . . ." and she proceeded to give me the same kind of fucked-up directions with hills and trees. I was looking at her like she had to be kidding, but she wasn't.

I turned around and we got back into the car, still trying to figure out what it meant to be a spell away. Close, I guess. But what the fuck is a spell? And how far is down yonder?

So we headed off again, down this narrow two-lane road, trying to figure out what the heck this secret country code was all about. Only a few minutes went by when out of nowhere a cop car came up on us. It was one of those older models with those old big ball lights on top.

Hey, I was driving okay, not speeding or nothing. Why get lost faster? Anyway, the guys get riled, arguing, "We ain't done nothing." I told them to just keep their mouths shut and relax because I'd handle it. Sure enough, those big old lights on the cruiser got bright and started spinning. Son of a bitch.

So I pulled over and again told everyone to keep their mouths shut. We sat there and the officer got out of his unit. A big, beer-bellied Smokey the Bear sheriff approached with the wide-brimmed hat and real dark sunglasses that made it impossible to see his eyes. He lugged his almost three hundred pounds over to my side, eyeing the car and us as he lumbered up.

Believe me, in the South, people do not like us. We had a big fancy car with New York plates. We were kids dressed in beautiful slacks and shirts. Nice jewelry. Typical hoodlum gangster kids.

I already had the window down. "How ya' doin' officer?" I asked. "As for us, we're a little bit lost . . ."

"Boy, do you know what you just did?" he interrupted.

"No, I didn't do nothing."

"You crossed the line and you didn't use the turn signal."

For a second I was speechless. I looked at the road. This was a two-lane country road, without any painted line.

"There is no line," I said.

"Are you calling me a liar?" he answered back.

"Absolutely not," I said trying not to sound smart.

But there was no line.

"Good," he said, trying to stare me down.

So then I said, "All right, you want to fine me, okay. Can I pay it now?"

He glared at me and asked for my driver's license. I handed it over with the registration.

"Oh. New York City."

"We are a little lost . . ." I tried again, but now one of my cousins rolled down the window and yelled out, "Whatever you do, you can't fucking open the trunk up. You need a fucking warrant."

I turned to Anthony and yelled, "Shut the fuck up!"

Smokey looked at me and said, "Boy, don't you cuss. What's in that trunk?"

"Nothin'," I said, but of course, he didn't believe me, but I added, "They're just trying to bust your fucking balls."

"There you go again with that mouth of yours," he said and raked under my chin with my license. "Shut up."

Anthony was still mouthing off. "You can't open the trunk."

Marcello piped up, "Whatever you think we did, we didn't do it. We weren't even around when it happened." I swear, they were acting like kids.

Now Smokey waddled back to the trunk and everyone piled out of the car. He had us put our hands on top of our heads, then told me to open the trunk. I did, and wise-ass Anthony said, "Geez, son of a bitch. I can't believe those fucking suitcases aren't leaking." I smacked him right in the back of the head as I reminded him, "Shut the fuck up."

Smokey reprimanded me for swearing again, called for his deputy and handcuffed us.

"What are you arresting us for?" I asked.

"Obstructing justice and intimidating a police officer," he said.

When his deputy arrived, they put two of us in each car and hauled us off to jail, where he put us all in one of the three cells in the building.

Before he walked out, I told him again, "Hey, you want us to pay a fine? Let's do it right now and get it over with. We will plead guilty."

"Oh. Okay. That will be five hundred dollars apiece," he said as he turned to me.

"Five hundred each? Are you fucking nuts? We are not paying no two thousand dollars. We didn't do nothing. You can just leave us here."

"I told you boys not to cuss!" he shot back as he walked out leaving us to sit on the benches in the cell.

About a half hour later, a nice chubby woman named Myrna came in and asked for our lunch order. Now this was something new. It was almost two o'clock in the afternoon, so we were starving. So when Myrna started telling us what she had on the menu, we started drooling.

Myrna came back in about twenty minutes carrying a picnic basket with our food: homemade meatloaf with gravy, green beans, cornbread, and apple crisp for dessert. Oh my God! We couldn't believe this. It was beautiful.

For dinner, Myrna made us southern fried chicken with mashed potatoes and gravy. We had coconut cream pie for dessert. This was feeling pretty good.

Later that evening, Smokey came by and said, "If you boys aren't going to pay that fine, you are going to be doing some time in here."

We told him we were not paying.

In the early morning, again he came in. "When are you paying that fine, boys? You are gonna pay it, 'cause I know you got plenty of money."

We all stood up and looked at him. Then I said, "What? Are you nuts? This morning Myrna is bringing biscuits and gravy. We're going nowhere."

He looked at us, took fifty bucks from each of us and kicked us out just as Myrna came in. Those biscuits and gravy sure smelled good, so we went across the street to her tiny hole-in-the-wall, greasy spoon restaurant and had our breakfast while sitting on old-fashioned pole stools at the counter. But the food was great, and Myrna was a sweetheart.

So we finished eating and got ready to get back on the road. But we were still lost, so I asked Myrna how to get back to the parkway.

"Well, boys, you're just a spell away. If you just go down by that gas station, turn left and go down yonder, you'll run into it."

We looked at each other and didn't say a word except, "Thanks, Myrna. Have a nice day."

We were the crime wave for that month.

Thank God, we found the gas station, and the attendant there was from Chicago and told us how to get to the parkway.

He said, "Go left for a quarter of a mile and take the road on the right. That will take you to the parkway."

Then I asked, "What is a fucking spell?"

He didn't know either.

WHEN WE GOT INTO NASHVILLE, Paulie asked what took us so long. I told him we got tied up down yonder, a spell away, and not to ask anything more.

So we went to work. We worked with a beer distributor out of Nashville who put in taps in the local taverns. He was kind of an associate who gave us leads to the bar owners who were weak, having trouble paying their bills. He got his kickback from us for doing that. We went and had meetings with them. We told these people, "Look, we can put these poker machines in here. If you have a good customer, you can give him a good payout on one every now and then. If not, hey, the poker machines are for amusement only."

At first the Southerners were hard to deal with. So many were churchgoing hypocrites. They prayed to hit the jackpot. They pretended not to drink in their dry counties and went over the Tennessee-Kentucky state line or to a wet county like Hopkinsville just a few miles away and loaded up on beer, and went to the local whorehouse. And they gambled. At first, they acted holier than thou. But the universal language was, and always is, money. We used sit down with a bar owner and after a few drinks, he'd admit that business was not doing so great.

Then I'd turn on the pitch. "Buddy, I'm not here to judge you. I know you're having a hard time and I can help solve your problem. Here is the deal: I can put poker machines and jukeboxes in here and I can help you out financially now and then."

I'd explain that the machines could bring in two thousand a week and—*ca-ching!*—their eyes would light up. That was all they had been making in a month. This was astronomical business to them. The cut was sixty-forty between me and the bar owner. They were my machines and I was the bank. If the joint was big, maybe fifty-fifty.

Putting in the vending machines was just the first step in a bigger plan. After we got everybody gambling, the next thing we did was bankroll these guys. The objective was to bring gambling customers in and keep them. So we suggested things like payday Friday fish fries to bring guys in after work. They'd cash their paychecks at the bars and spend their money.

At first the bar owners were, "No, no, no! I don't have that kind of money!" I reminded them that the businesses employing these guys are local and the checks are good. "No, no! I don't have the cash to put out!" they argued.

Well, that's when I explained, "We're going to bankroll you. I'll give you ten, fifteen thousand dollars, and you become just like a bank. You cash their checks and deposit them in the account we set up. And you make sure those guys put most of that money in the fuckin' machines."

Those bar owners recognized they had something good. Their customers not only cashed their checks and played the machines, but by the end of the night many took out a hundred-dollar loan so they could make it through the week. Paulie brought some girls out there, too. Asian girls were a big thing, very exotic for the hillbillies (and a few ministers, too). The local political people—the deputy, county clerk, assessor—were in our pockets in no time. They were ours before they knew it. When their loans started adding up, we went and visited them and let them know who they owed. After a short time, we manipulated whatever we wanted out of everybody.

At the same time, Paulie found old coal mines that were stripped, just holes in the ground. We bought up that land for five hundred dollars an acre. A whole area with coal mines cost maybe twenty thousand dollars. We bought up several large mining sites.

Waste management companies charged hospitals, clinics, and dental offices a lot of money to handle their disposal. And they, in turn, had to pay big money for an authorized place to dispose hazardous waste. Or they took it to us. A steady stream of semi-trucks rolled up to the mines, and filled them with waste. Bulldozers packed the waste down into the old mines along with sand and cement. When one mine was filled, we sealed it up and went to the next.

On a big scale, the operation brought in tens of millions a year. My thing with the bars was small by comparison but it gave us the political leverage we needed so there weren't a lot of questions asked about what we did with the mines. Town councilmen and people like that weren't going to get in our way when they owed us money. They were gambling, whoring, and owing money. I told them, "I don't care what you do, so don't care what I'm doing. Just pay your debts."

And with nice interest, too.

TOWARD THE END OF OUR BUSINESS in that area, five of us were sitting in a Louisville bar and some local cowboys swaggered in and got sarcastic about how we were dressed in suits and wore fancy shoes instead of boots. They were mostly addressing their remarks to Paulie, who tried to ignore these jerks, but a couple of us didn't like it one bit, got hot and wanted to kick ass.

"Don't let them talk to you like that, Paulie," we told him, but he stayed passive.

I was ready for a fight, but this was Paulie's call. I was aching to bust those rednecks' smirking faces and leave them all on their busted asses. It was hard for me not to start swinging at those sissies, wearing high heeled boots.

It was the first time Paulie realized he couldn't control me or protect me anymore. "Oh my God, you are just like Dominic," he said, kind of stunned. "But you can't just beat everybody up."

"That's how you get respect," I reminded him. "You can't let them talk to us like that."

Even though they said nothing, I could see Marcello, Ricky, and Anthony agreed with me, and were anxious to take care of those troublemakers on the spot.

"I'll take care of everything tomorrow," Paulie said. He wasn't going to raise a finger right there. I knew then that Paulie would never be someone to count on when the chips were down. I was quick to action; he was a talker, but hated confrontation of any kind. In that respect, he was weak.

One of the cowboys turned to me and asked, "You got a problem?"

I was only sixteen, but I was very husky and already looked like I was in my mid-twenties. With Joey and Anthony, I knew we could handle these guys if we had to make them eat their words. I stood square, looked him in the eyes and said, "No, *you* got the fucking problem."

He sized me up, chilled out, and backed off with his buddies.

So yeah, I was just like my father. I said what I had to say and would've done whatever I had to do because I didn't take nothing from nobody. That was the first time Paulie and I were together in a situation and I took control. He used to keep an eye on me, try to protect me as I was growing up. Things were changing and he knew I wasn't the same kid anymore.

A BULLET TO THE SOUL

Back in Chicago again, Paulie and I would meet for several hours every day at the candy store on Rush Street. It had an adult bookstore behind it and that's where we did a lot of our plotting. Quite often, we had dinner together, enjoying ourselves. He was always good company and we would talk about all kinds of stuff, from broads to politics and religion, mix in some business plotting and often end the evening with some hot women. There was never anything I couldn't discuss with him. He never judged me.

I matured very quickly. Being around adults so much, I had a large vocabulary and I always acted older than my years. I had also become very aggressive in my early teens and learned the business very quickly. I made deals with bar owners in Tennessee and

Kentucky; I helped with the coal mine negotiations; I knew how to conduct myself in any situation. Paulie could see I was growing up fast, and it was no surprise that I soon changed my attitude toward him. He just wasn't mean enough for me. He was smart and took no shit. He would talk another guy down, but if that failed, he had nothing to back it up.

But the man had a good heart. He loved his father, loved his mother, and was very family-oriented. He came to all the functions; he never disrespected us or failed to show up. He was a very caring man and we had to respect him for that. I think that outweighed and overshadowed everything else. But it always came down to covering for him, and we doubted he could be counted on if we needed him to cover our backs.

Whenever my dad was away, Paulie would come and take my mother to dinner. He bought my parents a Jacuzzi and threw parties for them. He loved people and worshiped my dad. My mother knew he was a playboy and would always be a womanizer, but he was a handsome man, and he had to do his thing. My dad loved him. Paulie was a good earner. People would complain, "Paulie did this, Paulie did that," but we loved him anyway.

SAM DiNAPOLI AND NICK NAPOLITANO were my truest mentors. Nick, who was born in Italy, got into this Family at an early age and became a hitter, an assassin. He was a specialist and did the jobs that no one else could do. His orders came from bosses in Italy, although for a time, he took orders from my grandfather D'Angelo. About the time of my grandfather's death, Nick got connected with the CIA and other political people and nobody would touch him because they never knew for sure who he was working with. He was so dangerous that nobody wanted to fuck with him. He did business worldwide. Nick could tell any boss in the States to go fuck himself.

Sam couldn't do that, but he didn't follow the rules as closely as most other guys. He was an in-house cleaner, another hit man, who got away with working for several different bosses and doing freelance hits as well. Everybody accepted that because Sam had the balls to do it. At the same time, he made enough money every month to kick money up to the bosses. So everybody was happy.

Both Nick and Sam were serious personalities, respected for their ability to get any job done, not just hits, and were often asked for even benign favors. They liked doing things for people. I learned a lot from them, and I learned it fast. I wanted to prove myself in the eyes of my childhood heroes. I didn't always know they were killers. It's not like they bragged about it, but I saw how people reacted to them. I knew they were important men, and both Sam and Nick became very significant influences in my life.

Joe Figorelli, one of the best bosses of Chicago, commented that an associate who was causing trouble for the Family had to be eliminated. I knew what he was talking about. The problem was a guy called Yani, who was involved with bookmaking and was stealing from the Family. He was also arrogant and ignorant, with a big mouth. That's always a potential danger. Yani was married to one of the bosses' daughters and was not only unfaithful to her, but he beat her. That was the final straw.

When the daughter came to her dad for help, it became a Family matter. When someone's private matters become Family business and known to everyone, it's embarrassing to all of us. It's a problem that has to be taken care of, one way or another.

Before I could fully digest what this really entailed, I stepped up to the plate. I heard myself say, "I can take care of that."

There was a brief moment of silence. This reaction was not what I had expected. It was as if I had stuck my nose in the wrong place.

"Oh? Okay, you go ahead," Joe said, with doubt in his voice. "Let's see if you can take care of this problem."

He obviously didn't think I was up to the job. It was now not only a challenge for me but a situation from which I could not back down. The only way out was to do the job.

I had listened and learned a lot from people around me. Everyone remembers the one mistake they should never have made, so I had to make sure there were no mistakes. It had to be perfect. There was no room for concern about what I was actually going to do. Taking a life was much further back in my mind than what I had to do not to get caught.

There were three intense days of planning. I knew Yani's routine, and studied it more carefully. At nine at night, he closed up his furniture store and counted his day's take. He never got home until after eleven. This was the prime opportunity to get him alone.

I went to his store about nine-thirty at night and knocked on the back door. He unlocked it and let me inside. I told him I had to use the restroom and talked about maybe playing some cards later that night.

My heart was beating a thousand times a minute, but I played cool. I hung around the store, telling him I was interested in getting some new armchairs for my parents. He was doing his count. We were making small talk. I wandered around the store looking at things. The point was to have the opportunity to be behind him as I did the job.

Finally, the moment came. I came up quietly behind him and raised my .22 with a silencer attached. As my arm came up, he turned around and faced me and looked stone cold into my eyes. There was no time for him to be anything but totally shocked. Before he even gasped, I pulled the trigger. His face, blood and brains splattered all over me. We had been too close.

I felt my blood pressure rising, my heart pounding. I felt hot, sweaty. I could barely control the shaking coming over me. But I was in control. I took the cash, making it look like a robbery. I left the body for the police.

Yani had a shower in the back of the store. I ran the water and stepped, with all my clothes and shoes on, into the heavy spray. I stood there until I felt the mess was off me, and left soaking wet.

Nobody was home. I changed and tried to burn the clothes in the fireplace. Because they were still wet, they wouldn't catch fire. It pissed me off, but I had to laugh. I pulled them out again and put them in the dryer. Finally, I got them to burn to ashes in the fireplace before I headed out to the club where I knew I'd find Joe.

I sat down at the card table with him and played a few hands. We talked about nice things, the weather, the business. Then after about twenty minutes, I commented, "I took care of that problem you mentioned the other day."

"Good," he said and nodded. Good. No more discussion about it. There never was. He ordered us a drink. I drank it and left.

JUST DAYS AFTER I TURNED seventeen, I had made my first hit. I did the job, and to everyone around me, it seemed I handled it without a sweat.

Only when I got home again did I start to understand the weight of what I had done. Only then did my mind keep going over the moments that had led, one by one, to that eternally irrevocable second when the bullet left the chamber of my gun and bore into the brain of "the problem." Only then, when I was home alone, did the problem become a man with a wife and a baby. And finally, by the time the sun rose again, after a night of pounding down the images, it had become merely a problem, eliminated, and to be forgotten. But I could not forget that I had sold my soul. It was done. The rush, the power, the promise of wealth and status swept me, quite willingly, along. I put aside my emotions, closed down my thoughts, and followed my fate.

9

FRED'S SPECIAL FUNERAL

After I took care of the Yani problem, I kept up my usual routine, but I hung out with Al and Tony more because they made me laugh. As part of their vending business, they had loaned money to Fred, a bar owner who became five months behind on his payments. Since he not only had been a customer for a long time but brought in a lot of money from the poker machines in his joint, cashed checks for everybody, and was an all-around good guy, Tony and Al cut him some slack. Still, it got to a point where they decided to sit him down and have a friendly talk. They called him and arranged to meet him at the bar at seven in the morning. Since Fred was a boozer, they wanted to talk to him while he was more likely to be sober and really hear what they had to say. They also called me to meet them at Fred's bar so that after they collected some money, we would go have breakfast.

I got there just after seven, walked in, and nobody was around. So I called out, “Anybody here? Where’s everybody?”

There was a noise from the back and in a few seconds, Al and Tony both came out. No Fred.

“So what’s going on?” I asked.

“You’re not gonna believe this,” Tony started.

“Lemme tell Michael,” Al interrupted.

“Wha? I can’t talk?” Tony voiced his annoyance. “We came in here right at seven . . .”

“It was six-forty,” Al interrupted again. “I know. I looked at my watch.”

“Your watch is fucked,” Tony shot back. “And I’m tellin’ this story.”

“You’re tellin’ the story. So tell it, big shot,” Al said as he threw up his hands and pulled back a barstool and sat down.

Tony looked at him and shook his head and stepped behind the bar as I took a stool, too.

“So like I was sayin’,” Tony started again, shooting Al a glare. “We came in here this morning and we see Fred, sleeping on the bar, like this,” and Tony put his head down on top of his crossed forearms.

“No,” Al corrected. “He was on this side, sitting on a stool, with his head down on his arms.”

“Well, yeah,” said Tony, “Of course he was on that side. He couldn’t be standing behind the bar and sleeping like this and not fall down! He was sitting on a stool, but he had his head down like this,” he showed me again.

“Sound asleep,” Tony said as he lifted his head. “So me and Al walk up to him real quiet so we can make him jump.”

“That’s when I stuck my finger in his back like it was a gun and jabbed him,” Al piped up.

“But Fred don’t move,” Tony added.

"So I smack him in the head and yell, 'Wake up!' and Michael, get this, he falls off the stool," Al said.

"He's dead!" Tony cut in.

"He's dead!" Al echoed.

Now I'm surprised and had to ask, "Com'on, did ya whack him? He didn't pay?"

"No, honest," Tony continued. "He was just dead. No holes. No strangle marks . . ."

"He's just dead," Al repeated. "Musta been a heart attack or a stroke or something."

"No shit! You're not puttin' me on?" I asked, still skeptical.

"No way," Tony insisted. "A stroke or heart attack for sure. He was already cold."

"He was just fuckin' dead! Comon, lemme show ya," Al said as he got off his stool and gave me a move-along shove.

The three of us went to the storeroom and, sure enough, Fred was definitely dead, without holes or any other marks from what I could see.

Back out in the bar, we sat down at a table.

"So now what?" I asked, more to make conversation than anything else. "What about breakfast?"

Both Al and Tony just sat without saying nothing for a few seconds.

"Yeah, I'm hungry, too," Al finally said.

"You two are hungry? We gotta figure out what we're going to do here," Tony said.

"Can you believe that fucker died? Geez," Al said and shook his head. "And he owed us money, the sonovabitch."

As soon as Al said that, Tony got up and went behind the bar again. He opened the cash register, counted out the cash, and found the keys to the place.

"I know what to do," Tony said. "Let's go. Put up the 'closed' sign. I wanna have breakfast."

"What are you gonna do?" I asked.

"Have pancakes, eggs, and sausage," Al answered before Tony could.

"I mean about this?" I asked.

Tony flipped the sign on the door around and came back to the table and sat down. "We're gonna keep this place. It's ours now."

"No shit!" said Al. "I like that."

"Fred had nobody," Tony said. "He had this place for, what, forty years? The old guy didn't have family, not even a girlfriend. Who's gonna complain?"

"Nobody," Al agreed and smiled. "Yeah, I like that idea. But I ain't tending bar. We gotta hire a couple of guys."

"Yeah, we'll stay closed for a few days," said Tony, "and then open up like nothing happened. Fred's gone. That's all."

So they locked up the place and we went to breakfast.

Three days later, we came back. They were there to meet some people who wanted to work there. We were in there maybe a half hour when the beer guy showed up to make a delivery.

Al was going over some of the books and just waved the guy off with, "Just put it where you always put it."

Tony finished talking to one of the guys that came in looking for work and came to the table and sat down. He picked up some of the bank statements and read them.

The beer guy came back. "The storeroom door is locked," he told us. "And it stinks back there."

I realized what the smell must have been. So did Al, who looked at Tony, who looked at me and back to Al. The beer guy just looked at the three of us and waited.

In whispers, Tony turned to Al and berated, "You forgot!"

"I forgot?" Al tried to shout in a hush. "*You* fuckin' forgot!"

The beer guy was only four feet away, wondering what was going on. "Are one of you gonna unlock the storeroom?" he asked. "I got other deliveries to make today."

"Ah, no," started Al.

Tony finished for him, "No, we forgot the key. I gotta go home and get it."

"So just dump the beer inside the back door," Al picked up the rest.

"Yeah, don't be late because of us," Tony added.

The beer guy unloaded and left.

When we opened up the storeroom doors, oh my God! There were flies buzzing and maggots crawling all over his face. Fred was the worst-smelling corpse I ever knew. The three of us wanted to gag. We went back to the table.

"What are you gonna do with the body?" I asked.

Al suggested, "I think we should have a funeral for him. He was a friend of ours."

Tony barked, "He fuckin' owes us money. You gonna shell out money for a funeral?"

"We should do the right thing," Al protested.

It was hard for me not to laugh. These two men, who were really very vicious, were a couple of comedians and didn't even know it.

"Do the right thing?" Tony barked again. "He didn't do the right thing. He owed us money."

"I still say we should have a funeral," Al insisted.

"Wait a minute," Tony said with a big smile. "I gotta idea."

He got up and made a phone call. When he came back he said, "I just arranged for Fred's funeral. You happy, Al?"

"Yeah, that's the right thing," he said, placated.

Tony made the arrangements to have Fred dumped that night in a cemetery hole, one that was going to be used for a funeral the next day. He paid the gravedigger a hundred bucks to throw enough dirt over Fred to cover him. The digger knew Fred, drank in his bar all the time, but didn't recognize him anymore. And we didn't tell him who it was.

But Al did ask him, "What time is the burial service tomorrow?"

The next day, Tony and Al decided we should go pay our respects. So we went to the burial of the guy who really had a funeral. There were maybe forty, fifty people there at the graveside service and we just mixed into the crowd and sat down.

Tony and Al got emotional. Al sat next to some guy and said out loud, "Poor Fred. He was a good guy."

The mourner looked at Al and said, "Fred? It's Brian McManus."

"Yeah, yeah, I know," said Al, sniveling for effect. "I'm so upset, I got confused. I'm just a little emotional over this whole thing."

Tony pitched in to cover, "Brian was a good guy. We're gonna miss him. May he rest in peace."

The other mourner kept talking to us. Soon he asked if we were going to the buffet after the service.

"What are they serving?" Al asked with a straight face.

"We're supposed to be across town in an hour," Tony tried to get Al to shut up.

"Where's it gonna be?" Al persisted.

The mourner gave him all the information and said it was going to be a real Irish feast with lots to eat and drink. There would be music, too. And singing. The guy was really trying to get us to go reminisce about dear old Brian.

Al was really getting into it and Tony kept jabbing an elbow into Al's side, saying, "We really have to keep that appointment across town."

Finally, the prayers were said and the casket was lowered. Right on top of Fred. People moved by in a line tossing flowers. Fred got his funeral.

I think Al really wanted to go to the luncheon. But Tony made sure we just left when everybody else did. We didn't go to the Knights of Columbus Hall.

Back at Fred's bar, business went on as usual without him. After a few months everybody stopped asking where Fred had gone. Any time anybody asked, they were told, "He won the lottery and left. Who the fuck knows where he went?"

Nobody ever knew what happened to Fred. Nobody ever came looking for him. Nobody.

10

BECOMING A BIG SHOT

At seventeen, I already had many responsibilities. I was working in Family restaurants like Fellini's and the Ashford House; at Frank's Produce; in liquor stores stocking shelves; and picking up money from different businesses. I also started helping at my dad's men's clubs. He owned a dozen, and another sixty were under his supervision; he also had fifty adult bookstores. I would work behind the bars at the clubs, and eventually, I managed some of them. Louie and Lenny always told me, "You got to start coming up with your own projects if you want to make it in this world. Be a producer. Produce money and you'll be somebody."

There are a lot of different ways to make money in Family businesses. I did my homework and watched people around me.

Bookmaking, gambling, loan sharking, and creating businesses that were certain to be repossessed by the Family were a few of the ways to bring in revenue.

Bookmaking is still just a way of placing bets with an outside source, a bookie, instead of at the racetrack or a casino. It's a convenience for the bettor and brings plenty of money to the bookie. Everybody loves to gamble, whether it's sports, bingo, or blackjack.

When I was young, there were private gambling clubs, which were not the same as the social clubs where we just hung out. Gambling clubs were set up with blackjack and craps tables, and an entire room for bookmaking. These were in every city, and in New York, they were spread out all over Manhattan, Brooklyn, and Queens.

When people gambled, they drank and then got horny. If a guy scored really big, he'd want a couple of whores, so the manager made sure there were enough of them around. The point was to always get as much of the money back again. If a guy won big and he didn't want a whore, it was good to get him drunk so he'd gamble more. Some of the games were fixed. With blackjack, some important cards were taken out to make sure the odds favored the house. With craps, either the dice were loaded or there were a few shills, guys who were playing but worked for the house, manipulating the attitude of the game.

The government quickly realized the best way to stop the black market from making money on anything was to legalize it. That's what happened. Gambling is still very profitable, but because it became more widely legalized, the syndicate had to find other avenues to generate revenue. Still, people get addicted to gambling, and eventually they're going to bust. If a guy who bets on a regular basis owns a construction company and is into the house for five thousand dollars, the manager kept a marker on him. It's important to keep him going as long as he pays the vig, the juice, the interest on a loan. On five thousand dollars, that might be five percent per week, or two hundred fifty bucks. One thousand dollars a month. The guy doesn't have to pay back the loan too soon, but he's gotta pay the vig every week. He keeps playing, keeps losing and pretty soon, his marker is up to twenty or thirty thousand dollars. Keep this guy on a string. Let him pay only the vig and let the principal get bigger and bigger. Before he knows it, he owes fifty large and he can't pay it. But he owns a million-dollar company. Guess what? The Family takes his company. That's the difference between the syndicate and a casino. A casino can't collect so easily.

In winter, a lot of guys in New York and Chicago who are in construction businesses are slow, so they go to the social clubs and the gambling clubs. They're hard-working guys, bricklayers, carpenters, and other tradesmen. Not everybody is a mobster who hangs at the clubs to play a few hands of cards. By spring, their money has been depleted and they're looking for jobs. They might have some big projects they want to bid, and they need loans, so they come to us. A lot of these guys don't have the world's greatest credit, a lot of their equipment isn't up to bank standards, some of it isn't licensed, doesn't have the proper title, things like that which keep them from getting conventional loans. When one of them asks for a hundred-thousand-dollar loan, he gets it because he has equipment and is going to be getting city contracts. Connections will make sure of that. And once they're into the Family for money, the Family gets a piece of their business, and will always get its money back. Not only that, the guy's likely going to be grateful forever. He's hooked and he's always going to come back for favors.

Loan sharking is more than loaning money and collecting interest. You gotta get a part of what the guy's got. Loan sharks don't give money out to just anybody. They give money out to a guy that can make them some money, who has something valuable, whether it's a business, house, boat, or car. It's collateral usually worth twice as much as the guy's loan.

There was a neighborhood guy who owned a small concrete company. He made a pretty good living, and he was getting ready to put his bids in, and he needed a little help. So he came to my uncle Mario, a judge, for fifty thousand dollars and some political help. Maybe we could fix the city contract to pour the curbs. He got the money to help him get through the summer and Uncle Mike took twenty-percent action of everything, not just laying the curbs, which brought him about one-hundred-fifty-thousand dollars net. He had projects all over the city and suburbs, both city and private. A fifty-thousand-dollar investment that year brought a two-hundred-thousand dollar return.

My dad loved it when a guy came to him for a loan if he owned a business. He got his hands on plenty of small pizzerias, hot dog stands, and limousine companies. He'd give a loan, and when a guy couldn't pay the note, the place was his. I even became a good pizza maker working for my dad. If a place made some money, it was extra income. When it didn't, it would be insured and burned down, or would be robbed or just sold. What my cousin Frank sometimes did was place an ad in the newspaper, have an accountant cook the books so his business looked profitable, and sell the place for maybe fifty thousand dollars. He often held a note on the place, and if the new owner couldn't make the note, he'd take the place back and sell it again.

That was done a lot with arcade rooms and restaurants, and in Las Vegas with strip clubs. A Family member would open up a beautiful strip club, get the zoning set and everything, put maybe sixty thousand into it. Then find a guy who wants to be in the titty business and get a hard-on. They would sell the club for two hundred thousand dollars knowing that the rent was ten thousand a month, there were no girls working who had a good following, and the new owner wasn't going to get any cabs to come over because he didn't know how to juice anybody to bring customers. The pit bosses weren't going to work for him. The casino managers weren't gonna do nothing for him. Why? Because the Family stopped them from helping him. The whole idea was to set the guy up for failure. This way, he lost his front money, he'd soon be out of business, the Family repossessed the club, and ran the scam all over again. That's how money was made.

I learned all these things while I was a teenager. And I started feeling the energy of the people I was hanging around with. It was time I made a move of my own. I was filled with ambition, so I started my own vending machine company and a janitorial business. The vending included not only the legitimate jukeboxes, pinball, and cigarette machines, but also poker machines. I made two, three hundred dollars off every legit machine every week. The poker machines brought in two thousand each a week. I had accounts for the machines up and down the avenue. I had nearly eighty pieces of wood on the street. By the end of the year I had almost five hundred pieces. Some of the money I made with the back-room poker machines was laundered through the cigarette, jukebox, and pinball machines in the front of the bars, social clubs, and my arcade.

The janitorial service took me into a lot of different companies, after hours. One of my big accounts was an electronics company. Soon I came up with a plan to rip off over one million dollars' worth of electronic products. I figured out a way to clean out the place with four semi-trucks over a holiday weekend. But what would I do with the merchandise? Where would I sell it? Who would I take it to? I couldn't take it to my father. It was the wrong time because he had enough of his own action going on. Besides, I wanted to make my mark without his help.

So, I laid out my plan for Louie. He then called a guy in Detroit, a semi-big boss who was buying this kind of merchandise. He flew into Chicago. Now, I was sitting there, barely seventeen, with three heavy-duty guys, planning out this million-dollar heist. They told me, "If this goes down right, it could change your life."

There was a lot of pressure. All eyes were on me. They seemed to say, "The kid's got moxie, but does he have the smarts? Does he have what it takes for the long haul?"

Luckily, the heist went down beautifully, smooth as can be.

But not without a hitch. The guy who was going to fence the merchandise ripped off two trailers, half the haul. I waited about a week for my money. I knew they were good for it, but it took a while for them to find the guy who crossed us. The bum had sold the merchandise, but didn't give up the money. It didn't take too long before Louie's friends found him. They arranged an afternoon meeting on the closed loading dock of an abandoned warehouse and brought him to me.

This sorry bastard stood in front of me, scared and ashamed. One of the three guys who brought him leaned in close to his ear and yelled, "See that kid? He's the one you fucked."

Then, to me, he asked, "What do you want to do with him, Michael?"

I didn't really know what the hell to say, so I just said, "Fuck him!"

It was the tough thing, the thing I knew I was supposed to say. Deep in my heart, I wasn't sure what the right thing to do was. I was angry. After all, he tried to fuck up my first major heist. The loser, standing there between two soldiers and one behind him, couldn't look anybody in the face. He knew nothing good was going to happen. He lost it and pissed himself.

They handed me almost a half-million dollars in cash and left. It was the money the guy had on him after selling our merchandise.

Four days later, the guy they had brought before me was found outside a high-class hotel, shot to death and left as a Confirmation in the trunk of a car. Allowing him to be found, making a statement of him, is called a Confirmation. If his body had been disposed of in a way that he would never be found, it would have been a Communion.

TWO WEEKS LATER, I got another six hundred thousand dollars. That was just my cut. The merchandise the guy had stolen from us and then sold was resold after it was located. Since the guy's fence was not reimbursed (as a lesson on knowing who to deal with), we came away with a larger chunk of cash than we expected. Right away, without anybody saying a word to me, I did the right thing. I took a piece of my money and gave it to my dad and the other bosses. I showed them I was more than productive. I kicked up more cash than four crews kick up in a month.

I bought a house in the Kings Point subdivision of Addison. It was a real mob neighborhood, with mostly Italian and Greek residents. At least every other house belonged to a gangster. There was no crime in our backyard. I also bought a couple of game rooms filled with arcade machines in Addison, and Elk Grove Village, and on North Avenue in downtown central Chicago. The one downtown also had a Las Vegas–style crap table in a back room for after-hours gambling. I also opened another vending company. These guys looked at me and realized I knew what I was doing. They didn't see a kid who went out and blew money on a room full of hookers and bubble gum. I made more money, and kicked more money up. I didn't have to, but I did.

All of a sudden the word was out: The kid was fucking good.

11

THE STAKES ARE RAISED

Dreamway Lounge is a club on Roosevelt Road in Cicero, just outside Chicago. During the eighties, it was one of many strip joints I ran for my dad, and the most sleazy; a real dive where the air inside smelled of cigarette smoke, stale sex, and dirty fantasies. The floor was sticky with spilled cheap soda, spit, and, very likely, cum.

The club serviced the low end of the blue-collar trade with girls you'd never want to see in the light of day, or even by candlelight. But, for what the clientele wanted, they were fine. The customers were, after all, no gentlemen. But there were a few middle-class guys, and one or two big-shot politicians, who showed up every now and then. Dreamway was always kept very dark. No one wanted to see too much, or be seen. Walking into that club was like slipping into someone else's bad wet dream.

Bay was a better-looking hooker than most. In the middle of the no-booze, five-hundred-foot-long bar, there was a stage about five feet by five feet square with a pole in the middle. Some of the girls were so stoned, they needed to hang on to it to stay upright. But Jamaican-Creole Bay knew how to work that cylinder. She would stroke it, hump it, wrap her long caramel-colored legs athletically around it. She'd gyrate and dance, and like most of the customers, never even notice if the music skipped or faded as tapes gave out. She was usually a little high, but always aware of what she was doing, and seemed to enjoy her job. After the ten-minute routine, Bay left the stage while Hall and Oates's "Maneater" still pounded through the speakers, sauntering to the tables crowded with leering men. She was all business.

"Hey, doll," one of the regular customers called out. "Hey Bay! You're looking fine tonight. Come join me."

She knew the guy for a good tipper, so she sidled up to him and rubbed her thigh and hip against his shoulder, then straddled his lap, pushing her breasts close to his face.

"Wanna have fun tonight, Georgie?" Bay really didn't have to ask. Georgie was ready.

The transaction was handled by Pete, one of the bartenders serving up ten-cent soda for three bucks a can. He also collected the fees. It was fifty bucks to use the back room. Had he wanted oral fun, it would have set Georgie back only thirty-five, but he would have been serviced at a table in another room, among other johns. After he was paid, Pete took Georgie to the room that was a honeycomb of eight smaller ones inside. Each of those had a mattress on the floor, and a curtain across the doorway. Georgie handed Pete the customary ten-dollar tip, and then he stripped and waited for Bay. Twenty minutes later, Georgie got off the mattress and went home. Bay added her twenty-buck tip to her stash hidden in her wig before heading out front for her next dance.

We always had two dozen, maybe up to forty girls working on the weekend, so there was always enough to go around. When friends or relatives came to the club for the first time, I warned them not to get playful with anything they saw on the streets around the club. It was just too dangerous. Remember what happened to my cousin Marcello and his pals, and what I had to do to make that situation right? Besides, a guy never knew what he might get out there. Some of those bitches were guys, for crissake.

Our girls might not be pretty, but they had all female parts. Some of the girls made two hundred bucks a night. Dreamway kept them off the streets in a neighborhood where they would be dead or beat up by pimps within a week on the pavement. Inside, they had our protection.

Even some of the clubs we didn't own had our protection. When someone wanted to open a club in this area, he had to come to us. First he would talk to one of the crew, then the crew member would go to his lieutenant, and the lieutenant would go to the capo with the request. No one opened a joint without getting permission. It was impossible. We controlled the zoning board, the fire marshal, the Business License Bureau, and a lot more. If we granted permission, protection from other competition, and the police, came with it. It would cost the owner a street tax, or tribute, which amounted to a piece of the action. It was a respectful arrangement for everyone concerned.

Most of the money the girls made went to drugs and to the hotel where most of them lived. We owned that, too. We didn't provide drugs, but we knew who was selling in the neighborhood. Drugs were a big taboo. Mostly Mexicans and South Americans sold to blacks, who peddled for them. Although it wasn't Family policy to deal drugs directly, we had to address the issue. Drugs were out there; people were buying and using them. How do you get involved but not be too involved? It's like any other business conducted in our cities. If someone wants to do business, like opening up a bookmaking place or place of prostitution, he has to pay the tax. So we taxed the drug dealers. We were not selling the drugs, but we taxed the dealers for selling on our turf. If others wanted to bring that stuff into our cities, there was no stopping them but every time something was sold, we got a cut of the profit for protecting them from the police, politicians, and other gangsters. To this day, for every kilo that goes into New York, at least fifteen hundred dollars goes to the syndicate. Are we drug dealers? No. Drug dealers rent pieces of our cities.

The girls, mostly in their twenties, but a few in their forties and even fifties, were straight-up whores. Some stayed at the club, a few went back to the street. Some girls had pimps, most didn't. I learned you can't go the extra mile for any of them.

There was one girl, Sharon, who had been on the streets. After she worked one night at the club, she showed up the next night with her face all beat up. Her pimp was still taking her money. I got all bent out of shape. I told her she would be better off getting away from her pimp, keeping her money, and living at the hotel with the other girls. She was petrified, so I took her home, something you just don't do. I felt sorry for her. I wanted her to stay the night in another room, get cleaned up, get a good night's sleep and figure out if she wanted to go back to this pimp or not. My mother lived in the same cul de sac. She came over and met the girl, helped fix her up, made her look nice and took her shopping. Sharon decided she wanted to break away from her pimp, so she worked at the club for three or four nights. Then she went back to the same bastard. Trying to help any of the girls didn't work. Try a few times, and you stop. You learn.

The girls would fight among themselves all the time. "You stole my john!" would start it. They sometimes got into it bad. Like one night when Dawn and Leticia got into a drag-out, down and dirty fight out in front of the club. One of my workers, Sal, and I went out. Sal made the mistake of trying to get between the girls. He wanted to end it in a hurry. It's not good for business to have fights right there in public. Leticia pulled off Dawn's wig and when Dawn bent down to pick up her money, Leticia pulled a switchblade knife and tried to cut Dawn. When Sal stepped in, Leticia stabbed him in the heart. He died right there. Over nothing.

But most nights were routine. Once a week I made special arrangements for our local boys in blue. I would call up a half dozen girls and one of my assistant managers. They would wait in the back of the building for the paddy wagon. The cops would pick them up and haul them off, not to jail, but to a motel a few blocks away. All night long, cops would stop by that motel and have fun with the girls. They didn't pay. Instead, each cop got laid and on the way out, was handed an envelope stuffed with two hundred dollars in cash. In exchange, if we had any problem at the club, or anywhere else, we could get help from the cops with one telephone call.

There were times we called the cops to help us out. And many times we didn't. We handled our problems ourselves, but not always the way people expected. For example, my dad owned a legitimate restaurant called the Ashford House. Dad and I went over there one morning for an early meeting before the place opened up for breakfast so we would have some privacy. We planned to discuss some things about Dreamway and some other clubs. Dad decided to make us some coffee, bacon, and eggs so he went over to one of the stoves and was about to turn it on when he saw some movement high above him. There were feet dangling out of a ventilation duct, about eight feet above another range with the fryers.

Some idiot had tried to rob the restaurant by coming in through the ventilation system that looked pretty wide on the roof but tapered to only two feet square at the inside ceiling. He expected to be able to drop through, but the column was deeper and narrower than he expected, so he jammed himself stuck, unable to get through the bottom and unable to climb back up and out. He was stuck like that for just over twelve hours.

My dad couldn't stop laughing as he yelled out to the guy some suggestions about what he might do to him even as he dangled there. But, eventually, when the others guys came in, some of us went to the roof and others pushed from the bottom and we got him out. It turned out to be the restaurant manager, Matt. He worked for us but wasn't one of us and didn't even know exactly who we were or how we did business outside of this one joint. And he obviously wasn't smart enough to have checked out the vent system better before pulling this stunt.

Once Matt was out of the vent, I started to call the police, but my father stopped me and said we'd solve it internally. Matt had no idea what that meant and it made him even more nervous. I took him to the office where my dad found it really difficult to yell at this guy without cracking up. All dad could think about was this poor schmuck stuck in the vent all night. I think Matt's situation made Dad remember when he and his old partner in crime, Vic Romano, who died when I was a small kid, were young and screwed up a heist. Dad got locked in a huge vault and when it was opened the following morning, Dad leaped out and dove through a window to get away. So he had some compassion for this kid.

Matt was scared, didn't know what to expect, and hadn't realized he had been trying to rob gangsters. He had no clue.

Matt, a young-looking twenty-year-old guy, pleaded, "Please, please, Mr. D'Angelo, don't call the police. Please let me go."

"I ain't going to call the police," my dad yelled. "I'm going to fuckin' whack you!"

At that point Matt almost passed out. And nobody there could keep a straight face.

Finally, after making Matt sweat for over an hour, Dad decided to put the guy to use. Matt was just a small-heist robber trying to make some money. He wasn't a drug addict or anything like that, so instead of whacking him, my dad gave him a pass on the condition that if Matt ever scored some good merchandise, he would give him a call first. You got to give a guy some credit for trying to make a living. Not everybody has what it takes to be a good criminal but those that give it their best shot are allowed some respect. It worked out okay, and Matt did come around a couple of times with some halfway decent stuff. We made a little bit of money off of him. My dad was not one to ever call up the cops and put somebody in jail. This guy was not too smart, but he had learned a lesson.

I MADE A MISTAKE HERE and there, and learned some lessons, too. Dreamway was a stepping-stone for me. I used it to make money, and a name—beyond Mike the Match—for myself. Then I got a little too cocky, and a lot too greedy. I made ten, twenty thousand, and more a day shaking down a few customers. I was being investigated, ready to be indicted on a number of charges, but it was my shakedown scam that got me pinched.

It started with one guy who walked in wearing a suit. At first I thought he was a cop. I looked outside and saw he was driving a Mercedes. This was definitely out of the ordinary, so I took down his license plate number for future reference. He sat at the bar, bought a soda, paid to take a black girl in the back, did his thing with her, and left after tipping her well.

A few days later, while I was having a meeting at Seneca Restaurant with some guys, a Cook County cop walked in. I asked him, as a favor, to run the license plate number of the Mercedes. It turned out that the john was a big executive with the IBM Company. He lived in a big, million-dollar house in Oak Brook. About a week later, my Golden Boy came back in. He sat with the same black girl (who I quietly told to detain him a while). I hooked up a video camera and taped his session. What big-shot executive wants his coworkers to know he's banging a black girl for fifty dollars?

The next day, I blatantly went to his house with two other guys and had the tape in my hand. I had my beanie hat on, a long leather jacket, and looked every bit the gangster. I told him I had a tape of him having a good time in the back room with the black girl and was going to show it to his wife when she got home unless he paid me twenty-five thousand dollars. At first he said he didn't have it, so I started to leave. Then he ran after me and we made arrangements for him to call a number the next day and bring the cash in exchange for the tape. We met, I got my money, and I gave him the tape. Two or three weeks later, he came back to the club. I guess he figured he was already taxed, so he took his chances.

Meanwhile, I had that same Cook County cop come by the club on Friday and Saturday nights when we were most busy, and keep an eye out for guys with nice cars. He'd run the plate and we'd get a feel for the guy's finances. Lo and behold, he got the tags of an alderman for one of the city wards. I had no idea this guy was coming into the club because he dressed really scummy and didn't bring attention to himself. This alderman came in a few nights later and the cop took pictures of his car outside the club. I didn't get a chance to hook up the video, but I bluffed it when I went to see him. I showed him the Polaroid of his car at the club. I told him I had a friend who would need a zoning favor, and I wanted ten thousand dollars cash. No problem. I told him he had paid his dues and not to think twice about coming into the club again. He came back.

I got greedy. I also had a local circuit judge and a couple of other businessmen I shook down. By then, the word had started getting around to the older guys and my dad. They didn't want this going on, even though I was bringing in maybe fifty thousand dollars a week in shakedown money. They explained that I was actually hurting business because people weren't going to feel comfortable coming to the club. I was making money, but killing business for the long term. Here and there, my being young and inexperienced showed.

Anyway, one of the judges told his story to the cops, and I got pinched when I went to pick up the cash. I thought I had my own insurance because I was also blackmailing the District Attorney and I threatened to open up my little black book and tell everybody what names were in there. Still, the D.A. played tough, figuring he could take the embarrassment of his visits to the club becoming public knowledge and make a name for himself as a hot-shot prosecutor. But the witnesses didn't want to come forward. Even the judge shut his mouth when one of my lawyers pointed out to him that he was stupid. Some people knew what he had done and that he had lost some money, but he could save a little dignity by not telling the whole world the details. So I took a plea bargain and took a total of a year-and-half sentence with six months in prison. Going to prison was an inconvenience, not a life-shattering event. Apart from that night in Tennessee, it was my first time and I didn't give any thought as to whether this would only be the beginning. Like going through a rite of passage, serving this time would make me more of a man in people's eyes. I knew I could do it. No sweat. Easy crime, easy time.

I SERVED THE SIX MONTHS in Federal Correction Camp Marion, a medium security facility. There were no fences. A hundred inmates were housed in each barracks. From that location, we could see the hard-time prison at Marion. Many of us often said we were lucky not to be behind those walls. We had all heard the stories of how bad it was inside. Here, we had soda and ice-cream machines on the property and we were allowed to carry up to twenty dollars in quarters every week. We would buy the roll of coins at the commissary that was pretty well stocked with snack foods, some clothes, personal items, magazines, a good variety of everything really. After we did whatever assigned work we had, we could roam the grounds from seven in the morning until ten at night. It didn't feel so bad being there. I found it amusing that one of my baseball favorites, Pete Rose, who I had met when I was a kid, had done time for his gambling scandal in this place before me.

First I worked as a clerk, and then I got into the kitchen, which is the best place to be because you control the food. Food is what every inmate wants. If a guy has no money, he will do your clothes for you, clean and iron them, for a sandwich every day. If we had chicken, he'd get a chicken sandwich later, too. If we had beef, he'd get a beef sandwich. He'd always get a sandwich in addition to his regular meal. It was a good arrangement.

The inmates at the camp were there because of lesser crimes, so we were a better class of criminal than the guys in the state prison. White-collar crimes got us pinched. Some were, like me, in for extortion. Others had investment scams, insurance or mail fraud, bookmaking, or tax evasion convictions. Some guy burned his car up to get the insurance money. He was caught. It became a federal charge because of the federal stamp on the insurance report document he signed. There were a couple of doctors in there with me, and even a police chief from Detroit who had been involved in some police department scam.

There were long visiting hours every day and family and friends could bring picnic stuff. My mom, the only woman I ever let come to see me in prison, brought me plenty of meatballs, sausages, and lasagna, whenever I wanted it. You could eat with visitors outside on picnic tables. When there was a holiday like the Fourth of July or something, families would come and there would be a big barbecue picnic and a softball game. It was all pretty laid-back. Even the inmates were tame. There was very little violence and only minimal drug use. The population was segregated, by choice. Blacks stayed with blacks, Latinos with Latinos, whites with whites. That's just how it is in any prison. You stick with your own. You understand your own language and rules.

I had my own circle and my own things going on, like poker

games. That's where the money was, and from money, comes the power, and with power, respect. If the inmates respected you, the guards respected you. That's what it was all about.

It might sound like a piece of cake, but it was scary. For the first time ever, I was out of my element, in controlled surroundings with strangers. I felt anxious, out of control. It was constantly nervewracking because I felt I had to always stay on guard. Luckily, I had no problems with anyone. Problems don't happen too often in federal.

After a little more than six months in prison, I was sent to do four months in a halfway house in Chicago. The federal system is great because they don't just kick you back to the street. The return rate on the federal level is very low, like twenty percent. Of all state prisoners, about seventy-five to eighty percent go back to crime and land back inside prison again. The federal system gives someone who made a mistake the opportunity to get his life back together. So after a certain length of time, they put a prisoner in a halfway house, find him a job, and help him to start earning an income. All he has to do is stay out of trouble and report back to the house by a certain time every night after being out no more than eight hours during the day.

Of course, I had a way around that, too. I was actually there, at the halfway house, maybe three hours a night (at the most) just to make an appearance. My pals and I set up a legitimate business that didn't actually exist while I continued doing my regular street business. Only on paper, I was spending my time carpet cleaning. With money and the right contacts, there was always a way to get things done.

Compared to doing hard time, federal prison is easy. Most of my family and associates considered it no big deal; it was a short bit. But it also served me well within the organization. The powerful people saw that I could take my sentence without bringing anybody else into my problem. I didn't talk about anybody else, didn't make any deals to make things easier on myself. They also knew it was a short sentence and I'd be back, producing for them again real soon. So people stayed in touch. And they didn't want me to be pissed with them when I came back out. It's only when you're away for several years that people forget and don't give a rat's ass about you.

But for me, being in prison was like earning an important badge. I had made a mark, and the right people noticed.

Soon after, I got summoned.

12

INITIATION

Because I did so much work in New York, as well as Chicago, I also kept a Manhattan apartment. One morning there, without any warning, someone knocked hard and loud on the door. They had gotten past the doorman and the concierge hadn't announced them so, at first, I thought it was the cops. But no, two of my kind of fellas were telling me to get dressed, in a suit and tie, and come with them. We had to go to New Jersey. Now. They spoke in a very serious monotone voice, not leaving much to read. I knew these two men, but this was all business. I was caught off guard. I was nervous. Hell, I was scared.

It was late morning and I was with my girlfriend, Angela, at my apartment on Fifty-Second Street and Park Avenue in New York

City when this summons came. While I dressed, I debated twenty things in my head. Did I somehow, unintentionally, fuck someone over? Did I make a mistake in doing business? Maybe wrongly stepped into someone's territory? Who had I pissed off? I also wondered if this was my moment. I had heard all the stories about it happening to different guys. My mind was racing with crazy thoughts.

During the hour-and-a-half drive, the three of us made small talk about sports, broads, the weather, anything but what I wanted to know. I knew I couldn't ask. They wouldn't do anything but shrug and say they didn't know anyway. So why bother? I didn't know what the fuck was going on but I told myself it couldn't be anything horrible or they wouldn't take the trouble to drive me to Atlantic City. So I hoped.

The driver and his buddy drove me up to the main entrance of Trump Castle on the marina and let me out after telling me to go to a particular penthouse. I was in a hyper daze as I walked through the casino. It was like the people, the noise, the lights, and the colors didn't exist. I saw myself as if I were moving through a dream. During the ride up the elevator, I could hardly breathe. My hands were all sweaty and shaking, my heart was pounding and my mouth was dry. At the same time, I was trying to talk myself calm, and appear cool and composed. As I stepped from the elevator and into the hallway to the penthouse, I felt like I was walking my last mile.

As soon as I knocked on the penthouse door, one of Joe Figorelli's men opened it. Behind him, I saw over a dozen other men in the room, heads of families from New York, Chicago, Detroit, and Philadelphia. Among them were: Joey Antonetti, Anthony Spilotro, Sam DiNapoli, Joe Leonardi, Jackie Cicero, Nick Napolitano, all from Chicago; Nick's brother Ralph Napolitano and Nicky Scaletti from Philadelphia; Albert Tucci from Detroit; and Paul Farentino and his brother Tony from New York. They sat at a round table, a symbol that everyone is equal and united together. Some of the lieutenants of these Family bosses were in the room, as well as my cousin Paulie D'Angelo. Each one of these men wore his most expensive clothes and the jewelry—there must have been a half-million dollars of it in that room. Everything was first-class. There was food all over the place and even an ice sculpture. My dad was there, too. I took everything in at once. It had to be something positive. Still, the air was charged; their attitude was solemn. It was no tea party.

Immediately, as I stood at the table, Joe Figorelli started the ceremony by asking, in a very formal voice, "Do you know why you are here, Michael?"

By now, I had surmised, but the respectful reply was, "No." I was thankful I was breathing normally again. It was all very serious, but I was calmer.

Then Joe, looking right into my eyes as if reading my heart, told me that I had been brought before these respected men so that they could make me a member of the Honored Society. Joe was leading the ceremony because he was the one who sponsored me. Next to him sat Nick Napolitano, one of the most feared and respected members of the Family.

Joe was the boss of all Chicago bosses and he talked about the foundation of the Honored Society. He spoke of loyalty, honor, and devotion. He explained that it was a secret society bound by our own justice system. Then he asked if I was willing to accept the society's rules and regulations.

I said, "Yes."

He further explained that the Honored Society didn't accept any form of government except its own. Members did not respond to any government authority. We were our own authority. And he asked if I agreed to these laws.

Again, I said, "Yes," never letting my eyes drift from Joe. I didn't even look at my dad. It was all very intense, and I was proud.

Joe continued. He asked if I would take a vow that Cosa

Nostra would be a priority over everything and everyone else in my life. He asked if I was willing to put the Family over my wife and my children if I were to marry. The Family of the Honored Society must always come first. Could I live by that?

Again, I solemnly swore, "Yes."

The next question, the one they always ask, was intended to test my loyalty. Was mine true and complete loyalty?

Joe kept his eyes steady and spoke: "If I asked you to kill for me, would you kill for me, without question?"

It was a tough question. A very important part of the ceremony. Although the weight of that possibility hit me with sudden reality, I didn't hesitate to say, "Yes, I would." I meant it.

At that point, they took a holy card—this one happened to have St. Christopher on it—and put it in front of me on the table. Next, Joe took my trigger finger, as a symbol of how we live our lives, and pricked it with a pin. He did it painfully, on purpose. My blood dripped on the holy card.

That's when my dad became an active part of the ceremony. As they burned the holy card with the picture of the saint and my blood, Dad explained that it was a symbol of how I would burn in Hell if I divulged any of the secrets of the society, or became an informant. The card burned. The ceremony came to its end.

At that point, at 18 years of age, I was a made man.

Applause exploded from the table. The atmosphere in the room became relaxed and animated. Everyone congratulated me. Soon, the bodyguards that were in other suites on the floor joined the celebration, which lasted the rest of the day and evening.

Getting made was an honor. It's not something that happens every year. Sometimes there was nobody made for several years. Then maybe in one year, the bosses would want to recruit new blood and make maybe up to ten guys, not more. It's a very serious thing. If things are going well, they leave things alone. If there have been a number of deaths and they need more men, the bosses open the books. Men are submitted and some are chosen to be made by the committee of bosses.

It was very hard to find the right kind of blood, brains, and balls. Everyone had to agree with the choice. If someone disagreed, they'd tell their boss why, but the final decision came from the bosses together. I was one of the youngest men ever made.

The buzz that I was a mover and a shaker had been going around ever since the electronics heist. Being a moneymaker is a big deal. They saw I was handling my own businesses, that I was becoming recognizable, and that people were paying attention to what I said. I did this without anyone directing me. So the Family decided to bring me in. Of course, they wanted their cut of my action, so getting me made was a way to tax me legally, within the rules. That's what it was really all about.

At the time in Chicago, Anthony Capelli was still the boss, but he was in very poor health, so he was largely retired. We used to call him The Tuna. He was a tiny man who had a cane with a big tuna on the handle. He had worked for Al Capone and was allegedly one of the shooters at the St. Valentine's Day massacre. Joe Figorelli and several others took over Tony's active duties. Joe was Tony Santoro's boss and was in charge of taking care of him when Santoro got caught skimming the skim for the Las Vegas casinos. Both Joe and Nick had sponsored my initiation.

When a guy got made, he got put into somebody's care. He belonged to somebody who was responsible for him. Joe had chosen to give me to Nick, who would thereafter be responsible for me. In structure, I was under my dad who was my boss, but Nick would be the one I'd go to if I had a beef with someone, not my dad. Nick was the one who would help me settle a situation. My dad had bigger responsibilities.

Nick was a man who had earned a lot of respect; as he got older, even bosses feared him. Nick's orders always came from high above. He was a very serious man, and technically, he didn't work for anybody but himself. He didn't have to produce anything to bring to anybody. He was part of the Family, a crew member, but he had a top status. If one of the bosses was out of line, it was not easy to dispose of him because of ranking and respect. One crew member could never kill another crew member, one boss could never kill another boss, unless there were orders. If orders came down from above the boss level, they would go to Nick. He answered to the Mustache Petes of the old country and sometimes, it was rumored, to the CIA for special services.

If you killed someone in the Family without getting permission, you would most likely get whacked yourself. That's not allowed, no matter what you see in the movies. John Sotto should not have had Paul Farentino whacked; he had no permission. Sotto did have enough people behind him because there was a rumor that Paul was going to say things, rat on a lot of people, so Sotto got away with it. Chances are, if Sotto had not ended up in prison, he would have gotten whacked, too. You had to have the okay of everyone in the chain of command to make a move. That's how it was.

Everything in the Honored Society had rank and rules. At the top, there was the Boss of all Bosses, the Capo di Tutti. Each of these men ruled the Family of a particular city. The capo was next in command, then the lieutenant, then the skipper, who was in charge of a crew of men, and then soldiers, men in the crew. When the Bosses of all Bosses got together, they formed a Commission that set policy for the Family in the U.S. They sat together and decided which boss stayed and which one went. One Family boss could have several lieutenants. A lieutenant had a skipper, like his own underboss, and a crew of soldiers who worked for him. Soldiers, or crew members, never discussed business with the boss, only with the lieutenant. The lieutenant talked to the boss.

After being made, I was a soldier; after a short time, I became a lieutenant. I had to produce for Nick and answered to him. Not only do the bosses command respect, they get a cut of everything produced by members under them. Like any pyramid, the cuts get bigger as they move upward. A cut of all the money made in the United States goes directly back to Italy, to our roots, our foundation. Just the way a crew kicks money up to the bosses here, the U.S. bosses kick money up to the bigger bosses in Italy. The majority of the Family-owned clubs in downtown Chicago are on property owned by key players in Rome. They are silent partners in a lot of U.S. real estate, which is a major part of their money laundering. Each year, hundreds of millions of dollars goes back to Italy so it can be returned again to grow in legitimate investments.

In Italy, the organization knew I was made. It's a secret society, but I was in the books that supposedly don't exist. They do exist. That's what's meant by "opening the books" for me.

There was a high sign, or code words, too. For example, if someone was with me who wasn't a member of the Family, I introduced him as a friend of *mine.* If he was made, I introduced him as a friend of *ours.* No business was ever discussed in front of a civilian. There can be no mistakes.

These are the little signals that a lot of people don't know; these were the things that you learned, like there's Sicilian and Italian. In Chicago, the syndicate is called the outfit; in New York, everyone connected is a Wise Guy. It's like calling a soda, a pop. In Philadelphia they pretty much follow New York and use the term Wise Guys. In Las Vegas, it's like Chicago. Nobody uses mob. It's "syndicate": a group of people who join together for financial and industrial business undertakings.

In the circle, made men are given a lot of free things. Lots of guys go to nice restaurants where they're known as being in the syndicate. They are not going to get a bill; that's disrespectful. But then the guy should tip with a hundred dollars cash. It's just how things are done.

Sicilians sometimes greet each other with a pinky-to-pinky handshake. It forms like a circle with no beginning and no end.

Most important meetings are held at a round table to make everybody all equal. No one is sitting in a more powerful position than another. But like so many things, codes of behavior and ethics have changed over the years. They keep changing.

To grow a mustache or a beard is considered not only unclean, but also downright disrespectful. Everybody is very physical. When a guy meets with his crews or his capo, he often gives a hug and a kiss. It's an old-world sign of respect. Any kind of abrasiveness against the cheek is a sign of disrespect. It's like a slap in the face. It's also a sign of unity that we all stay clean-shaven. Years and years ago it was the opposite. The original guys back in Sicily were called Mustache Petes because they all had very flamboyant mustaches. It changed here in the States. Grow a beard? Forget about it. Maybe a skipper, a lieutenant can get away with a mustache but not a beard. No way.

And most guys will not use money clips or wallets. Using a simple rubber band around cash or credit cards is like a trademark. Part of the uniform.

Never be sloppy. To be well maintained is to be organized. A guy has to look and present himself as a businessman. No one could respect a man who didn't take care of himself. A man who dresses like a million dollars and has a self-assured attitude is a guy to respect immediately. What a guy can produce, what he actually does, counts more, but being well groomed is expected.

Once I was made, the respect that was paid to me was much greater. Everyone knew. I became untouchable within our system. Some guys, fifty years old, never got made. They didn't have the balls, or the common sense to be a producer. They were taking orders from me.

Money and power made a big difference. Gangster girls hung out at the bars we owned and were always looking for good fellas. These broads were very well-manicured, gorgeous girls who were attracted to the dangerous lifestyle. They were groupies, and we dated them even though we knew they weren't interested in us, only the life. A girlfriend of another guy used to be off-limits even if they broke up. It was another respect thing. Unless, of course, she was the kind of woman who'd been with everyone. Then it didn't matter. That all got old fast. It was never love, just party time.

Eventually, after the ceremony and party, some of us were taken back to Manhattan in a limousine. On my ride back, I thought about Angela. Everyone I knew loved her. She was totally acceptable, and her father was in the life. Angela was a girl who cooked dinner and took care of my clothes. I could take her out anywhere and be proud, then take her home and she was exactly the woman I wanted her to be. She was good, very good.

I was, however, very proud of my new status, and I knew things would be different from that day on. I had the green light, and different aspirations. I wouldn't have time for Angela the same way anymore. Now a made man, and with the Family connections I had, I would be doing business not only in Chicago, Detroit, New York, and Philadelphia, but other cities, too. That was just for starters.

While I was being driven back to Manhattan in the limo, there was plenty of business talk. I was told what I got every week and from who and why. I would be going into some new territory, too. At this point, the New York pizza connection was starting to come into play. There were a number of pizzerias that belonged to associates who used the business to move heroin. It was big action. It became my job to go in and tell them they now belonged to me. I would be collecting their tax. They belonged to us, and they had to pay. They had no choice. Neither did I. It was the job I was given to do. I was told I could do whatever was necessary to get them to comply. I could mess with them any way I wanted to get the job done. I was young, I was tough. Messing with them was something I was good at.

There was also big money in vending machines, all kinds: cigarette machines, poker machines, pool tables, and jukeboxes. When somebody opened up a bar, I had the right to go in with the jukebox company and become part owner of the bar. I also had the right to put poker machines in place. The bar might make maybe fifteen hundred dollars a week, but the poker machines were making three or four thousand a week. So, with the New York territory I was assigned, I had the right to come in and say okay, "I am gonna give you the money for the bar, but you're gonna use my vending machines." And I would do just that.

That was all in New York, and every week I would go back to Chicago because I still had my own deals working there: prostitution, limousine services, bookmaking, juice loans. I wasn't really supposed to have them, but I was ambitious. Once I got those deals going on my own and cash was coming in, I kicked up some money to the right people and nobody bothered me. I was moving up and I wanted my own businesses. Because my family was in both New York and Chicago, I got away with stuff like that. I was always trying to figure out how to get the best of everybody. Besides, Nick and Sam taught me that I could get away with a lot of things if I had the balls.

In the limo, I was finally one of these guys. They were my enemies, and they were my best friends. I was ahead of the game because my father already told me these were my people but not to ever take my eye off of them. Like the old saying: give a man a living but don't let him get too fat. And of course: keep your friends close, and your enemies closer.

13

LOVE IS THE FIRST SACRIFICE

Keep your friends close, but what about the love of your life? I had to make some decisions about that. There was no doubt I loved Angela. There were times I imagined myself doing the whole thing with her: marriage, nice house, kids, everything. But that kind of life is hard to do right, especially when you got Family business. And I had just given my vow to put nothing before Family. Not a wife, not kids, nothing. It didn't seem so hard to give those things up because I didn't have them in my life just yet anyway.

So what about Angela? As we drove into Manhattan I felt a little sad thinking about Angela and I didn't understand why and I didn't want to know why, so I pushed the feeling away. I wanted to stay happy, riding the high of excitement that being a new made man brought me. One by one, the driver dropped off the other guys. Alone, I sat in the limo, enjoying thoughts of how I'd get to the top, be in charge, be the person who everyone feared and respected.

As we crawled through Park Avenue traffic, I decided to just keep my thoughts to myself for a day or two until I figured out how, or even if, Angela fit into my new life. For the rest of the late afternoon and night, I just wanted to celebrate. I called her on my cell phone and told her I'd be in front of my apartment in a limousine to pick her up in about ten minutes. She said she would be ready and waiting when I pulled up.

She was. As the limo stopped, the uniformed doorman opened the lobby door, and Angela walked out. She was beautiful, in a fitted, tan cashmere coat that blew open in the wind that pressed her short silk dress against her breasts, her flat middle, and her sleek thighs as she hurried to the limo just ahead of the scurrying doorman. She waited, he opened the door for her, and as soon as our eyes met, her face lit up with that dazzling smile that made me melt every time.

Angela eased in and pressed herself against me. I gathered her into my arms and kissed her on the forehead; she kissed my cheek and we settled into the soft black leather.

"Onward, James!" I called to the driver with a carefree flair. I was determined to keep things upbeat and fun, no matter what that whispering voice in my head wanted to say about love, and how it can be a man's downfall. But it was there, muttering in the dark places of my brain.

Angela took a pretty silk scarf from around her head and neck, shaking out waves of dark hair. She had a confused look on her face and sensed something was different now.

"Sooo, tell me!" she started. "Where did they take you? What happened?" Then she whispered against my ear, "Was it the 'ceremony'?"

"Ssshh, sshh, later," I begged off.

"But was it?" she persisted.

"Yeah, it was," I gave in. "I'm official now. But let's not talk about it. I can't talk about it. You know that. Let's just have a nice time together."

Already I felt pressured by her. I looked at her big brown eyes and felt something stir. I looked away. I had to look away. Still, I was sure she knew something more than just my status was changing. We sat in silence as I stared out the tinted windows.

"Hello in there? Anyone home?" she asked, as the driver turned left from Park onto Fifty-Ninth street.

I snapped out of my greedy thoughts for a few moments, looked at her face and wondered, What am I going to do? How can I have the life I want and Angela, too?

"What are you thinking?" she asked.

"How beautiful you are," I only half-lied and she giggled in her teasing way I loved. I felt uneasy by her wanting me to be more attentive. I felt myself slip deeper into myself even as I squeezed her hand, hoping the gesture would replace the words she needed.

"I know you've got a lot on your mind," she cooed, stroking my face. "It's all right. We'll have a drink, a nice meal, go back to your place and I'll show you the surprise I have for you. It's red. It's lacy and . . ."

The limo pulled up to the steps of a large hotel facing Central Park, and the doorman helped us out. I felt rescued. When we walked through the lobby, Angela wrapped her arm around mine. I loved her there on my arm. A beautiful woman with a heart of gold and sexual hunger that matched mine. Angela was absolutely striking and she turned men's heads everywhere we went. We made a great couple. I know I looked good in the way I dressed, and walked, and talked. A self-confident attitude is what it's always about. With Angela, I felt proud. Like a king.

We had cocktails, and I found myself starting to unwind. The tension that had grabbed me by the shoulders in the limo started to ease. I enjoyed watching Angela sit in the barrel chair across from me, her long legs crossed, showing a peek of stocking top. She knew I was a sucker for a garter belt and dark nylons. Angela was the perfect woman. Drop-dead gorgeous, smart, very presentable in any situation. Men loved to look at her. I loved the way she let them know she was mine by ignoring them. I mean, she did everything right. Cooked, cleaned, kept herself trim and fit, and was passionate in the bedroom. Angela loved me. I never had any doubt about that.

But as I swirled my brandy, sipped, and savored the taste, my thoughts wandered as Angela talked about her sister Isabella's upcoming wedding. I watched her talk, even nodded my head often enough, but my mind was listening to that dark voice in my brain again. What would it take to get all I wanted, all I ever dreamed about? Everything. Could I sacrifice everything, including Angela, even though I knew she loved me and that I loved her? Sitting across from her, touching the smooth skin of her forearm, watching her eyes dance with expression, I stared as she talked. About what? Bridesmaids' dresses? Honeymoon? Bachelorette party? I only heard every few words. She looked so happy talking about the wedding. It almost broke my heart. I wasn't sure why. So I downed my brandy, snubbed out my cigar, and told her I had a great idea.

"Let me take you on a carriage ride," I said as I stood up, interrupting whatever it was she was saying. She loved carriage rides in Central Park and gave a little squeal of pleasure as she jumped out of her chair.

"Oooh, good idea! Let's go through the park and down Fifth Avenue to the restaurant," she said planning the route.

I left a hefty tip on the table. There was no tab. The manager knew me, and my connections. A made man doesn't pay among our own.

Outside, carriages were lined up in every direction. I asked

Angela to pick her horse and buggy. She picked a black horse with a braided mane and white blaze down its face. I haggled with the coachman, paid him and helped Angela into the carriage. As we were pulled forward, the evening air hit us with a chill, so I pulled a seat-side blanket over our laps.

As we rode through the park, listening to the steady clip-clop of the horse's hooves on the pavement, Angela rested her head on my shoulder and stared up at the twilight through the trees.

"It's so romantic," she whispered. "I love you so much, Michael."

"I love you, too, hon," I answered, loving the thought that the park with its lake was going to be my private backyard. Even with Angela resting on my shoulder, I thought only about the new projects I wanted to start, the moves I was going to make back in Chicago and Philadelphia as well as here in New York.

"Michael? What's the matter?" she asked while stroking my thigh under the blanket.

"Just thinking, that's all," I told her.

"Well, I guess that's what's the matter. That's the problem, Michael," she said, "too much thinking. Start feeling like I'm feeling," she coaxed. "Baby, come here, honey."

Angela took my hand and moved it just above her knee. She had black nylon stockings on. I felt the lace where they ended and the soft warm skin of her inner thigh began.

I felt myself get aroused. I wanted her bad. I nuzzled her hair, and turned her face to mine. Her mouth was delicious. At that moment, I wanted to make love to her and never let her get away from me. I sucked in the smell of her, sweet and musty. I could get drunk on her. But as my right hand floated up her thigh and touched her panties, the finger that got pricked in the ceremony dragged across some lacy fabric and hurt. I pulled back, chilled by the reminder of my new life.

Angela felt me recoil.

"Baby, why don't you want me? What's wrong?" she asked.

"Nothing. I just don't want to do anything right now. Not here," I said, without looking at her. I knew the look on her face but didn't want to see it. I'd go weak. "Not now."

"Not now, like this minute, or not right now, like in this, this . . . lifetime?" she sputtered.

"Oh stop it," I scolded her. "Your sister's wedding has got you thinking crazy."

Angela was someone who, more than anything, wanted happiness and security. All her wedding talk at the hotel had only added to her expectations, and my discomfort.

Angela stared at me, then pulled her skirt back down, yanked the blanket to herself and moved away from me.

That little voice whispered inside my head, "It's all right. She's getting angry. So what. She's making it easy for you to tell her to get lost."

We rode the rest of the buggy ride in silence. It wasn't turning into much of a celebration evening. We trotted down Fifth Avenue until I told the driver to let us out, not at Rockefeller Plaza but around the corner, on Avenue of the Americas. I got out and helped Angela, giving her an extra hug and a kiss on the cheek as she stepped to the curb. I was feeling guilty and thought I could get her a little something to make up for being kinda shitty to her.

"Let's go window shopping," I said with a smile and led her into the Diamond Exchange. I moved to the back where an old buddy of mine had his area.

"Hey, Solly! How ya' doin'?" I called out to the jeweler.

While Solly and I talked, Angela got lost in showcases filled with diamonds and gold jewelry of all kinds. Angela loved shopping and helping me choose my clothes. I loved to watch her try on clothes I would sometimes buy for her. She knew what was going on, where the money came from. It didn't matter to her. Her father and brother were associates. Jewelry shopping was rare. She started bouncing from case to case ooohing and aahhing over bracelets, rings, pins, and earrings. "Oh, honey," I heard her say, "isn't this gorgeous?" But then she'd continue before I could respond. "No, no, no, I take that back. Look at this one!"

I continued to do business with Solly. We exchanged some cash. First from him to me, then after he brought a couple of items from the back, from me to him. I put the box with a diamond tennis bracelet into an inside pocket of my overcoat, collected Angela, and we left.

Over dinner at La Reserve on Forty-Ninth Street we sat close to each other in a booth. During dessert I presented Angela with her gift. She startled and her eyes went wide even before she opened the box. When she did, she gasped, "Oh Michael! I didn't see you buy this! It's beautiful!" and threw her arms around my neck and kissed me. Then she settled back, cradled the box in one hand and with the other, ran one finger across the stones, treating it like it was something alive and fragile.

"I wanted you to have something very special to remember a special day," I said.

And she cried a little, quietly, a single tear. She touched the stones again and closed the box, put it deep into the bottom of her handbag.

I was surprised as I expected her to put it on right away. "Aren't you gonna wear it?" I asked. "Don't you like it? What's the matter?"

We looked at each other, talking with only our eyes, and I saw something sad, disappointed, but Angela leaned toward me and kissed me again, on the cheek.

"Thank you, Michael. It really is beautiful."

"And so are you," I answered. "You deserve the bracelet. Put it on."

"I'll wear it for the first time at Isabella's wedding next week," was all she offered, not making a move to take the bracelet out of her bag.

"Suit yourself," I huffed and we left within minutes.

We walked out of the restaurant and headed for Fifth Avenue. As we turned the corner together, arms hooked at the elbows, an older man stopped in his tracks, smiled, tipped his hat to Angela, said something quietly and walked off.

"What the fuck did he say to you?" I asked her.

"Oh, nothing."

"Nothing? Tell me what he said to you!"

"He said, 'It's a pleasure to see such a beautiful face.' Something like that. Forget about it, okay? He was being a sweet old man."

I stared back down the street, wanting to kick his old ass.

We walked some more and Angela asked, "Why do you have to get so mad, Michael? You've been tense all evening."

"I'm not mad," I insisted. "Strange men shouldn't talk to you. It's not respectful. And he didn't even say nothing to me, like I wasn't here. That's not right."

Angela and I both knew I wouldn't be around much longer anyway. And that was the real issue we didn't talk about, that had us both uneasy. Everything had changed since that morning when we made love. Before the knock on the door. She knew it. I knew it. Instead of pushing anymore and forcing that conversation to happen right then and there, Angela got mad and quiet.

"Let's get a cab," I said. And we did. We sat with plenty of room between us. Only in sideway glances, I watched her pout as she stared out the window at nothing in particular on the sidewalks.

She's beautiful. Sexy. You love her, a part of me was saying.

But the dark voice whispered back, "Money and power are the only things you need. You can't keep Angela and have that, too. At least not now. Give her up. There are plenty of broads around."

I loved Angela and resented her at the same time. If I didn't love her so much, it wouldn't hurt to leave her. There would be no conflict. Simple. But I knew deep down that the closer I kept her, the more I'd hurt her. The life I was leading and was going to conquer was hard enough without having a woman making demands, too.

If a guy is banging his broad and gets a call to meet someone downtown, he's got to hang up the phone, zip up his fly, put on his shoes and socks, and go. That is what Family life was like. If a guy doesn't do like he's told, forget about it. He'll end up getting whacked. I had to ask myself what kind of life would that be for Angela? I couldn't put her through that constant abandonment. What would it do to her, and what kind of marriage would we have?

Back in the old days, women in the Family were very tolerant. My mother, for example. She never questioned my father or anyone for that matter, about anything. Women are different now. Even Angela, as good as she was, could never be as completely, unquestioningly supportive as my mother was with my father. And I saw how my father's work affected my mother. I saw the sadness on her face when Dad was gone for a few days, or a few weeks. I didn't want to be responsible for someone else's unhappiness, even for a few weeks at a time. I didn't want the pressure.

The cab dropped us off. We rode up the elevator to the fifty-second floor. At my apartment, I turned the key in the lock and I said, "Baby, we gotta talk." I didn't look at her when I said it, and she didn't look at me because I think she really knew what was coming. She probably knew after a few minutes in the limo when I first picked her up.

We walked through the foyer area, still not saying a word to each other. I helped her off with her coat; I took off mine. Angela kicked off her shoes. I unbuttoned my jacket, took it off and walked to the bar. She only shook her head "no" when I asked if she wanted a drink, too. She walked to the stereo like she was going to put on music, then, without touching it she walked back and sat in the corner of the sofa with her legs drawn under her. We were both just wasting time, fidgeting.

"What?" she said, with her arms folded in front of her chest.

She quietly sat on the couch across from me, knowing this could take a while. She looked like a little girl on the verge of crying.

"Things are changing for me, gonna be different now," I started.

"Different? How 'different'?" she said softly, without anger. That made it even harder.

"Different like I can't give you what you need anymore. I won't have time for you no more," I said, laying it on the table, pushing for a fight. I got a rise.

"I knew this was fucking coming," she said almost under her breath because she knew I hated it when she swore. She was on her feet in no time, pacing to the windows and back, shaking her head, at a loss for words, or unable to say them.

"Baby, it ain't about you," I went on. "Right now I'm just not capable of having a relationship with anyone. There's too much going on with me. It is not you. It's me." And my Family, my needs, my career echoed in my head. That dark voice was laughing in my brain now. It liked where we were headed.

"So I'm just out?" she asked. "Just like that? We're over and I'm replaced?" She started to cry, but tried to hold it back.

I couldn't let her work the tears on me so I went a little bit crazy on her.

"You're not replaced, you can't compete," I spat out. "Besides, I'm sick and tired of watching you flirt with every guy in the room whenever we go out. I'm sick of thinking who you're with when you're not with me. That wimpy guy, Will?"

This was untrue, I knew, but I wanted her to be mad, to stay away from me, not try to pull me back with her pout, and tears, and sexy body.

"But I love you, Michael, you know that," she begged.

Everything she said was true. About loving me, wanting to be with me for the rest of our lives, having been there for me. I loved her. But love is not enough. I knew she'd make a great wife, a wonderful mother. But I wouldn't be a good husband, not the husband

Angela deserved. I could only love one family at a time, and I made my choice.

"Yeah, well that don't mean shit no more. I got to move on and make something of myself and I can't have you around to think about all the time."

She started to cry again and sobbed, "How can you talk to me like that? I love you. I've been here for you for what? Since we were kids."

"Oh bullshit," I growled. "You were under a lot of guys in high school. I wasn't the first, just the best you ever had. You're gonna miss the sex, that's all."

I slammed her with my words again and again, while something inside me pushed me further and further. Sometimes I'd been mean to her in the past, to test her a little, but never like this. I wanted her to walk away from me.

Then she brought up her father. He wasn't made yet, but he was on his way, finally, after a lot of years. Her older brother was a pretty good producer, too.

"So, what? All the men in my life put me second or third to . . . what? This big-deal thing, this life, this so-called business? Is that the way it's always going to be with every man I ever love?"

"Yes."

"Yes? Just like that, yes? *Vaffanculo,* Michael!" She swung her arm back and tried to slap my face, but I caught her by the wrist. I held it as I grabbed her close, turned her around so her arm was pinned backward; my other arm came around her waist and held her other arm against her body. I knew she hated to be held like that. But I wouldn't be held tight in *any* way.

From behind, with my face in her hair, I growled against her ear, "First, don't ever talk to me like that! No one tells Michael D'Angelo to go fuck off, got it?" She struggled against me. I went on, holding her tight. "It's always going to be the Family first. Love doesn't work with us the same way it does for other people.

Remember that, Angela. People like me and your father got more important concerns."

"Bigger than daughters and wives and real family? Blood family?" she bawled, starting to sag in my arms.

"Much bigger. Remember who puts the food on the table, brings home the furs and jewelry. Who pays for the kids' tuition, clothes, everything? The men do. Yeah, I could do that for you, but I'm not ready for that life. We got a different kind of Family, and it ain't no good for you. Go back to that guy Will. That milk-toast, sweaty palmed sonavabitch."

"So what makes you think you know what's good for me, Michael? You! You sorry *asshole!*" she did her best to fight back with words.

I smelled her hair against my face. Her scent was warm, wild.

The dark voice inside reminded me, "Don't fall for it! Don't give in. She's the only thing that stands in the way of everything you want."

Then I felt myself go cold. It was like watching myself, and Angela, from somewhere else. I turned her around to face me. I looked into her tear-stained face, the makeup-streaked cheeks. The woman I loved? I felt nothing. I had won. I could leave her. For her own good, yes. But mostly for my own. I opened my arms. I let her go. I let her go in every way.

Still looking at me, Angela backed away as I released her. She looked at me as if she had never seen me before. She had had enough.

"I'm going to bed," was all she said.

I said nothing, just looked away as she turned and walked toward the bedroom and slammed the door behind her.

Alone, I poured myself a stiff drink and sat in my favorite armchair. It faced the best panoramic view of the city I had. The dark voice in my brain was quiet now, because it was the only voice left. It was my voice now, completely. No more second thoughts.

I stared out at the city that I would own someday. Every building and business, every cop and judge. Lights sparkled from buildings like stars in a concrete galaxy. I sat counting as many lights as I could. Each one represented another piece of money and power that would be mine. I counted them until I fell asleep, dreaming of my new life.

When I woke up, it was still dark. I heard Angela making loud, banging noises in the bedroom. I knew she was packing and I still drifted in and out of sleep. I was relieved that she didn't wake me up to say good-bye.

Eventually, my eyes opened to the morning sun. As they focused, they fell upon something sparkling on the side table. I leaned forward, picked it out of the open box and sat back again. It was the bracelet. I held it, fingered it and put it down again. I had the receipt. I'd take it back later. Or give it to another broad someday.

14

NEW YORK, MY KIND OF TOWN

When I split up with Angela, Paulie said, "She's just a broad. There are plenty others." He knew about women. He had them from east to west, up and down each coast. Paulie put his dick in front of everything. He'd stop by the side of the road with a broad to get a blow job. He'd go through maybe ten women a week, two or three in a day. I was no saint. Especially after Angela, I had two or three women a week myself. I liked cocktail waitresses, because they reminded me of showgirls the way they were dressed. Paulie and I loved to go to the Playboy Clubs. Oh my gosh, when I think of the Hugh Hefner girls I banged! There was something about those cottontail outfits. We belonged to the private membership area and whenever us Bad Boys came up the elevator, those women fell at our feet. It was that easy.

COLLECTING THE TRIBUTE, or taxes, for the Family was not always easy. In New York, the areas of Brooklyn, Queens, Bronx, Long Island and Manhattan are each controlled by a different Family head and his crew. But each boss got a piece of the action in every area. For example, the D'Angelos controlled Manhattan and all the hospital and restaurant linen supply, the docks, and a few other things there, and plenty of other business in each of the other boroughs. The Sottos controlled Queens, all the gambling and prostitution in Manhattan, and some business in the Bronx. Each Family group pays the others in the area a little piece of the action. Nobody gets to keep one hundred percent of everything; everybody brings some protection or expertise.

I collected the gambling money in Manhattan. A Turkish guy, Suleyman, controlled gambling houses for the Sotto family, who had to pay us a piece of the action because we gave their late-night gambling clubs police protection and kept the fire marshals off them. Suley hated the sight of me. He did not like to pay because his boss felt they didn't have to pay us even though they were under our protection. Every time I had to see Suley, and it was too often, it was always a quiet battle. I went to whatever club he was at on a particular night and he welcomed me with a lot of phony courtesy. Then Suley dragged things out, kept me there all night, tried to get me drunk hoping I would forget about the money and leave without it. Fat chance. I never drank with him, never broke bread with him. I wanted as little to do with him and his bullshit as possible.

Suley only ran the gambling clubs; he was the front man. He wanted to be a boss, but he was only the patsy who would take the pinch if everything came down. He just wanted the envelope. I had to let Suley think he was the boss most of the time, but I had to remind him every now and then who the boss really was. That usually came with handing over the money.

"You give me the envelope because I am the fuckin' boss and you are working for us," I would say. "Remember that."

He didn't want to hear that. Too bad.

Inside the Sotto gambling places, we had our broads. If I wanted to put twenty in there, I put them in there. If I wanted to pull them out, they were gone. These women were our spies and kept an eye on the gambling action, passed on the information we needed. Sure, sometimes they lied, but even a lie can lead you to a truth you need to know. I asked them how much gambling had been going on last night at any particular club. Maybe there was a lot of action. And maybe the next night, when I went to pick up the envelope, I might see the cash was a little short compared to the action I heard about. I put Suley on the spot about it.

I had a reputation as a dangerous man because not only could I deal with my own kind, I dealt with Wall Street brokers and heads of industries. I learned to manipulate business and the stock market. I had balls, and smarts. I produced plenty of money for myself and the Family.

While I was in New York, I got an education in the stock market through a brokerage firm, Hatfield and Delaney. It was the responsibility of the brokerage firm to keep felons out of their business. However, the head of human resources, who was supposed to do a background check, was connected and got me into the firm's stock market courses and sponsored me for my series seven and thirty-six series licenses. She was also the mistress of the firm's general manager, a crooked former athlete we had worked with on other deals before he got into Wall Street. I would never have been able to work on the stock market floor because the Stock Exchange did their own background checks on people there, and anybody with a criminal background is banned. But I could go a long way without being on the floor.

It took me a couple of months to go through the full-time classes through the brokerage firm. It was pretty intense and I learned a lot. They sponsored me for the brokerage test and I did really well. I didn't even cheat.

Then the firm put me on sales, cold calling. They didn't know, but I didn't cold call anybody. I had my own little book and called up my guys and I brought in over fifty thousand dollars in my first two weeks. Nobody else did that. I made a million dollars in trades within the first month. The commissions were nice.

My supervisors asked, "Who are you? Are you a broker? Do you have a clientele? Where are you getting these people?"

I just looked at them and said, "I got lucky. I'm a good salesman."

Then I started to hang out with the more experienced guys at the firm who knew about hot trades and investment banking. I told them I was working toward getting my full-series stockbroker license. Sometimes they were helpful, sometimes not. Sometimes I got myself some leverage with them and they opened up.

While I picked up money from the gambling clubs, I ran into a few brokers and other investment bankers having a good time with the games and the broads. Some of these brokers were from other firms, some from Hatfield and Delaney. Sometimes they bragged about the hundred-million-dollar deals they were making. Not in detail, but they talked.

So, I introduced myself at the club, and if they were at the same firm, I stopped by their office the next morning.

"Hey, remember last night? Great fun," I said. "So, how's your family? Oh, two kids, got pictures?"

And while I looked at his wallet photos and maybe a framed picture of his average-looking wife, I threw in, "I wanted to talk to you. Maybe you could give me some information on some good deals."

"Oh, ah, yeah, last night," they remembered. "Yeah, it was fun, but, ah, I can't help you with information . . ."

"Eh, sure, you can do it," I pushed. " What you were doing last night, you weren't supposed to be doing either, but you did it, so you can do this."

Some got nervous then and maybe thought about what I might

say to whom. Or just figured, "Okay, we can talk," because we're two of a kind, both like to gamble and party a little.

These Wall Street guys never came back with, "Eh! Are you threatening me or something?" No, they said nothing, but knew what was happening. They gave it up right away.

I usually took them to lunch at a fine restaurant that same day or the next. We would chit-chat and then I said, "I'm interested in making some investments. I'm curious about which stocks are going to move soon."

Then we talked about how this company was going to merge with that company although it wasn't official yet.

"So when do you think it will be official?" I kept asking.

"The merger is in preparation right now," he would say. "Maybe a month, six weeks, max."

"So it would be a good time to buy those individual stocks wouldn't it?" I kept pounding, all casual and social.

"Yeah, it would," he would say.

Those Wall Street guys were hungry. They all wanted money. They were young and looking to make twenty million dollars by age thirty so they could retire and live well. They were married and vulnerable to being embarrassed, or worse: if the wrong people heard they were having some kind of inappropriate affair or gambling heavily, they would be fired. Maybe they were using company expense account money. Maybe using a little dope. You got them. They were not going to lose a million-dollar job to some petty indiscretion.

At that point, they were in bed with me. I was going to fuck them as often as I could. A little inside trading information goes a long way because I then called up everybody and bought up the right stocks. After the merger, after the stocks doubled—sometimes even more than doubled—we sold them. Pump and dump. Plus, I got commission on the stock sales and a kickback on the tip from everybody I told.

Hanging around big investment bankers, I learned about

bearer bonds. They're like cash. Whoever holds it, owns it. There is no coupon or registered serial number on it like on a stock certificate or regular bond. The bearer of that bond is the owner.

When the Family needed to move money to different countries, I couldn't take two or three million dollars on a plane, but I could carry bearer bonds in my briefcase and make the deposit to a Swiss bank. I bought these bonds through the brokerage house after I brought in almost a dozen guys on the Stock Exchange floor. I had them buy up a million dollars in bearer bonds and threw them some cash. They called all over the world to find them. It was a great way to launder money. Of course, the government started to figure that out, too, and there are far fewer bearer bonds in circulation now.

Opening new avenues, this was new-generation Family business. It helped our old businesses, too. Some of our guys in the construction business took their companies public. We put the company on the market, did an initial offering, built up the stock, and watched it rise. When it hit its high point, we sold the stock, the company went out of business—at least on paper—and we got rich off of it. Pump and dump.

New pharmaceutical drugs were a good way to make money, too. Before the FDA approved anything, the drug company was worth nothing, maybe six, seven dollars a share. After the drug got approved, it was worth sometimes over a hundred a share. We had an inside track through the investment bankers and brokers in finding out if the drug was going to get approved or not. So we would buy thousands of shares. When it got approved and the share value skyrocketed a couple weeks later, we sold it. We didn't hang around to see if the drug was going to make it in the long haul. Buy low, sell high, period. That's the basic rule to follow, and especially powerful with inside information.

However, the stock market has its own monitoring system to watch who buys and sells. They look out for those trends, for someone, or some firm buying and selling in a pattern that suggests insider trading. We got greedy and a little careless, making too many trades, and burned out that firm. The head people at the firm didn't care because they all made money.

By that time, I had learned what I needed to know on Wall Street. I continued doing it through my contacts from wherever I was and made good money. Hit and run. I had learned enough, and felt the stock market would decline before it hit about two years later, so I didn't get hurt.

I LOVED MY APARTMENT in Manhattan. The building was full of diplomats from all over the world. I chatted with a few of them in the elevator and before I knew it, I was invited to parties. After I went to one party, I met more people and went to more parties. That might sound like a lot of fun, and it was, but it was good business. It was part of my job to make connections with the right people with power, influence, and information. It was also good to go to these parties alone, without a date, so I could talk to the women more easily. Sometimes the best way to meet an important man was through his wife or girlfriend.

About a month after I broke up with Angela, I was at a party full of international diplomats, many from Korea, Japan, Peru, India, Mexico, and a whole bunch of other countries. At the official country-sponsored parties everything was very hush-hush. I would meet people who would invite me to other social gatherings. I would become an acquaintance and four or five meetings later, we talked a little more about each other's lives and would eventually bring up business.

I took these politicians to the best clubs and showed them a good time. I mean, we walked in the door and twenty women waited for them, made them feel like kings, and took care of their sexual pleasures by the end of the night. The next day, I called them up and found them glowing from the night before. They went on and on about the terrific time they had and how they wanted to do that again. It was all business, no matter how much fun. The more I mixed with these people, the more information I got, the more juice I had. They knew who I was, who my buddies were, and they wanted to do business with me. There was never any, "Oh no! You're a gangster!" in those circles. Politicians are the biggest criminals in the world.

As often as possible, I would let them bring up the idea of us doing business together. If I came to them, they were very hesitant and didn't want to discuss it. It was always best to let them feel comfortable; let them bring up business. Before I knew it, they were talking about manipulating the whole world.

Mexicans always liked the idea of import-export business. Diplomats from Indonesia and Peru were all about drugs. They wanted to know what they could invest in to bring money back to their countries. They talked money laundering on a huge scale—tens of millions of dollars.

A guy from Ethiopia, where everybody was starving, needed restaurant equipment to set up centers to feed people. He had a massive budget and wanted to skim some cash for himself from it. I found him large numbers of used restaurant equipment. He needed rice and clothing, like jeans and gym shoes. We had our guys on the docks. We got him two truckloads of jeans and at least twenty tons of rice. He paid garage-sale prices on a huge scale, in cash.

The Japanese were the most crooked when it came to real estate. They were buying up land all over the city and building new structures.

At a party they would complain, "Oh, it is so difficult to build in America."

"No it ain't," I told them. "You just need the right connections. What you need is someone to help you with zoning, building permits, and getting the right construction companies."

Several meetings down the road, the business of real estate and construction would come up again.

"Oh, you can help me with this?" they would ask.

"Absolutely, I can get you all kinds of building breaks," I convinced them.

Within a few months, these Japanese guys were putting up five-hundred-million-dollar buildings. They couldn't do it without pouring concrete, putting steel down, having windows installed. That was all union work, and union workers belonged to us. I knew before many others and had the inside track on getting bids in. I found out which properties were involved and where they were going for financing, information like that. I went to one of the bosses and before the Japanese even started getting licenses and permits, I made sure my organization had its hooks into them. We got a good piece of the action from the offices and apartment buildings constructed from Sixty-Seventh Street up through Spanish Harlem.

Dealing with international people was a great rush for me. I loved the social circle they moved in, the certain kind of power they had—I mean, geez, they have immunity from most of our laws. Ambassadors had the attitude they could do anything. They can. They could commit murder in the U.S. and get away with it. Usually, the worst thing that happens is that they're sent back to their country and banned from this one. Talk to them about anything that could make them hundreds of millions of dollars and they listened. They had nothing to lose. It was just a profitable power game.

I earned the reputation of being one of the best connected guys. So I went to plenty of parties. I made sure I met as many influential people as I could, or at least the people who worked for them. Even a secretary or aide often offered up good information. Senators and congressmen liked to talk about themselves and their work. And everybody likes to have a good time.

AT THE SAME TIME, there was a small but vicious drug war going on in New York. Drugs, no matter how the Family tried to avoid them, brought in good money, but they always involved some dirty dealing. The drug war became an out-of-control situation. There were too many low-level people involved and too many drugs flooding the streets. It was a rule that no drugs were to be sold near schools, and never to kids. The penalty was death and everybody knew that, but certain lower economic groups didn't care. They sold dope to ten-year-olds, and we couldn't control it. When rival factions started fighting over the street territory, each side asked us for help eliminating the other because we had been collecting taxes from them for protection. We wanted both sides eliminated because if we couldn't control a problem, we had to contain it. You can't control a wildfire, so you light a backfire, a controlled burn.

Sam DiNapoli didn't give a damn about anybody involved in the street dealing. They were giving him fifty thousand each for every guy whacked. So were the guys in the rival gang. One didn't know about the other. Sam was making money off everybody else's problems, plain and simple, and solved ours, too. He took the opportunity and made a lot of cash on the side.

When more than one or two bodies had to disappear over a short period of time, it took some work to make certain they didn't get found. Getting rid of the evidence was sometimes more gruesome than doing the hit. There was a florist shop on the lower east side of Manhattan, near Mulberry Street in Little Italy. The guy who owned it used it for gambling, for making book. When we had to, we used it as a chop shop. When we had a chop shop for cars it meant we took the car apart and sold its parts separately or used them in other cars. It's a way of getting rid of the evidence in pieces. The chop shop in the florist's back room was a little different. His grandmotherly-type manager didn't have a clue what was going on. We would drag a body in a bag right under her nose and she'd think it was a big delivery of decorative moss used in flower arrangements. She just stepped over it; she was really that naive.

After closing, she'd leave. That's when me and Stavros, an Italian Greek, went to work. Stavros was a personable, well-dressed, and vicious guy in his fifties. He was great at hotel heists; he'd get into the safe deposit boxes inside the rooms. He was also a friend of Sam, who paid him to get rid of the corpses.

There was a lot of blood in the bodies because they were usually pretty fresh. Anything older than a day, and it smelled worse than it already was. The nice thing was, the florist had a table in the back that was similar to the kind used for autopsies. It had deep drainage ditches on the sides, so when we tilted it, the blood and other body fluids just flowed into a bucket and then we emptied it down a drain. It worked well.

We wore outfits like a couple of surgeons. Those green suits like they use in a hospital came with booties, so we covered our shoes, too. We used electric and manual saws and hatchets of different power and sizes to take the corpse apart, limb by limb, piece by piece. Then we would wrap each piece in aluminum foil or cellophane before we put them into a fifty-five gallon drum and finally poured cement into it. It would take us anywhere from forty-five minutes to an hour and a half to finish a body, depending on how much meat, muscle, and fat there was. A large guy's bones were always the hardest and we needed the power tools. After the body was packed up, another guy with a pickup truck helped us get the drum in the bed of the truck and then drive it out to the New Jersey Meadowlands, or Canarsie, or some pier, and dump it.

It usually went pretty smoothly and without interruption, except for one night when there was a knock at the front door. A local cop had seen the light from the back and figured someone was working. Luckily, Stavros hadn't suited up because he was talking business with the pickup truck driver, but I was up to my elbows in blood, guts and, bones. If I ever felt panic, this was the time.

But Stavros was cool. He let the guy in. It turned out that the cop had just gone off duty and when he saw the light, he figured he could surprise his wife with some flowers to make up for some argument they had earlier in the day. The cop was real chatty, giving Stavros his life story about his wife, their kid, and the bills while walking around the front of the store looking at plants and stuff. But while I thought Stavros was going to whack the cop, he started putting together a fucking bouquet for him. All the while, Stavros talked like he really knew something about "the language of flowers," wrapped them up and handed them to the cop who probably thought he was going to get them for free, but Stavros told him, "Ten bucks." The cop shelled out a ten and left. If I hadn't been so scared, I would've died laughing.

15

SOUTH AMERICAN INTRIGUE

Nick and I were put in charge of setting up some bookmaking, poker machines, and other gaming for the mob in Bolivia and Colombia. I knew lots about gambling, and Nick knew the territory and had major contacts. Nick also had some business of his own down there, although he didn't tell me much about it. I figured it was a hit but I never asked. I rarely knew if he was doing Family business or his own freelance contract work for the CIA or some other international group.

The Colombian drug cartel had so much cash they could get away with anything; they could buy anyone. And they did. Their criminal organization had plenty of politicians from the United States to halfway around the world in Malaysia in their pocket.

Using them, they could get their own people into key positions in customs and all areas of local government. Often their ambassadors, who had immunity, helped transport their drugs. Hell, people with immunity could get caught with a hundred kilos and the worst that would happen to them would be deportation. And because of their political clout, ambassadors could call in favors if their drug-smuggling pals were arrested. They even had people who let them know when DEA officers were undercover or giving a push to their anti-drug campaigns.

We were using Nick's contacts to meet some of the high-level cartel members and scope out who was helping them. If we were lucky, we could convince them to help our Family, too, in ways other than drug trafficking. Nick was using our gambling business proposal to get closer to his assignment.

Nick taught me a lot about keeping my guard up at all times and to always be very aware of my surroundings. He wasn't comfortable on the flight from New York to Miami and was even quieter than usual. I don't think he liked being confined in a plane with nowhere to hide, and being too easily tracked coming off a flight at an airport. I didn't like to fly, so I ordered another straight Absolut, downed it in two mouthfuls and nodded off until we landed in Miami. At the gate, we transferred to another airline and a smaller plane for our flight to Bogotá.

When the plane's door opened, we were among the first passengers out and were met by two Latin men in suits and dark glasses who greeted us with a polite but formal handshake. Nick made the brief introductions in Castilian Spanish before the guys drove us in a private car and silence through the city of Bogotá. They dropped us off and made sure we got registered at Casa Medina in the business section of town. They didn't hang around after that.

It was a beautiful landmark hotel, and there were curvy ladies in the lounge who looked delicious, but it was already nine o'clock and we were jet-lagged, so we turned in for the night. Besides, I didn't want to go wandering around the streets of "Locombia," as some people called this crazy land. The police are more corrupt there than the average criminal.

Before the sun came up, Nick pounded on my door. At five, Javier and Raul picked us up and, after a twenty-minute drive, brought us to a small helicopter pad surrounded by tall sugar cane. Because the roads were always bad, filled with potholes and prone to guerrilla activities, anyone connected to the cartel used helicopters as their favored way to get around. There was no train service. Using cars and motorcycles would've been too dangerous and slow.

While I was like a kid looking out each side of the Jet Ranger III, Nick was his usual cool, calm self. I wondered if he had done this trip before. Nothing seemed to interest him. If he hadn't been here before, maybe he saw photos. He's always well briefed by his other organizations. I also remembered that he had once told me about an assignment from who-knows-who that sent him on some mission that brought him from Panama through the Darien Gap, the jungle that interrupts the Pan-American highway. The trek took several weeks of evading guerrillas who would have loved to kidnap someone like Nick, hoping somebody would make a high bid on his important butt to bring him back alive. As it was, when he came back from that assignment, he was way too skinny and had contracted malaria, something that came back periodically when he'd least expect it.

We were flown above miles of Amazonian jungle, along the Rio Magalena, and after about forty-five minutes of flight time, we began to descend into a narrow valley on the east side of the Andes Mountains. I was stunned to see a castle. Yeah, a huge castle, actually reconstructed from an original one in Ireland. It was so strange, suddenly popping out of the dense jungle all around it.

We landed on the roof of an annex to the main building. As the blades were slowing down, I watched three heavily armed men rush toward the helicopter. I didn't say nothing to Nick, but I got tense, thinking, "Oh shit, now what?"

I hadn't said the words, but Nick responded to my expression with, "No sweat. They're security men. Let them search you when we get out," instructed Nick.

They did, quite completely.

No guns. That was one of the most important rules of the house. Only El Jefe and his men were allowed to have them.

From the helicopter pad, I had another look at this guy's entire compound. Oh my God, it was amazing! There was a full eighteen-hole golf course, at least three guest houses that were bigger than any normal house I'd ever lived in, and two out of three of them had their own swimming pools. The garage area had two Rolls Royces, a Bentley, several Land Rovers parked outside, and I couldn't imagine what was behind the garage doors. Between the two areas, closer to the golf course, there were stables and several large paddocks.

Before we walked down the stairs, the helicopter took off again and I could see another, and two more behind it in the sky headed in our direction.

We were shown to our rooms and after our bags were delivered to us, we freshened up and we were invited to watch Jorge Menendez, the second-in-command of the cartel, show off his birds. Or we could go for a horseback ride or play golf. Nick and I got into a waiting Land Rover with two Mexican diplomats.

As we were driven away, our escort asked if we knew anything about hunting birds. None of us responded, so he explained that falconry uses birds of prey to hunt quarry in a natural environment. The guy went on and on about long-winged birds and short-winged ones. Which ones were good to use in the jungle and which were best in the open area of the compound. I had a parakeet as a kid; I hated pigeons. That's all I knew.

Not far from the house, we found Jorge had just returned in an open Jeep. Almost before his driver stopped, Jorge stepped out with a hawk on his gloved hand and arm.

"Hello, my friends," he greeted everyone as a group, then waited for Nick to introduce me.

That done, he told us about his just-finished hunt.

"I usually take Dracula here with me on horseback," he said of the goshawk, "but today I've let Ricardo use my favorite horse to escort our other guests for a ride."

We followed Jorge to a small building, bigger than any chicken coop I've ever seen. He put Dracula into a private section and took out another bird, Medusa. Assistants scurried with a cage of pigeons as Jorge explained, in far too much detail for me, how a hawk can catch another bird and break its neck in midair. Killer birds. Cool. Jorge loved his hawks and never let anyone else take care of them or hunt with them.

Nick paid close attention, coming out with comments that made my head turn. When the heck did Nick learn so much about falconry? Within a few minutes he had won over Jorge as a bird buddy. When Nick asked to put on the glove and hold the peregrine, Jorge obliged. After a pigeon was released, Jorge let Nick cast off Medusa. She did a good job soaring high and then swooped downward straight at the pigeon that was DOA when she landed back on Nick's arm. He and one of the Mexicans got into quite a conversation with Jorge while I chatted with the other one from Guadalajara. He was interested in finding U.S. outlets for his export company which, he indicated, "delivers all kinds of valuable goods, with a Mexican police escort," through the U.S. near Yuma.

After Nick was satisfied with killing three pigeons with two different hawks, Jorge showed him how to put the last bird away. He did, with more questions and interest in birds than I imagined he ever had. He took off the glove and put it away in the area Jorge indicated.

We got back to the house in two vehicles and were told that luncheon would start in an hour. I was glad to get back to my room and change into something that didn't smell like the great humid outdoors.

The luncheon was served in a ballroom filled with buffet tables piled high with all kinds of food, pastry, and ice carvings. Waiters eased through the crowd serving champagne or retrieving whatever other drink was ordered. It was hard for me to believe we were in the middle of nowhere surrounded by guerrilla rebels and elbow-to-elbow with some very powerful and dangerous men. I was only disappointed there were no broads. Not a one. I realized that even the staff was all male. Butlers everywhere; no maids. Just several hundred men; heads of state, ambassadors, corporate big-wigs, a big-weapons dealer, and a mobster or two, all there to discuss cartel business of one kind or another.

Nick looked off in a direction and held a stare. I followed his look. He told me the man in the middle of a conversation with several military types—out of uniform but unmistakable anywhere—was Enrique Luis Barrello, El Jefe himself. An impressive man, short but powerfully built with an attitude that oozed lethal charm.

As I mixed and mingled, I expanded my circle of contacts, as did everybody else, and I loved it. Soon, I saw two men I recognized from recent New York parties. They had been rather unapproachable in Manhattan, even antagonistic, and I suspected from the start that they had their own action going. As they approached me at this party, one had a funny grin on his face which could mean, "You're fuckin' dead," or "It's great to see you." It was a heart-stopping moment. They came over and we shook hands and they immediately introduced themselves to Nick as the Malaysian emissaries to the U.S. No one was playing games with their identities at least. I was just surprised that they didn't even seem shocked to see me there, when I couldn't believe it for myself. It was a quick conversation, because everyone was into schmoozing and moving around. There were a lot of really major guys there.

Ambassadors are the most sought-after international contacts for the drug dealers because they are exposed to fewer risks with their diplomatic immunity. They mix in the right circles to gather information and influence higher-ranking government officials. They can demand as much money as the cartel is willing to pay.

Eventually, Enrique made his way over to Nick and me. As he walked across the ballroom, everyone watched him move; they watched every move, if only through the corner of their eyes. He commanded attention. And he was friendly enough. Men made a path for him and turned to glance as he walked by them, giving him a pat on the shoulder and a quick "thank you." One or two nodded or winked at Enrique in a familiar way; he'd point back at them as if acknowledging some secret or inside joke.

"Michael D'Angelo," he addressed me, right after nodding to Nick. "I have heard a lot about you. Glad to have you with us," he said, shaking my hand.

"It's a pleasure to meet you," I answered, "Thank you for allowing me to join Nick for this wonderful event, Mr. Barrella."

"Enrique, please," he indicated. "I hope you enjoyed Jorge's killer hawks. This afternoon I want to show you some of my personal playthings."

"I look forward to that," I said.

Then Enrique turned to Nick. "Let's have a few minutes alone before we have too much champagne," he said, and the two of them walked away, out the French doors to the balcony, leaving me with Jorge, who looked annoyed to be excluded from Enrique and Nick's company. Still, he and I had a productive conversation about setting up gambling clubs while Nick was conducting business with our host.

I knew that Nick and Enrique had been close for a long time. They both shared a special interest in Manuel Noriega. This was just before allegations surfaced that the Panamanian leader was involved with drug trafficking, money laundering, and acting as a double agent for both the CIA and Cuba. Much later I found out that Nick was working with the CIA to rein in Noriega. Enrique wanted his drug-dealing competition eliminated so he could expand his own power. Jorge, who was starting to pull together his own power circle, was pro-Noriega.

The openly discussed topic for just about everybody at the party was cocaine production and distribution. Jorge introduced me to the guys in charge of transporting the cocaine from Colombia through Peru.

When Nick came back, we had a talk with a judge from New York who told us that it took two drug busts a month to keep things cool with the District Attorney.

Much of the U.S. government's slush funds came from money from drug dealers. Cooperation between certain government bigwigs and the cartels made certain national politicians look good in their war on drugs, while drug kickbacks and hush money helped them get elected and others build new wings on their Virginia headquarters. There were important individuals in the DEA and CIA who were crooked. The CIA allowed seventy percent of the drug trade to flow smoothly. It was fascinating to see how corrupt members of the government were involved in drug smuggling; the war on drugs was a bullshit political smokescreen. It wasn't about us against the drug smugglers; it's always about us against us. There was no way out of it with all the money that people made. They'd hate to lose it.

An hour and a half into the party, Enrique addressed his guests. "Gentlemen, enjoy yourselves here at my home. Use any of the facilities here. They are all at your disposal."

He went on about how valuable everyone in the room was to him, how happy he was to have such important men working with him. Enrique referred to product and profits without using the words drugs or cocaine. Everyone understood what he was talking about. Soon after, some headed for the links, others the stables or the pool.

Only a handful, including me and Nick, were driven to the weapons bunker. There were cases of M-16 and M-60 machine guns, grenades, rocket and grenade launchers, and missiles. Plenty of nine-millimeter pistols, too. It became obvious that one of the guests from the party was Barrello's supplier. He was happy to give us some demonstrations of his latest goods. I wanted to get my hands on some of those big guns. I did. From almost a mile away, I shot a tree in half with a sixty-six millimeter Law training rocket. I had no doubt it could've taken out a tank, and the recoil could've taken off my face if I hadn't been prepared for the jolt. I'd never handled so much firepower in my life. What a rush!

When we got back to the main house, Nick and I returned to our rooms to change for cocktails and dinner. I went to his room to get him later, but he wasn't there. We caught up with each other in another huge dining room.

Dinner wasn't as business-oriented as I thought it would be, basically because there were over twenty guys sitting at a huge long table, most of them talking to each other all at once. There was a man from the office of a West Coast governor, one from Costa Rica and South Africa, too. I overheard bits of interesting conversation. There was talk about wives and girlfriends, trips to exotic places for work and fun, and heavier subjects like private paramilitary groups working unofficially for multinational oil companies, terrorizing Indians to get them to move off their native land. Someone in the group said the leaders of those groups were often Colombian guys who got their training from the U.S. Army's School of the Americas in Fort Benning. Down here they called it the School of the Assassins. There was talk about rival drug cartel conflicts, cultural cleansing, stuff like that. Some believed that many of the civilian deaths here were the result of the Colombian army, which got

American arms and supplies to fight the drug war. Some crazy politics. Listening to this made my Family business sound a lot safer.

But this kind of talk didn't interfere with anybody's appetite. Lots of great food and plenty of drinks disappeared. There was food there I had never heard of. Most of it was good; I wouldn't touch the entree with eyes still in its head.

After dinner, Nick suggested I turn in early, since I looked so tired and had had a few drinks during the banquet. He had some things he wanted to do alone.

"Are you sure? I'm fine. I could stick around and . . ."

"No, I'm fine," he said and cuffed me on the shoulder.

"Get me up if you need me, all right?"

"Sure," he said and walked away.

I got to my room and found the bed turned down, and water bubbling in the marble hot tub. What a life.

In the morning, before the sun was completely up, a butler knocked and wheeled in a cart with my breakfast. He opened the balcony doors and set up the table overlooking the pool. I hadn't ordered anything but there was juice, coffee, eggs Benedict, and toast. And a reminder to be downstairs in forty-five minutes.

Several SUVs and Jeeps drove us to another section of the plantation where they grew and processed the coca leaves for cocaine. It was like a field trip. Enrique greeted us at the factory and turned us over to Jorge to be shown the whole production process from leaves to brick.

For starters, there were wood frames laid flat with chicken wire on it. The workers take hundreds of pounds of coca leaves that have been soaked in lime water and kerosene for several days and lay it across the top of the chicken wire. I thought it was to dry out the leaves, but no. Men and women got up on the low platform and walked across the leaves barefoot. It made me think of those old movies with people stomping grapes in Italy. Anyway, they walked and walked until all the leaves turned to paste. About two hundred fifty pounds of leaves made a little more than two pounds of paste.

Then they scraped the paste off the wire and put it into big tubs. At another location, it was treated with sulfuric acid and potassium permanganate. This was then filtered and dried. Next, they used another chemical, ammonium hydroxide, over the mess and dried it again. That makes about twenty-two pounds of base cocaine from the original bunch of leaves. But they still weren't done.

The next thing all these short, little, brown workers—like busy ants running all over the place—did was dissolve the base cocaine in big vats of acetone mixed with the same kind of acid you use in your pool. White stuff settles out after about six hours. The mixture was poured through cloth to trap the crystals and then the remaining residue was wrung dry before being put into trays that looked like large ice-cube trays or loaf pans stuck together. That was all put under huge heat lamps or the sun to bake into two-pound hard, white bricks of pure cocaine.

Jorge looked like he enjoyed showing us this whole process. He was like a happy tour guide. But by the end of it, he was anxious to get to his hawks. He wanted to kill a few more pigeons. Nick and I were scheduled to leave on the first set of three Jet Rangers.

Enrique met us at the take-off structure and we made our good-byes with promises to continue our gambling venture. He and Nick exchanged a word or two and we were off. Two escorts joined us. Again, I loved watching the jungle, the waterfalls, and the river beneath us. Nick was his usual quiet self. We landed at the airport and were shuttled to our flight.

During our change of planes back in Miami, Nick got a call on his cell. He said only a few words, "Hello . . . Good . . . Yes . . . 'Bye."

Nick turned to me and said, "Jorge is dead."

"No shit?! What happened?" I was totally surprised.

"He was hunting Dracula and had a massive heart attack," Nick offered. "He had just released the hawk and dropped. The bird came back with its prey and hopped on Jorge's gloved arm anyway."

"Geez," was all I could say. Later, I found out what Nick's other business had been. At the time of his death, Jorge had had plans for a quiet coup against Enrique's cartel, the largest not under the protection of Manuel Noriega. Jorge was a hindrance to U.S. covert plans for Noriega in which Nick played a part.

Nick never told me the full details of his work, whether inside the Family or outside of it. He was a total pro. Only years later did Nick explain his smart-ass trick with Jorge's falconry glove, some liquid nicotine, and a self-dissolving release gimmick. He set it up to release inside the lining when Jorge stuck his hand into the glove. If he felt the dampness, it would've been too late anyway. By the time Jorge fell to the ground, Nick was halfway to Bogotá with not a whisper of suspicion coming his way. What a guy!

16

NEARLY KILLED, ALMOST REDEEMED

A Chicago winter is as far from the South American climate as you can get. It had started to snow as I drove home from a meeting with some of my guys at one of the social clubs. I was glad I'd be home for the night, before the weather got really bad, and I looked forward to seeing white-covered ground and trees in the morning. I always loved winter. The sharp air always made me feel awake, alive, ready to move.

A classical station was playing Beethoven on the radio as I drove my hard-top convertible Corvette—the one Sam had given me as a birthday gift when I turned sixteen—along the parkway service road near the airport. I felt a little hungry and sorry I hadn't grabbed at least a calzone before I left the club. There was some leftover lasagna at home that made me hungrier when I remembered it. My stomach growled as I saw a truck come up behind me on the two-lane road. He was in far more of a hurry than I was, so I realized Mr. Federal Express was going to pass me. Not much traffic anywhere. No big deal. I slowed a little, he veered into the oncoming lane, made his pass and came back into my lane. Too soon. Too close.

Thunk! Screech!

In a heartbeat, the truck cut me off, its rear end butting my left front end and throwing my car to the right. Hitting the brakes on the wet pavement, I went into the spin that started on impact. In slow motion, I felt my car spin again and then fly off the shoulder. Airborne, my adrenaline level surged as I waited for the impact of landing. The slam came sideways; me and my car rolled and rolled some more. It rolled eighteen times, taking down an old chain-link fence as it went.

All I saw lit up by the headlights were trees, branches, and bramble in a blur. All I felt was my head knocked repeatedly against the side window, the seatbelt digging into my neck when it slipped as I was jostled. The horn blasted spasmodically. The ravine went deeper. In a flash I wondered if I would burst into flames or be crushed. Before my car flew again, the seatbelt came undone, and I was thrown left and right and finally through the windshield, battered into unconsciousness when the car slammed into a sturdy, old tree.

Most of us like to think we'll die at a ripe old age in our sleep. Safe and peaceful. With the kind of crazy life I was leading, with all the dangerous things I did, in all the unsavory places I worked, I didn't expect to be killed in a simple car accident. I was a safe driver, no thrill-seeking race car demon. So what was I doing in a car rolling endlessly down a fuckin' ravine? You can never guess what you will be thinking when you just *know* you're about to die.

It was over an hour before firemen and paramedics got my broken and bleeding body untangled and hauled back up to the road. I remember only parts of this. The first thing I vaguely recall were noises, sensations of movement, a few dreamlike specks of flashing white and red and blue light. I don't remember feeling pain, or anything, not even scared. I don't think I could've talked if I wanted to. Then noises got louder. And I saw, but not through my own eyes, not from the body lying on the gurney being wheeled into the emergency room.

I was watching from above, six feet over everything. It was like I was being pulled along, like a balloon in a kid's hand. I was somehow attached to the body I barely recognized as my own as the gurney was pushed down the corridor. But I felt none of the injuries. I saw the nurses and doctors, the paramedics. I saw my mother, and Nick and my dad holding her back, hugging her for support. Paulie was there, too. He was nearby trying to talk a nurse into letting my mom go to me.

I heard her cry, "My baby! Michael! My baby! Let me go! Let me go! I have to be with him!" But they didn't let her go, just held her tighter as she struggled.

As the paramedics wheeled the gurney around the corner and through the next set of doors, a doctor rushed over. An EMT told him, "He's DOA. We lost him. No vitals for the last twelve minutes."

"Let me take a look," the doctor said, pushing the EMT aside as he lifted eyelids, felt for a pulse. "Get him into Number Three with the code blue cart."

At the nurses' station, someone was talking about getting off duty in a half hour; she had a date. Another nurse was calling the lab for results on a heart attack patient and was pissed that she was put on hold. An X-ray tech was coming on to a unit secretary until an intern told him to get the patient with an injured leg to X-ray. This is what I saw and heard as my unconscious body pulled me through the air to Number Three treatment room.

There, two nurses started cutting the remaining clothes off my body. My chest was bare, my slacks cut free. An older doctor came in and repeated the exam the first doctor made.

"He's gone. Official time of . . ."

"Wait a minute, let's shock him," interrupted the doc, who had met the paramedics at the door. "He's my patient!"

"Okay, Lloyd, do what you want, but hurry up. It's a full-moon Saturday night. We're awful busy," chided the older doctor who shook his head and walked out asking someone in the hall, "How's the food poisoning in Eight doing? Keep the saline going until I get the labs. And call a psych consult. There's something else going on with that one."

I'm still watching from the ceiling, curious and confused as the doc and nurses were busy around my bloody body. There was a tube down my throat. The paddles were readied. The doc called, "Clear!" and zapped my body and it jumped. I didn't feel a thing. He did this two more times and seemed happy with the results he saw on a monitor. He ordered some shots; they were given. But something happened and he called for the paddles again. I felt myself rise higher; I saw the room and I saw the other rooms. I saw my mother crying, with Dad holding her and Nick nearby. A nurse asked if she needed something to calm her. But everything got brighter, then images went fuzzy. I was dying. I knew the other guys were right. I was dead on arrival.

Forget what they say about a peaceful white light, about a warm and happy glow. I started feeling again. First, a dull slam like I was knocked to a wrestling mat. And then I started seeing different things. Not the hospital room, not the nurses and the doctor that wouldn't give up. I knew they were there, but what I saw was straight out of Hell.

Fire and all. Red, blue, yellow flames were crawling all over my body like snakes. I can't say I felt the heat. I felt terror and wanted to scream, but no noise came out. My mouth was wide open and straining, my throat burned, but I couldn't make a sound. I heard laughter, different voices in each ear.

"Yo, Honky! Hey, Mike the Match, remember me?" a black specter wielding a crowbar whispered.

"Smell something, white boy? Yeah, it's regular unleaded," said the other as the first one gouged out my left eye with the pointed end of the crowbar and the other sliced my right eyelid off with his switchblade. I smelled gasoline burning flesh, as blood oozed down my face.

Through the flames, the kind doctor's face came close to mine. The pimps disappeared, and the doc leaned into me while two topless nurses, no, they were dancers from Dreamway, pushed me horizontal. Doc had paddles in his hands. No, his hands were Freddy Krueger blades. Oh no! He jabbed hard and fast into my chest and razor fingers scooped out my stomach and intestines that slipped through his metal fingers as he placed most of the gore on a hanging scale. I was dead and in Hell. I was sure of it.

I felt like I must've peed myself.

"Oh God! Let me wake up. I gotta be dreaming. This can't be Hell. I can't stay here forever!"

As if in answer to my cry for help, Stavros appeared. He had brought me flowers. Smiling, he held them out to me with bloodied hands, but the next thing I knew, my leg was sawed off at mid-thigh, right below where an ice-pick protruded. He hacked off the foot and dropped it into a fifty-gallon drum. I felt no physical pain, but I was aware of a heaviness against my chest, like a huge vice holding me. It was hard for me to breathe; I was strangling in undying death.

Yani came to me next. With his disembodied face floating in front of me he asked, "Who are you to judge me? Why did you play God? Everything you do, have done, or will ever do again, you do to yourself. Remember that."

I turned away and back again. He was gone. I looked up and saw nameless faces hovering above me, calling, "Mi-chael, Mi-chael.

Hell-ooo," over and over again. I turned my one-eyed gaze away and found Bruno, with his demented smile, firing shots from his nine-millimeter pistol into me. I didn't feel a thing but raw terror. With pliers, another ghostlike demon was methodically snipping off the toes of my remaining foot. There was someone behind me coldly chanting, "Fuck-him-fuck-him-fuck-him."

"Oh God! What's happening? Where am I? Let me out of here!" I screamed in silence. That was the closest thing to a prayer I had uttered in many years.

Again, I thought my cry was answered when beautiful Angela touched my cheek, leaned forward and kissed my lips. "I love you, Michael, and I'll never leave you," she murmured as she ran her fingers down my neck, across my shoulder, down my arm.

"Help me!" I pleaded. "You can save me from this, Angela. Help me!"

She took my hand and kissed my palm, then took the red and swollen finger pricked in my initiation and kissed it, and drew the blood from it. I remembered, but couldn't feel, the rush of excitement we shared in lovemaking.

"I love you, Michael, but you should never have left me," she spoke while kissing my finger. Then she took it into her mouth to the base knuckle.

Crack! Blinding pain, real fuckin' pain exploded, shattering me into a million pieces as Angela bit off my finger. A flash of brilliant cold light blasted the darkness. Nothing more existed. No one was there; nothing, not even me.

Slowly, I came back to ER Number Three, floating closer to my body, practically touching it. The doctor looked drained as he turned and walked away from my gurney. A nurse pushed the code blue cart with its paddles and wires out of the room.

At the door, another nurse told the doc, "They're ready for him in ICU. Jamie will take him up the first chance he gets. Can his mother come in now?"

"No, tell her . . . no, I'll talk to her," he said and disappeared.

I couldn't see so much anymore. I felt like I was in and out of my own body. But I could hear, I swear I could, as the doc told my mom I was likely going to be all right, that the next twenty-four hours would be critical. I think that's when my spirit relaxed and I went back to myself and slept without dreams, without ghosts.

When I woke up the next day, over twenty-four hours after being brought in DOA to the emergency room, I found Sam had managed to sneak into my room and sat at my bed all night. That's how he was. I was glad to see his face.

"How ya' doin', kid?" he asked, his eyes red from being so tired. "I just wanted to make sure you didn't do no talking in your sleep."

I was so exhausted I couldn't talk. I just reached for Sam's arm and he put his hand over mine until I fell back to sleep. A few hours later, I woke up again. Sam was gone. I asked for my doctor.

"You are the one who saved me when everyone else gave up," I said. "I saw everything. You, the nurses doing stuff to me. Thank you."

He believed me because he had heard things like I was telling him before. But he tried to explain it all with scientific reasons. I let him talk, but I knew what I had gone through, and that it came from something more than traumatic stress and chemicals in the brain. Even the action at the nurses' station was verified. I had seen it all while DOA.

After the doc left, I thought about everything that I saw while I was dead. I saw the ghosts clearly, but the terror had subsided. It was weird, but I felt like I had learned something important. I felt like I was allowed to live again. It wasn't the first time I had escaped death. This time Someone was telling me, "This is what you have done. You've done it to your soul as well as to the people in your life. Take a good look at what you are doing with the rest of your life."

A parish priest came up and talked to me when I was in the

hospital. I told him I was having bad feelings about my life. He listened, never asking questions. He didn't have to because he had known my family for years. I felt like I could redeem myself. For the first time ever, I actually felt bad about the things I did. I was so sorry, so very sorry. I learned what it's like to have a conscience. When I was alone, I wanted to cry, but I knew if I let myself do that, I would break. I would never be the same again. Something would be totally lost. I didn't know what, but I couldn't let myself break down and cry. It would be the end of me. Maybe I should have let that happen. But I didn't.

For the two weeks I was in the hospital, I swore I was never going to do anything bad again. I had been given yet another chance at life. When I got home, my mom took care of me. I had so much money, I didn't need anything and I really thought I was through. I would quit. I didn't need the crazy life anymore. I didn't need to create more ghosts.

People came to visit me every day. It was terrific, especially as I started to feel better. My parents had this humongous custom-made bed, bigger than king-size. I swear, it could fit ten people across it, and sometimes it did. I had a whole harem of girls who loved to take care of me, brought me things, cooked for me, pampered and fussed over me. I felt like a sultan or something. They were all great friends. And guys would come over, too, often bringing me money.

The guys who visited me most were Nick, Sam, and Paulie. I loved them for being there for me. Nick kept a lot to himself, but whenever I was hurting or in some trouble, he was there for me. Sam, on the other hand, always had good stories to tell me. He had made a big name for himself as an independent. Bosses would contact him from everywhere when they needed in-house cleaning. When Sam showed up in another city, people were petrified, wondering who was going to get whacked. Even bosses got nervous. He wasn't answerable to any one boss. If someone had a beef with him, the committee of bosses got together and one would become responsible for talking to him. If Sam or Nick were not on my side, I would be scared to death. I found it impressive how they made assassination an art form.

Paulie always had some story about his latest broad when he came to visit me while I was recuperating. During the first week I was home, Paulie brought two of his latest playmates into the house one evening when my dad was out doing business and my mom had gone to dinner with Uncle Frank's wife, Maria. One was a hot redhead and the other had the longest, blackest hair I'd ever seen. The two of them definitely lifted my spirits and made me forget my pains.

As I got healthier and stronger, I started thinking about what was going on without me taking care of business. It was time for me to get back into action. I had survived; I was okay. But I felt sad, like my life had changed in a way I didn't understand, and it was uncomfortable. It felt good to be looked after, to be around people who were so loving and lovable. I was nowhere near any violence of any kind for over a month. But I didn't know what to do with myself.

When you hang around doctors and lawyers and stockbrokers, those are the kinds of things you talk about. You talk about medical science and corporate life and the stock market. You talk about the law, court cases. Hang around a bunch of gangsters and you are talking about your next score, you are talking about whacking. Your environment dictates what you are going to do with your life. That is what happened with me.

My first day up and out I took care of a little problem we were having with an adult bookstore in our area. They didn't want to pay tax for our protection. So I went in there, right in the middle of the day, and took care of the misunderstanding. I made a killing, about thirty-five thousand dollars that day alone.

I also had to deal with an arrest. I was charged with trespassing on federal land because my car broke through the airport fence when it rolled off the road. Crazy as that was, I had to go to court. When I went before the judge, he thought the prosecutors were nuts. He saw the report of what happened. It was a hit-and-run with witnesses. One witness came forward and gave a statement about how the Federal Express truck was going too fast and moving erratically. The judge also saw from the reports that I had spent a couple of weeks in the hospital and a month bedridden at home. He not only dismissed the case, but pointed out that I had an excellent lawsuit not only against Federal Express, but the government for wrongful prosecution. But when I followed up and filed lawsuits, background checks on me gave everybody ammunition against me. It was like they were trying to blackmail me and I decided to let things go.

The old life was a bitch, but one I knew how to handle. My ghosts were shoved back somewhere I didn't have to see them. I had work to do.

17

REDEFINING MOB POLICY

Because Philadelphia was so dysfunctional, I had a lot of opportunities to do new business there. There was no local leadership out there, no real boss in play because Ricky Delgado and his next in command, Ralph Napolitano, were both in jail and Joey Bellini was acting boss. Of course, Bellini wanted to be boss, but he didn't have the know-how. Delgado had been a pretty good boss, ran his own town. But when he got put away, Philadelphia was pretty much an open town.

Overall, Philadelphia fell under the jurisdiction of New York, where my grandfather's influence outlived him. Las Vegas is under the control of Chicago. Anybody who wants to start something in Las Vegas or Philadelphia has to get permission from Chicago or

New York. I had bloodline connection to both. I did a lot of things other people couldn't do because I wasn't stepping on people's toes. I had a lot of influence in Chicago because my dad Dominic had so much business there. I'd start up a number of my own businesses—pizza parlors, carpet cleaning, arcades with something going on behind the scenes, like bookmaking or making loans—on the sneak. I could get away with having businesses of my own by spreading them out all over. Fewer people knew exactly what I was doing. Whenever I opened up a new legitimate venture, it started with Family money that came from some illegal operation. It was always a matter of money laundering. So it was necessary to kick money up to the next level of the organization. The more businesses I owned in more cities, the fewer people I had to answer to. One boss would think I'm kicking money up to another boss. Doing things on the quiet, my personal businesses brought me more money. After I was in play and making money, nobody cared. I made sure everybody who was supposed to got what was coming to them. I always remembered the advice, "If you want to be somebody, you gotta produce. You gotta make money." Money is always power. So I had a reputation for getting things done. I didn't go into Philadelphia like a gangbuster. New York knew what I was doing. They knew I did good work in Chicago and New York, so they let me do what I could in Philadelphia. As much as any Philadelphia boss wanted to believe the city was on its own, it always answered to New York.

The one guy in town that I figured had some moxie was Joe Delvecchio. He had a big bookmaking business that was doing very well and a lot of other action, too, so I started to work with him a little bit. There were a half-dozen things in that city that I wanted to get into. I thought about bringing my crew into Philadelphia and becoming the boss. I could have, but I didn't. I came in quiet and simple. Still, when I got there, the streets were talking. Everyone wondered about what I would do.

First thing I did was buy a pizza joint at a great location not far from Pat's Steak House, a hangout for the New York D'Angelos, near Tenth and Carpenter. I bought the place for fifteen thousand dollars. The rent was six hundred; I brought in a thousand a week profit. It was a gold mine. We made great pizzas and used it for a gambling front. I also bought into a towing company so I could start a chop shop for hot cars. When I took over that pizzeria, I had neighbors dropping in all the time. People started asking me for favors, and I had never said a word. They just knew who I was and what I could do. Like I said, the streets were talking even before I actually showed up. They knew I was coming.

At that time, we were partners with Robert Sterling, who was one of the biggest adult bookstore owners in the city. With him, we took over more bookstores and got into other things like clubs and gambling. I also had a piece of a little restaurant in Rittenhouse Square.

But the Japanese were in my way. They had virtually all the massage parlors, maybe a hundred, with over a dozen in one tight area in the heart of our turf. They were really whorehouses. We had a few, not many. The thing was, nobody was taxing the Japanese parlors.

"What the fuck is up with that?" I asked Bellini over dinner, just between the two of us. "That's money we're just letting slip right outta our hands. They are in our territory."

"Oh, they're in a world of their own," said Bellini.

"Yeah? So what! We gotta go in and take their joints and let them know they're in *our* world, pal."

Bellini was lazy. He just shrugged, "We don't want to deal with those guys. Nobody cares about them. Not even the cops."

"Fuckin' great!" I was getting hot. "So if no one bothers them they're just pulling in the cash and keeping it all to themselves. What's the matter with you?"

"Fuck 'em, D'Angelo," he blustered. "It's not such a good idea. We got enough of our own action."

"Hey, you said the police don't bother them. Why not? The department belongs to us. The Japs don't have them in their pocket, so why should they get a free ride?"

"Oh those parlors don't make much money," Bellini insisted, but when I asked "how much?" he couldn't answer.

I could see I was getting nowhere with this acting boss, who wasn't acting like one at all. I didn't care if the Japanese were making a little or a lot of money. Some of it belonged to us. So I brought this situation to the attention of everybody else in New York and a few sharp guys in Philadelphia. They all wanted answers from Bellini about why he hadn't been taxing the Japanese massage parlors, but he had no answers. Bottom line, he was afraid that moving in on the massage parlor action would cause a big battle with the Yakuza, and he was afraid of them as a group. Like we didn't have our own organization, and on our turf. Geez.

Like I said, the Japanese had, just in one small area, about a dozen massage parlors, open twenty-four hours, seven days a week. Each one of those joints had maybe ten to twelve girls there all the time. These girls didn't get much money. In fact, they lived right there in one or two back rooms and were treated almost as bad as slaves.

So I structured a plan. I got some local cops and paid them off a little bit. They started to put the heat on the Japanese joints, hassling them every day. They lost some of their girls because they were arrested. It cost them money to get them out of jail, for lawyers, everything. It was a big pain in the ass for them. This went on for only a few weeks before we got word that the Japanese leaders wanted to have a meeting with us. Of course, when the Japanese started to break, everyone including Bellini wanted to take credit for changing things.

Generally, Japanese guys were hard to deal with; horrible really. They took shit from nobody. Yakuza. These guys were tough and had been around a long time, like since about 1600. They started out as a bunch of young guys who rebelled against the Samurai warlords. They were more like Robin Hoods than street hoods then. But most of them were rounded up and killed about a hundred years later. The idea of a rebel group still hung around. After the Second World War, everyone, everywhere wanted to have their own gangster group like the Sicilian Mafia. The young Japanese gangsters started copying our look: tailored dark suits and sunglasses. But underneath their clothes they also had hundreds of tattoo designs all over their bodies. By the sixties, some agencies considered them as big as, if not bigger than, the Cosa Nostra. One of their biggest gangs started out on the waterfront in Kobe and really took off when Taoka Kazuo, Japan's Al Capone, took over. To this day, they have such strong ethics among their own. You see very few of them in prison because they're smart and don't rat on each other. And they're tough, with their tattoos and their finger-chopping punishments.

Anyway, the Japanese finally realized where the heat was really coming from and sent a messenger to one of our social clubs to make some inquiries. Of course, everyone who wanted to take credit for starting their problems didn't want to take credit now. Someone told the messenger that I was the man who put the heat on them. So they wanted a meeting, but not on our turf, on theirs. Through this messenger, I negotiated the meeting. We would meet in a small neutral restaurant, La Rouge, downtown. It was rented like a private party for a few hours in the afternoon. Nobody else would be there, just some of us, and some of them, and no one would come armed. Sure. They left their Uzis home, and we packed light and discreet.

Five of us pulled up in two cars. The Japs were already there and by the number of cars outside, we figured there were a lot of them.

"Geez, four cars with a waiting driver each," Joe commented. "How many of 'em does it take to screw in a light bulb?"

"There are two over there," Johnny noticed, "And there goes one inside to announce our arrival."

"They're obviously nervous," I huffed. "We got the upper hand. They're the ones who've got the problem right now. Nothin' horrible is gonna happen."

One of their guys stayed at the door, but he didn't make a move to open it for us. He was trying to save face already.

"Alfie, you stay out here and keep this nice gentleman company," I said to our driver as four of us entered.

The French restaurant was very chic, with paned glass doors that opened to outdoor tables. Inside it was very intimate, with silk and brocade fabric on the furniture. Classy. The Japanese guys, ten of them, were all impeccably dressed in dark suits and, even in the low light inside, sunglasses. None of them smiled; they hung on to their unreadable non-expression as they sat at a cluster of tables that inadvertently put them in an audience position I used to my advantage.

"So, how ya' doin', guys?" I blustered, in a subdued manner by my standards and over the top by theirs. I reached out my hand to the man standing, knowing he was the man in charge, Hiro. He almost didn't take it, but shook it with the slightest of wry smiles. He suggested with a slight backhand wave that we sit down, just the two of us at one table. Joe, Eddie, and Tommy sat at a table behind me.

"It's come to my attention," I started, dismissing any small talk before it started, "that you're having some trouble with your business here in Philadelphia. Perhaps you can use our help."

Hiro stayed as motionless as a lizard sunning itself on a rock.

"We do not need your 'help,' Mr. D'Angelo," he spoke in the loudest whisper I ever heard. "We have been doing excellent business here for several years now."

He paused and leaned forward, "We are here today because you have been trying to cause us a great deal of annoyance."

"Oh no, Hiro," I said with a chuckle that wasn't quite a laugh in his face. "We wouldn't want to cause any newcomer to our city 'annoyance.' You're still practically guests here. It wouldn't be gracious. That's why we're here today. To explain the way things work here . . ."

I sat back and took out a cigar, clipped it, lit it and took a deep drag. Hiro sighed but said nothing. Maybe he was seething. It didn't matter to me. Most of his crew were nearly motionless, too, except one who reached for the water pitcher on the table and poured himself a refill. My guys were on the alert, too. Just in case.

"We will not tolerate interference, Mr. D'Angelo," Hiro hissed. "You are going to back off from us, or we are going to cause you problems, too."

"No, you won't," I said, and pushed back. "You can't."

"Who are you to tell us we can't do our business undisturbed? The police are already involved."

"The police aren't involved," I made it clear to him. "They are not going to be interested in anything you have to say. We put the police onto you. The police are there to remind you that you are in *our* town. You think you can do business without us? I'll tell you how we work. You need to pay taxes to us every week."

Hiro didn't move a muscle. Then his thin-lipped mouth uttered, "We don't pay anybody. We pay our own expenses, the rent, and take care of our girls. We do everything and we do not have any need for partners."

"No, Hiro, it doesn't work that way," I said with a smile. "What you are doing is a criminal activity. That falls under our domain and if you want to continue doing business, we are going to tax you. Or you don't do business here. Period." The words were pointed. I wanted to see where his attitude would go.

Still stone-steady, Hiro argued, "You are trying to take our business away . . ."

"Oh no, Hiro, no, no, that's not the case," I interrupted. "We're taxing you, not putting you out of business. You are on our ground. If we were to go to Japan, you could tax me. That's just business. We make money together. Or we can go to war. How much would you lose then? Maybe we would both lose. That's not good thinking if nobody makes money and just suffers a lot of grief. I think it's better that we both make money."

Still, Hiro was immobile, thinking, analyzing his next words. I didn't say anything. Instead, I let the silence hang in the air, letting him know I didn't have to explain my point any further.

The Japanese are so different to do business with than anyone else. Take the Russians. With them, you have to sit there and party until you're ready to drop. They drink vodka like it's water. That can be helpful, because they talk a lot more than they should when they're drunk, and they like to be drunk. They're hardcore individuals who have been through prisons in their country that are a thousand times harder than ours, and you have to be buddy-buddy with them to do good business.

Gypsies, on the other hand, cannot be trusted at all. They are the bottom feeders, preying on the weak and old in their petty crime world. They hurt the poor. They are not murderers. They are not fighters. They are scam artists with their fortune telling and elderly care scams. They're heavy into recycling wiring, copper, metal. Petty people.

I knew the man in front of me would look at the bottom line, have a corporate outlook on the situation. Hiro understood business. I respected him. I liked the way he conducted himself.

I watched Hiro and knew his mind was sorting through the possibilities. He realized we weren't interested in throwing him out of town or strong-arming him out of business.

"And what privileges do we buy with the taxes we pay you, Mr. D'Angelo?" he ventured and went into business negotiating mode.

"We want what is rightfully ours," I said. "A percentage of your take every week. Every day I can protect you and your employees from being arrested, and your places from being shut down. I can keep the building inspectors and fire marshals from coming around. Think about all the money you save in fines and legal fees."

"I see," Hiro nodded. "How much of a percentage?"

"Twenty."

"That's too much."

"No it isn't," I said and stared. "Plus one-hundred fifty thousand in the next three days. You owe back taxes."

Hiro was in danger of losing some major face. Unconsciously, his right foot started to tap to an unheard rhythm.

I lightened up. "I'm your new partner and best contact here in Philadelphia. If you need something, you can call me. Heaven forbid, you get a traffic ticket, I can help you." I leaned forward so only he could hear, "Take the deal."

Hiro gave a sort of short laugh as if we had shared a joke.

"Throw in a Mercedes," he said, smiling for the first time, "and we can celebrate our new partnership."

I practically slapped him on the back as I got up.

We shook hands and I politely dismissed him with, "Hey, I look forward to doing business with you. Now go pick out the car you like and let me know the year, model, and color you want. I'll see what I can do."

He gave a glance to his men, and they all left.

In a half hour, I had handled my first "take control of the turf" situation and I had done it well. Without violence, using some business sense, I gained a lot of respect from everyone. Everybody got what they wanted. Nobody wants bloodshed.

I got Hiro the Mercedes he requested, and that opened up another little business. They wanted stolen Mercedeses, to bring back to Japan.

Business boomed from there. I gave the Japanese a New Jersey connection for the cars. The Jersey crew kicked back to me on the deals they made. So working with the Japanese was profitable in many ways. It turned out that their massage parlor tax brought us a cool one hundred thousand dollars a week in new revenue.

I was finished with my work in this city. I had redefined some of the ways things were done there. I had set up some of my own businesses. But unlike Chicago and New York, Philadelphia was not where I belonged and even though it was there for the taking, I wasn't interested. Philadelphia had been another arena where I could make another mark for myself, proving I could handle things anywhere—whether in a country like Colombia or another city here in the U.S. Taking Philadelphia wasn't my goal. I wanted to be more independent, like Nick and Sam. To do that, I had to prove myself in many ways, establish a power base that encompassed a lot of different territories. It also meant making a lot of money for the Family. As well as for myself.

18

A LETHAL LESSON

Some of the guys from my old Oak Park neighborhood thought they could be pretty good thieves. There were about five of them running around in an independent gang. There were a couple of Italian brothers and three Irish kids. They had made a few scores in middle-class neighborhoods and decided to raise their sights, so they started to hit on the high-end homes. They did well with the first one or two, getting about eighty thousand dollars worth of cash and jewelry over the course of a few weeks. But they made one big mistake. They didn't always check to find out whose house they were robbing.

They burglarized the multimillion dollar home of Chicago's crime boss, Anthony Capelli, and made off with a huge amount of jewelry, cash, and guns. When word spread on the street that

Capelli's home, his private sanctuary, was violated, these kids had nowhere to go. Everybody knew who they were; they were local. It wasn't long before they were rounded up one by one. One of them, Larry, a guy who used to try to hang with me in high school and was with me the night Mandy Lewis was almost raped, was actually wearing one of Anthony's stolen rings when some soldiers brought him to the boss. He was lucky Capelli's men didn't take his finger off with the ring.

Every one of the kids tried to deny the whole thing. That was another stupid mistake they made. Then they tried to get Capelli to agree that if they gave back everything, it would be all right. Like they had anything to be negotiating. Bigger mistake. Capelli was going to get his goods back regardless. Maybe if they had been real men and admitted what they had done, there would have been a chance Capelli would have given them a pass with a less severe punishment.

Some of the other bosses tried to sway Capelli, hoping he would finally give the kids a break.

"Make them bring your stuff back to you," one said to Capelli. "Scare the shit out of them. Torture them if you have to, but give them a pass," another suggested.

"They're just kids trying to make their way. Everyone starts somewhere," and "So they screwed up. They didn't know it was your house, " came from others.

It all fell on deaf ears.

What made it worse was that there was some question about whether the kids really didn't know it was Capelli's house. They were stupid and cocky and disrespectful, too. They had to be taught a lesson, so in the future other guys understood there was no way they could cross this powerful man and get away with it. There were just certain things that were never done. You never violated a fellow crew member; you never slept with another guy's wife; you never messed with another guy's blood family, no matter how pissed off with him you were; and you didn't touch his home in any way. The band of five renegades weren't part of our organization. They were total outsiders and they crossed one of the most sacred lines: the front door. And not even just the home of a soldier, or a lieutenant, but the boss himself.

Their deaths were ordered.

Over several days, the kids were found piece by piece by piece. One all chopped up in a trunk of a car; his brother, all chopped up in a garbage can; the hand of one showed up in a box in his backyard but the rest of him was never found. The paper on another was given to me. I had to take care of Larry, the kid I knew from high school.

The boss in charge of any particular city, in this case Capelli, has the right to bypass an underboss and give orders to anybody, even the lowest associate, or anybody in between. The underboss makes sure the order is followed out. The paper came to me directly from Capelli, but my dad, as my boss at the time, had to make sure the job was completed. Also, since I was relatively close to this kid, I possibly had more opportunities to get to him than anybody else did. Having me do the job was a statement on several levels. It didn't matter if the guy was somebody I knew. I had to follow orders. Not only was it a test for me but it showed everybody else in the organization that at any moment they too could be called upon to do something that, like it or not, they would have to do. Capelli was telling everybody that no one violates his home. He was also telling us that we could disagree with him—so many of us wanted him to give the kids a pass, myself included—but he was the boss, period. What he said was the final word. Making someone who disagreed with him do the job was a kind of punishment for questioning him.

After I got the paper on Larry, I left Capelli at the social club and went home to make some calls and figure out a plan. I was in my house only a few minutes when Nick dropped by.

"I heard," he said and grabbed himself a can of soda from the refrigerator.

"Yeah, I gotta take care of it as soon as possible."

"Wanna soda while I'm in here?" he asked, before he closed the door.

"Nah, I could use a double Absolut, but not right now. I gotta think."

Nick sat down in an armchair, put his feet up and didn't say very much. It wasn't his way.

I called Rico, who had a lead on Larry's whereabouts.

"The kid's been shacking up with an older woman in Hickory Hills," Rico filled me in. "He's been at her house for the last two nights. But I hear he's gonna leave town, alone, sometime late tonight. He's driving. Maybe to Los Angeles. He's at the house alone now, but the woman is gonna be home from work in less than an hour."

"Gimme the address." He did and I figured I'd wait until at least dusk before I headed out.

I took a soda out of the refrigerator, and my twenty-two from my safe. As I checked that it was clean and attached the silencer, Nick and I talked.

"Geez, Nick, I hung out with this guy in high school," I told him. "We played foosball, shot some pool, played cards every now and then."

Nick listened.

"We weren't tight like buddies," I rambled. "I thought the kid was someone who had no direction, no idea what he wanted outta life. Ya' know, he talked tough but didn't have any balls."

"He found the balls to heist Capelli," Nick said.

"I think he got suckered into doing the robberies by the two brothers. They always yanked him around in school."

Nick shrugged, "It doesn't matter."

I knew he was right. Whenever I've gotten the paper, I knew it was a justified hit. This time I wondered if giving me someone I knew was some kind of message to me. Like Capelli wanted to see if my car accident had done any damage to my balls.

"Justice must be served," I nodded, aware it's not my place to question a boss's decision. It's just easier to administer justice when I feel it's one-hundred percent deserved.

Nick watched as I adjusted my holster.

"I know what my role is," I said, talking more to myself than to Nick, the consummate assassin. "The guy has got to go."

I knew I had to shut up and set my mind to understanding I'm doing the right thing. While Nick relaxed, I told myself over and over, "Larry did wrong. This is the justice I have to serve him." I didn't like thinking about it so much. In the past, I usually didn't.

"Want me to come along?" Nick offered, maybe sensing something. He knew this was my first paper since the accident. He was one of the few people I told in detail about my near-death experience.

Geez, I thought. Now he thinks I'm gonna fuck this up. He was practically telling me he'd take this off my hands. I knew I could trust him not to tell anyone if I took him up on his offer, but he would know and I'd feel ashamed.

"Nah, I've got Rico on hold. He's staking out the house," I explained. "He'll call me again in a little while."

I told myself I could stuff my conscience into a little box and put it on a shelf. If it escaped again, I'd deal with it.

"Okay," said Nick as he raised himself out of the chair. "If you finish up before one, I'll be at the River's Edge. I'll buy you an Absolut."

"Thanks, maybe I'll see you later."

Nick let himself out, and as I heard his car pull away, Rico called.

"The broad got home and he's already put a bag in the trunk of his car," he said. "I think you better get over here. Looks like he's gonna make his good-bye real soon."

"Okay, you know what to do with his car. I'm on my way and I'll be down at the second cross street headed west toward the parkway. In the gas station, near the air pump. If he leaves sooner than fifteen minutes, call my cell phone."

I was on my way, a few blocks from the gas station when Rico called. "He's movin' in the direction of the parkway, driving a blue Camaro . . ."

"I see him," I interrupted. "Perfect, he's stopping for gas. Pull into the alley across the street, behind Carlo's deli."

Rico and I were in the alley at the same time. I got into his car, and when Larry pulled out of the gas station, we followed him at enough distance not to be conspicuous. We didn't say a word. We drove, and waited.

From Route 55, he took the 80. We drove an hour more before his right front tire went flat. Rico's handiwork and the vengeful gods of justice were on our side. He started to pull off a long exit ramp but was already riding the rim and stopped on the shoulder. So did we, almost a half-mile back. While he popped his trunk and got out his jack and spare, we moved steadily along the shoulder toward him, turning off our headlights as we took the exit. When we stopped a few car lengths behind him, I got out quickly so the interior light wouldn't catch his eye, and gently closed the door.

My adrenaline surged. I focused only on the target and felt nothing but my blood pumping, thumping in my ears.

I was at the rear of his car and he was straining at a lug nut when he saw me striding up to him. He looked up, he gasped, the jack slipped, and Larry stumbled backward as he tried to get up from his squat. Without missing a stride, I drew my gun from the holster under my arm, and straddled him. He reached up and I took his arm as if to help him to his feet.

He was almost standing when he didn't realize he had uttered his final prayer: "Oh my God! Mi . . ."

Pop! One shot between the eyes. He was silenced. I grabbed him around the waist before he fell back and wrestled him into the backseat of his car. Rico helped me finish changing the tire and I drove Larry and his coffin to the junkyard we used for special burials.

On the way there I thought about Larry. I hated the look of terror on his face. He looked so young. Damn. I remembered him as a decent kid, but if I hadn't taken him out, I would've gotten whacked because everybody knows you can't trust a man who lets his emotions get in the way. Thinking too much was getting me down, so I blasted the radio, but first I said out loud, "I'm sorry, God, for what I've done, but I had no choice."

After Rico and I used the car crusher, we picked up my car and I joined Nick for a drink.

Capelli saved face and instilled fear in everybody around him. Everybody recognized that if he could destroy these kids, he would be even harder on his own crew. No one wanted to think about that. So Capelli sent a strong message and I was one of the messengers.

It was clear what had happened to the boys and why. The police tried to investigate. They suspected the truth, but they had no evidence. The last two bodies were never found—Rico took care of the last kid—and the cases were closed. Capelli was a very powerful man. Nobody ever touched that man's house or neighborhood again. He could leave his doors and windows open if he wanted, and nobody came near his property.

As for me, any conscience I found when I had that car accident was in a box and beaten down harder than ever.

19

PAULIE SCREWS UP AGAIN

Through the years, Cousin Paulie remained one of my closest friends, even though I made advancements and he didn't. A handsome Hollywood-gangster type, he loved the broads, so he put lots of energy and even more personal attention into the prostitution end of the business. Even when I was still dating Angela, Paulie and I would go to dinner and spend the night checking out the women and having a good time. He had a gorgeous five-thousand-square-foot penthouse condo on Lake Shore Drive with a breathtaking view of Lake Michigan at Navy Pier and downtown Chicago, through floor-to-ceiling windows. A live-in, twenty-something maid from Puerto Rico kept the place spotless. Personally, I think her specialty was knob polishing. He loved living high in every way.

If he had twenty thousand dollars today, he would have five thousand tomorrow. Paulie really enjoyed the more glamorous side of mob life. He did well in the areas of victimless crimes. But life in the mob, and a lot of the work that was done, was not so much fancy fun. We didn't get pretty women and parties every day.

In a minimall where I had a game room, there was a burger joint run by a guy who was a compulsive gambler. He had borrowed so much money from loan sharks to pay gambling debts that he couldn't afford to pay the vig on the loan. He was into debt about forty-five thousand dollars. Then, he was stupid enough to borrow money from another shylock to pay part of his debt to the loan shark. That just wasn't done.

This creep was a wife beater, out of control on booze and drugs. One night he was driving a huge pickup truck while totally messed up. He hit and killed an eight-year-old boy. The boy's mother was devastated; he was her only child. She worked at a Family deli and everyone there knew what happened so, for a number of reasons, it was decided that action had to be taken.

Paulie was the one who got the order to whack the guy, but Paulie had still never developed the personality for doing this kind of thing. He could never admit that to anyone, like he did with me, but most of us knew. Every time it was in the air that someone had to be whacked, he decided to leave town, or he came up with a story about being followed, or said he thought his phone was being tapped. If Paulie did get orders, he usually screwed things up somehow. And he would come to me afterward and talk about what he had done. It was like confession or something. He was always petrified of getting caught, or going to hell, or both.

For this job, Paulie decided to use my game room. He had the keys because sometimes he'd open or close the place up for me if I was away. There was rubber mat flooring throughout the arcade so he figured it would be easy to clean up. He didn't use much sense, though. Paulie never planned things out, didn't think fast enough about what to do next. It was like him to wear a three-hundred-dollar jogging suit and white Reeboks to do a job.

For this job, his two biggest mistakes were first, that he didn't have a backup to help him and verify the hit, and second, he didn't put down any sheets of plastic. After the job, he had blood running all over the place and didn't even remember where to find a mop. The mark had shit his pants and the smell made Paulie sick. Between that and the blood, he was puking and nearly passed out. Then he realized one of the blackout shades wasn't totally down.

When a person is scared, mistakes are inevitable. Cold-blooded killers are very hard to catch because they don't have any kind of fear at all. All their energy is focused. Without fear you can accomplish a lot; but if you're shaking and nervous, your mind doesn't see everything and you fuck up.

Paulie finally called me to help him move the body. When I got there, everything was a mess. I'd never seen him looking so bad and I could see he had been crying.

"Mikey, he begged me," he choked. "He cried and begged on his knees. You shoulda seen his face. He said I'd burn for eternity in hell. I almost let him go, Mikey."

"But you didn't," I tried to console him. "You were a man. You did the job. Forget about it."

"I can't forget about it," he sobbed. "I can never forget about it. I never forget any of them. I swear, Mikey, they come in my sleep and haunt me!"

This I did not want to hear. I had enough unfriendly ghosts of my own. But this was the first time I didn't have the heart to argue with him. I put my arms around him and led him to my car without saying another reprimanding word. I drove him home and went back to the game room. I did what I had to do to get the body into a trunk, cleaned up the place real good, and dumped the trunk where it wouldn't be found.

I had covered for Paulie again. In the past, I covered for him, did the job myself and let people think he did it. I saved his ass a number of times. It was hard for me to say no because I didn't want anything to happen to him. But we all knew he wasn't the guy to back you up, or watch your back in a bad situation. This was the first time, however, that I really understood why it was so hard for him to do his job. Conscience is a bitch that grabs you by the balls, sometimes when you least expect it.

PAULIE HAD HIS STRONG POINTS. He controlled most of my dad's bookmaking and prostitution. Most of what we did together was overseeing The Playground, The Magic Touch, and Goldfinger's. They were each my dad's pride and joy, the gems of his whorehouses. The Playground alone brought in a hundred thousand every week. We did good business because we were smart; we were innovators. Back then, in the early eighties, we were already using credit cards for billing customers' business with the girls. Paulie was the one who brought credit cards to my father's attention. Credit cards later became our downfall, but at that moment we thought it was a brainstorm, Paulie's greatest idea ever. He helped us set up that system, and Telechecks too. Everyone spends more when they can charge a credit card. We took hundreds and hundreds of credit card payments every week.

My dad, Paulie, me, and everyone who was the least bit smart about business never passed up an opportunity to use a new angle. My dad bought a bar, River's Edge in Schiller Park. He bought the land, the building, the whole package. Then he renovated the bar and turned it into an Italian restaurant, but couldn't make a dime there. This was the first property of his that failed.

We learned that you never know where you might find a good idea. My cousin Marcello and I put condom vending machines into the washrooms of The Hunters' Club, a gay bar. The place was packed with hundreds of gay guys dancing with each other. I told my dad about it, and we turned River's Edge into a gay bar. We packed the place but everyone was drinking beer. They would have one beer, pick up on each other, and go somewhere to get it on. Then, a friend showed me a lesbian bar in Manhattan's lower thirties. It was not only packed, but women were hanging out the doors. And women spend more when they go out drinking and have a good time. We turned River's Edge into a plush girls' club, with lip-syncing transvestite shows, a sex toys boutique, and a twenty-buck cover charge to keep it upscale. The women who came into the club were fancy with nice clothes and well-done hair. There weren't many butch girls. Open only four nights a week, River's Edge became as big a moneymaker as The Playground in just one year.

Paulie spiced up the regular broad business by bringing girls from overseas, mostly from Japan. We also started a limousine service together. We each put up fifty thousand dollars, bought some limos, and put our better-looking girls in them. The escort service did really well.

We also did collection, picking up money from a number of establishments we owned, or were under our protection. We made a great team. I was more physically aggressive than Paulie. If someone mouthed off over something, I'd be the one to throw the first swing. Paulie was more diplomatic. He was the talker; I was the slugger.

His talking brought us into another area of business. One night a large group of Colombians came into The Playground and were spending astronomical amounts of money. Tens of thousands of dollars. The next night they came back, and Paulie thought there might be something we could do with these big-money men. It turned out that the Colombians, drug king Fernando Agular and his son Felix, were looking to launder between two and three million dollars. Paulie convinced them that we could do everything in the world, and made a deal with them.

When Felix and his men came into town again, they came with a suitcase full of fucking money, gave it to us, told us to do what we could with it and that, in a couple of weeks, they'd come by and pick up the checks. In five days the money was clean. The fee for laundering depended on the amount of money we handled. For cleaning a million dollars, it was about ten percent; for half a million, it becomes fifteen percent. The less money they had to launder, the higher the percentage. They were bringing us all big bills and that was harder to launder than tens and twenties, so the percentage went up a little. We laundered a lot through the strip clubs, and the vending machines. I could have a game machine that wasn't doing anything, but I could say it made a thousand dollars per week. Now, I have clean money. We set up a corporation and ran checks for the Colombians through that. Our corporation wrote checks to their corporation and the money was clean. The government collects tax on income, but it doesn't give a damn where it's going.

Of course, the deal had to be brought to my dad. He loved it. Because this was really major business and because of the amounts of cash involved, my dad told me to head up the project. He sort of took it away from Paulie, who, because he belonged to my dad, had to follow orders. I had been given to Nick, but this was a situation that came out of The Playground, which belonged to my dad. No one thought that Paulie could handle something so serious. He was a womanizer, and he liked to party. He was good with the broad business, but this was a whole different level. Dad kicked it down to me because I'd rather do business than go out on a date. I would rather have been around seventy-year-old men than twenty-year-olds I couldn't get along with. Young guys hated me because they thought I was too uptight. To this day, in my mid-thirties, people tell me to relax. I'm just very earnest about the things I do. And back then, I was both money and power hungry. That's why I was chosen to head up the Colombian money laundering.

If Paulie felt betrayed when my dad told him he had given me the power with the Agulars, he didn't show it. But Paulie told me of his disappointment, and it was clear he didn't know how to handle it. I tried to explain that I could get tougher with the Colombians than Paulie could. They scared him, and with good reason. They didn't just whack someone. Often, they would slit open a guy's throat, pull out his tongue and hang him by it. A helluva way to bleed to death. I knew they were serious people, not into party time. With them, it was all about more money, and more power.

I could see Paulie's attitude change a little, but I started to move up the ladder while he only revved up his party life. I wasn't someone who could be manipulated into partying all the time. That became something of an issue between us. I had less time for him on a social level, but we still had business together. For three busy years we saw each other every day. At times, I was even in the next room when he was getting laid.

Anyway, about this time, my psychotic cousin Bruno got out of prison again. As my dad's button man, he was the absolute opposite of Paulie. He loved killing. To make matters worse between them, technically, Paulie was Bruno's boss, but Paulie knew that Bruno was really taking orders from me simply because it went more smoothly that way. There was no respect between them, and they hated each other. They couldn't work together. Paulie was really afraid of Bruno because of his unpredictable tendencies. We were always careful with what we said when the two of them were in the room with us. If anyone even implied that Bruno should whack Paulie, he would've done it on the spot without a second of thought because Bruno hated Paulie's weakness when it came to killing. He didn't consider Paulie man enough to be his boss. Bruno was a scary guy sometimes, but I managed to keep him in line. I had a rapport with him, and he respected my dad as the man in charge of us all. Still, the animosity between him and Paulie got so bad, it was a good idea to get one of them out of town. So, because he was good with handling girls and gambling deals, Paulie was given some work to do in Vegas. Unfortunately, it went to his head. Once again, he spent more time partying than working. He should have been more like the rest of us. We got up in the morning and went to work. It wasn't corporate work, but it was our job.

It took a serious talk from my dad, Paulie's boss, for him to get his head back on straight after his Las Vegas escapade. A few days after Paulie was back, he was doing what he did best in Chicago.

20

MY HEART REMEMBERED

I had missed Paulie's company while he'd been in Vegas. Soon after he got back, we had dinner at Fellini's. Me, Paulie, Tony, Al, and Sam. Just some wine, pasta, and a little business. My favorite way to spend an evening. Al got there first, like he usually did, and sat at our usual table. He sat in a position with his back to the wall. The rest of us trickled in and got comfortable.

When I got there last, I saw the place was doing well for a weekday night. That made me feel good; making money always made me feel good.

"Hey, how ya' doin'?" I greeted everyone.

I looked at Al and Tony gave him a smack on the arm. Al moved from his chair to another. Sometimes he forgot that I liked my favorite position. The waiter came right over when I arrived.

"A bottle of that new Merlot I tried the other night," I told Jimmy. "And let's start with some calamari. Two of those and maybe, yeah, some mozzarella and tomatoes."

It had been a long day but a very profitable one. I picked up a dry cleaning business without even a threat. The guy was running drugs out of there, was into a loan shark for more than he could handle, was into us for some taxes, and was into his drug connection for a couple of thousand, too. He was a BDHP: a broken-down horse player. For the price of making things right, a small fraction of what he actually owed anybody, the guys he was beholden to turned him over to me. Nobody asked his permission.

I walked in at closing time, looked him square in the eyes, and said, "This is your lucky day, Julio. Your debts are paid. You got nothing to worry 'bout. Go on vacation. Or go look for a job 'cause this joint is mine."

Julio looked at me, dug out the keys from his pocket and handed them over.

"Everything is okay?" he asked hesitantly.

"Yeah, no problem, amigo," I assured him. "As long as you stay around long enough to sign some papers. I'll send someone to your house later tonight."

"Okay. Okay, Mr. D'Angelo," he said, practically hyperventilating. "Your friend Sam explained to me . . . Ah, thank you."

I took his place and he was appreciative. How fuckin' easy was that? Power was everything.

The wine had arrived and was poured.

"To Julio!" I toasted, and everybody joined in, even though Tony and Al didn't know who the fuck Julio was.

We were all feeling pretty good about the day, and over dinner talked about how business was going on all fronts.

"Hey, Paulie, my pal, you owe us some fuckin' money," Al said, and took a shrimp from Paulie's plate and put it on top of his sausages and peppers.

"Now what?" Paulie shrugged, knowing what was coming. Some of his hookers sometimes had johns who needed loans, and Paulie would send them to Al and Tony.

"That customer you sent us a coupla months back ain't payin'," Al grumbled. "If he don't pay, I think you should pay."

"No way," Paulie dismissed him. "That's just one of the risks of the business."

"Al's right," Tony piped up. "We give you a little kickback when things go good."

"You should give us some payback when you say a guy is good, and then it turns out he ain't," Al finished the thought for Tony, who took some tortellini from his plate and put it on Sam's bread plate, then took a half meatball from Sam's entrée.

Paulie put a shrimp on Tony's plate and scooped up a tablespoonful of tortellini for himself before he replied, "Fuck you."

"Goddamn Republican," Al muttered. "Next time, make sure the guy's solid."

A half-dozen mouthfuls later, everybody was talking about sports. And still sharing food.

Paulie, sitting next to me, acted a bit distracted and glanced over toward the alcove a few times. It seemed like he was maybe hiding something from me. He just kept looking in that direction without saying nothing.

"What's with you?" I finally asked.

"Eh, I didn't know if I should tell you," he started, and I didn't know what to expect. "Angela is here. She came in just before you did."

"Angela? My Angela?" I heard my own words and realized I'd never really let her go. And the thought of seeing her again made my heart pump. She was out of my life, but she still had this effect on me.

"Who's she with?" I asked.

"Her father, mother, and some guy, her husband I guess . . ." Paulie said.

It had been so long. I turned, but couldn't see much around the pillar. I had heard that she married Will, the mechanic she had been dating on and off when we had started out together. They had babies, twins.

"I should go say hello," I said but made a point of not getting up too fast. I took a few more bites of my veal parmesan and finished off my second glass of wine. I asked Paulie about the new girls at The Playground. I was glad to hear they were working out. Sam mentioned some work he had to do in Ohio. Al kept eating. My mind kept going back to Angela. I was practically in the same room with her. I had to see her.

"I'm gonna say hello to Angela and her family," I told the guys and got up. "Order me a tiramisu and a regular coffee. I'll be back in just a few minutes."

I got up from the table and walked across the room, around to the alcove. I turned the corner and was immediately at their table. Angela's parents and Will were there, but in that moment I saw only Angela. It was like there was a spotlight on that beautiful face. Her eyes met mine and she lit up. That smile. Oh, what that smile had always done to me.

"Michael!" her dad said and reacted by getting up, grabbing my hand to shake it, then instead threw his arms around me and gave me a warm Family hug. "It's been a long time!"

"Well, I've been busy, Sal," I explained. "Out of town a lot. Plenty of traveling."

I turned to his wife, Andrea, and made my greetings, said hello to Will, and turned back to Angela. She extended her hand. I kissed it and squeezed it, offering a special hello. The blush that rose to her face made her glow even more. Her eyes were gorgeous.

Our last meeting kept running through my mind. The anger,

the tears, the pain. Her leaving in the morning without a word. I knew I had done the right thing. Cutting her loose so she could be happy. I guessed she was happy now. I hoped so. I really did.

"It's good to see you, Michael," she said, finally taking back her hand.

"It's a treat to see you, too, Angela," I didn't lie. We could have been completely alone in that room at that moment. Our bond was still intact.

Her father gently interrupted, "Please, please, join us for a drink. Have you had dinner? Come sit down," and he started to motion to the waiter for another chair.

"No, no, Sal," I laughed. "I'd love to, but I've already had my meal with my buddies in the main room over there, so please, go on and eat while I spend a few minutes with you."

I looked at Will, sized him up, and felt he was doing the same to me. I knew all about him, and I was sure he knew about me.

"How's your work, Will?" I asked him.

Without blinking, he replied, "Couldn't be better."

I knew he was uncomfortable.

I turned back to Angela. "So how do you like being a mama? I hear you had twins, no less."

Angela looked beautiful, but my question dimmed her glow.

"Oh Michael," she started, "I love being a mom, but the boys." A sadness came over the table as she finished. "Their hearts are damaged. They need an operation. It's very serious, and they're so tiny."

I wanted to reach around and hold her, but I didn't move. I could only offer, "If there is anything I can do, please let me know."

Will quickly spoke up, "We can take care of everything ourselves."

He was protecting his own, being the man, and I understood that. I knew he took care of Angela and the twins well. I had heard he was making pretty good money, and he had always been a decent man. I couldn't ask for more than that for Angela.

Angela's mother told me a little more about the boys' congenital heart defect. It pained me to hear they were so sick. We changed subjects, made some small talk. I didn't even have to look at Angela; I felt her eyes on me. Our connection was still so strong. I knew what she was thinking. She wanted to be near me, and I felt the same.

"I need to go," I said and left the table with brief good-byes and empty promises to stay in touch.

As I passed their waiter, I told him, "Put that table's bill on my tab, your tip, too."

He nodded.

At my table, I sat down and let out a deep breath. I needed to be away from her, her smell, her touch, those eyes. It would be so easy to give in, but I couldn't let myself be drawn back to her. It wasn't good for her, a married woman, and it wasn't good for me.

My dinner partners were quiet. Then Sam commented, "I noticed she packed on the pounds. What? Maybe fifty? Sixty?"

"Shut up and eat your cannoli, Sam," I said, recognizing it was true. "She's a beautiful woman. And her kids are sick. She's under a lot of pressure. It takes a toll."

As we left, Paulie suggested, "Hey, Mikey, let's go find some broads and have some fun."

"That's a really good idea," I agreed. I wanted a distraction. Somebody to take my mind off Angela. Somebody totally different from her. It was safer that way.

21

TROUBLE CLOSE TO HOME

I never could figure out which was easier: forgetting a woman, or handling one. One night, months later, some of the guys had been playing cards at my house and everybody else had left except one of my crew members, Uncle Frank, because we needed to discuss some business. When we finished, his phone rang. He listened, and I saw his face get red, and he started breathing hard. No doubt about it; he was furious.

"When I find them, I am gonna kill 'em!" Frank yelled at the top of his lungs, as he snapped his cell phone shut.

"Benny, one of my number runners, says he saw my wife at a motel with another guy," Frank spat. "He talked to the clerk, a friend of his. Maria's been going there two, three times a week with the same guy."

I'd never seen Frank this wild. I thought he was going to have a stroke.

"Take it easy." I tried to soothe him. "Don't take the word of a guy who does nothing but pick up numbers. Check things out. Maybe he's wrong. My mom has lunch with her a couple of times a month. She's a good woman."

It didn't seem like he even heard my words. "She's my wife; she belongs to me. How could that bitch even think about screwing around on me? I am going to make her wish she were dead!"

Then he got calm, too calm. That's when he always got dangerous. He started plotting. Then he got up without another word and started for the door.

"Frank, don't do nothing rash," I called after him.

He must have cooled down between my house and his because I didn't hear nothing about it for a while. And I was too busy with Paulie to ask questions. Paulie had called me one morning, earlier than he usually gets out of bed.

"Mikey! You gotta help me out!" were his first words over the phone. Then he rambled, "I'm downtown. I'm in jail. Call my lawyer. I gotta get outta here. Mikey. What am I gonna do?"

"Slow down!" I yelled. "First thing ya' gonna do is calm down!"

"But you don't understand, they're gonna keep me here if you don't get a lawyer to get me out. They're gonna take everything I got. My penthouse, my car, my accounts. Mikey you gotta go to the safe deposit box—"

"Shut up now!" I yelled louder. "You say another word, I'm not gonna do a damned thing. Shut up and listen!"

"But Mi—" he started.

"I told you to shut the fuck up!" I was ready to hang up on him but I'd never heard him sound so pathetic.

Paulie went silent, but I heard his breathing and felt his panic. My heart went out to him.

"Paulie, listen to me," I lowered my tone. "Tell me exactly

where you are. I'll call my lawyer; he's better than yours. What happened and why were you arrested?"

He explained he had been getting letters from the IRS for some time but first he ignored them, and then handed them off to his accountant, who suggested Paulie go to a tax attorney. Of course, Paulie didn't bother. He was arrested for tax evasion.

I called my lawyer who arranged for bond, and by dinner time, Paulie was out. He looked like hell, but he was calmer. Or maybe he was in shock. His whole world was upside down. I tried to explain to him that it was no big deal. Our lawyer could make some arrangements. He might lose his penthouse and other assets, but he could build everything back again and probably not spend much time in a soft federal joint. Easy crime; easy time.

Paulie spent half his time during the next few days at my house and with his aging parents. It was so sad to watch him, a lost soul, needing help at every turn to move some stashed cash and hide a few valuables. The sentencing came exactly a week later. I was there for him, and as I predicted, it wasn't bad. Three years in a federal joint, a real country club kind of place with inmates serving time for a variety of white-collar crimes. With a little luck, our lawyer, and a few favors, he would be out in less than two years. I saw Paulie had tears in his eyes when he left the courtroom after the sentence was read. But I felt he'd be all right. I knew I'd miss him.

THE NEXT DAY MY MOM was going to have lunch with a girlfriend. I asked if it was Maria.

"Oh no," she waved me off as she left, "Maria's not allowed out of the house except with the kids now. 'Bye!"

So I figured Uncle Frank had given her a good talking to. Later I found out the situation didn't just blow over with a heated argument. I heard the details from Frank's brother, my Uncle Arty, and his pal Jimmy. Some other details came from Terry, Maria's little sister.

Frank set a trap after he did some digging and found out what Benny said about seeing Maria at a motel with a guy was true. A few nights later, Frank showered, got dressed up, and told Maria he was going out for the whole night. "Business," he told her, as he had so many other times.

Maria hardly waited for him to close the door behind him before she made three phone calls and got ready to go out, too.

"Hi, Eddie, meet me at the motel in an hour," she said provocatively, not realizing Frank had the phone bugged and his brother was listening. "Yeah, the Wayfarer. I called there already and got our regular room, 106. Everything's all right. I called Terry to stay with the kids. They're asleep."

On the drive to her rendezvous, Maria had no idea she was being followed or of the surprise that was in store for her. She got to the Wayfarer first, lit some candles, poured the red wine she had brought with her, and took a sip as she slipped into a short, black lace negligee, with her highest stiletto heels. She sprayed some perfume on her cleavage and on the bed, then turned and looked at herself in the mirror. She'd been working out and liked what she saw. Long black shiny hair, a round feminine body with a small waist and long legs. She knew she was one hot woman. What she didn't know was that two days ago, Frank had paid off the hotel manager and hidden a camera in the room. He was watching every move.

There was a soft knock. Maria opened the door and Eddie came in and wrapped his arms around her, whispering into her hair as he pulled her close, "I could smell your perfume outside."

"I want you, baby," she said nibbling his ear. "I've wanted you all day."

It got hotter between them fast. "Getting back at Frank makes this all the more exciting," Maria told Eddie, who didn't seem to care about her motives. He just wanted her, and slipped his arms around her waist and pulled her close to him.

He undressed on his way to the bed, leaving a trail of clothing.

"I can't get enough of you. You are all I think about," he said, pushing her back onto the bed.

Eddie kissed her neck as she threw her head back, letting him explore her with his mouth and hands.

Bam! The door crashed open and before their eyes could focus, Eddie was yanked off the bed and dragged out the door by two men. One stayed behind.

"Oh my God, Frank!" she screamed.

Instinctively, she jumped up and grabbed her dress, hoping to get away. Frank grabbed her.

"Where do ya' think you're going, you whore?" he said, throwing her back to the bed.

"What will you do to Eddie?" she managed to ask, in spite of her terror.

"Don't ever mention that name again as long as ya' live," he said with a clenched jaw. "You're mine, and will always be mine."

He moved back from her and opened the door.

"Jimmy, I want you to take her home and watch her. Don't let her out of your sight."

Jimmy dragged the half-dressed woman out, and Frank yanked the small camera from its hiding place.

Maria was taken home where she waited for Frank, with Jimmy in the house standing guard over her.

At a warehouse on the other side of town, Eddie, still naked, was tied to a straight-back wooden chair with Frank's brother behind him.

Eddie was praying, "God, help me."

Frank walked in and heard him.

"God can't help you now, you sorry fuck," Frank growled and stood quietly looking at him, holding something behind his back.

"Frank, forgive me," he begged.

"There is no fuckin' forgiveness for you, Eddie," Frank said as he turned half sideways, raised the bat from behind him, revved up a swing and smashed Eddie's left leg. And then his right leg, and then one arm, and the other. Frank hit Eddie in the chest, and the chair fell backward. A few strikes to the head and it was over.

Much later, Frank dealt with Maria, who was too scared to sleep and sat up when he came to the bedroom.

"I ought to throw you out on your ass, Maria," he said, poking his finger into the middle of her forehead.

Then he laid down the new rules: "You are not to leave this house without permission. You are not to talk on the phone. You will do what I say when I say to do it. Whenever you think you're too good for me, or you start talking high and mighty, I'll play these tapes for you," he said, showing her an audio and a video cassette. "Then you'll know I never forget. Never. If I find out you're not doing like I tell you, I promise, I will kill you."

Maria had betrayed him, the worst thing a wife could do to her husband, and Frank would never love her or trust her again.

She was a very attractive Italian woman. When Frank married her, he expected her to stay home, cook, clean, take care of the kids, and be there waiting for him when he came home late after partying with his whores. In return, Maria got a very generous allowance, drove a fancy car, had a gorgeous home, and wasn't deprived of anything but passionate and exclusive love.

Eventually, this kind of life takes a toll on women. They get a little hard, sarcastic, and cocky, too, because they enjoy the fact their husbands have some power and influence. They get bitchy when they find out about the girlfriends and whores. A guy can cheat all he wants, but God forbid a woman cheats on her man. That destroys a man's home, even if they stay together for the kids. Nothing can ever be the same again. A man's home is his sanctuary, his last place of refuge. Take that away and there's trouble.

This life is more than the average woman can handle. A lot of guys get married because they want to have a child and they want a woman who is going to take care of the child. They look for a woman who is devoted and who will keep her mouth shut.

Then they go and find themselves a whore. A woman who is going to do nothing but fuck. She is the girl you go out with all the time. She is the looker. She is the one you make a presence with when you're with all the fellas. The wife is the one that makes you look good with a couple of kids, a nice suburban home, and a family. She handles the image and you go along with it. But the wives in mob life have a hard time. They have some of the hardest lives in the world, because they don't get the benefits of all the wining and dining. The girlfriends do.

The wives get treated well. They have access to everything. As far as money goes, if they want something, they are going to get it. But they don't get the love and the devotion from the heart like they really should. The wives get to know each other, and it's like a little club. Who else can they really hang out with? It's like my mother. She couldn't hang out with a bunch of churchgoers; what is she going to say when they ask what does your husband do? When these women marry us kind of guys, they are marrying into a different world. They are sort of kept women.

Nowadays it is very hard to find that kind of woman, but back in those days men treated their wives much differently because they could get away with it. At least most of them did. Old-fashioned women are impossible to find anymore. Women today are more independent, with their own jobs and money. As things changed, men were expected to treat women like equals. A lot of the old-timers didn't like that. They wanted to come home and find their pasta on the table, clothes cleaned and pressed, the children taught respect and good manners. And if a man did something a woman didn't like, she should look the other way. But times have changed; loyalty has, too. Those old-fashioned women didn't see nothing, didn't hear nothing, didn't know nothing. When the Feds came knocking, they spit in their faces and slammed the door. Their loyalty was always with their husbands, who made a good living and supported them.

It was rare that a wife ever behaved like Maria. Most knew better.

22

CROSSING THE LINES

One night at The Playground, I stopped by to check on things. Fernando Agular was the head of the Colombian drug cartel doing business with us. The old man was smart, but his son Felix wasn't. Felix was at the club and I had a drink with him in a quiet corner booth so we could talk business. The money laundering between us was going well; everybody was happy.

"Sam DiNapoli is doing a very good job with the other money, too," Agular said, referring to the counterfeiting the Colombians developed as a sideline.

"Yeah, he's quite smart," I agreed. "He knows everything about paper and ink."

"He found us a good engraver, someone we are very happy to do business with. We keep him working overtime," he said with a smile.

"And earlier tonight I met one of your other men, Mickey O'Brien," Agular mentioned, while drinking his third Johnny Black. "He says he can move a lot of product for us. I'm happy to hear that."

My antennae went up immediately. I knew a small deal for the Agulars was not less than five kilos. When he said "a lot of product," he was talking major risk.

"First of all, I gotta tell you, Felix," I started. "O'Brien is a big-mouthed Mick who's just a low-level employee of ours. We bought his phone sex operation when it was nothing. We turned it into a fuckin' good operation and kept him on to manage the girls. That's all. O'Brien is definitely not one of my fellas."

"He struck me as someone I could make some money with," Agular shrugged. "Very self-assured. Like you say, he started the business you bought. And it sounds like he's got contacts."

"Do what ya' gotta do, Felix," I told him, trying not to insult the man, "but I'm telling ya' straight up, don't do that kind of business with this guy. He'll invite trouble. I can't vouch for any of the contacts he claims to have."

It wasn't more than a few weeks later when Agular set up a deal with O'Brien and the shit hit the fan. A whole bunch of Agular's men got pinched with a total of one hundred kilos of cocaine. Felix and his buddy Kenny got arrested, too. Immediately, Fernando called me up and asked me to help him get his son and his worthless pal out of jail.

O'Brien had gotten into trouble over a lousy few ounces of coke and a little speed. He panicked, and his way out of going to jail was to roll over on somebody else. He gave up the Agulars.

"Of course I'll do whatever I can," I told Fernando, in Colombia. "We'll get Felix and Kenny out in a few hours and we've got the best lawyers. Don't you worry about nothing."

I was mad about the whole thing. I had warned Felix, and I wanted to get my hands on O'Brien, too, but at that moment I was most worried about my own ass. I knew that Kenny was not a strong man. It would be like him to roll on us, so I did the best and fastest thing I could do. I went down to the jail with my old buddy Sam, and bailed the two guys out. There were still the problems of charges, sentencing, and jail time. Kenny could destroy everyone.

We took Felix and Kenny to the Agulars' local home in Bloomington. From their library, my next phone conversation with Fernando was tense. He was in his private jet on the way back to Chicago after doing some business at home and was very grateful for what we did, but he didn't want to hear what I told him.

"There is still a very big problem," I started. "The problem is that your man Kenny is a weak son of a bitch and I hear he's going to rat."

"He would not do that," Fernando said, trying to protest.

"Like hell," I said. "I know who he's been talking to, I know the kind of deals those guys will try to make with him . . ."

"You're wrong," Fernando insisted. "His family and mine have been loyal for decades. He grew up with Felix . . ."

"I don't care," I interrupted. There was no getting through to him. I got to the point. "You need to take this guy out now. Take him out right now. Tonight."

Fernando blew up. "Do not tell me how to deal with my people!"

"You take him out now," I repeated, "or we will take him out ourselves because he puts us in too much jeopardy."

"No!" he fumed, and spat some other things in Spanish that I didn't understand.

"Listen up, Fernando," I said, shouting. "The only reason your fuckin' son is on the street is because we got him out. We used our people and our connections and our money to do that. If we hadn't done that, he'd be in lockup for days and Kenny would be singing. Get your son back to Colombia. He can skip bail, it's worth the money to get rid of this problem, and get rid of this son of a bitch Kenny because he is going to rat on us."

While I was on the phone, Felix came into the room and heard me yelling and cussing at his father before I hung up. He didn't know exactly what had been said, but he showed us to the door with only the least bit of politeness.

As Sam and I left, I told Felix, "We're going to call you in an hour. Talk to your father because I expect a solution to this problem."

"What problem?" Felix asked, as Kenny came into the hall.

"He knows," I told Felix. "Expect my call. Have an answer. An hour."

Back at my house, Sam and I were agitated as we waited.

"I am not happy about this," Sam said. "If they don't take him out tonight, we're going to take him out ourselves. Now. That Kenny kid is too squirrelly and we can't afford to take a chance. There's too much at stake."

"I know," I agreed. "My downtown sources tell me he's already made arrangements for a meeting this week with the Feds."

"Yeah, I know, I know," said Sam, getting more nervous. "Call him up. It's over an hour. Call Felix."

I called, and Felix answered on the first ring.

"So, what's the deal?" I asked, without announcing myself.

"We want to talk to you," said Felix. "Come back to the house."

I agreed. But as Sam and I got back into the car, Sam shook his head and said, "This don't feel right. Something's not kosher."

"You're right. This ain't good," I agreed.

We decided to stop at Sam's place and as we drove, we called a couple more guys to meet us. At Sam's, we picked up some supplies and headed out again. Our guys would meet us at a Denny's restaurant not far from the Agular house.

When we were all at Denny's parking lot, I called.

"Hey, Felix, we're just down the street at Denny's," I said. "I think you should come down here. We'll have a bite to eat and you can tell me that you've already taken care of the problem."

"No, come to the house," he said, "We are going to work this out. Come up here and we'll explain."

"So you haven't taken care of it yet?"

"No. We have some ideas."

"Shut up and get down here!" I shouted at him. "Forget the restaurant. I've lost my appetite. We'll meet you in the warehouse parking lot farther down the street. It's still neutral ground. It's close and we can get things settled. Get the fuck down here before this all gets out of hand."

"Okay, but I'm telling you right now, my father is not authorizing the action you suggested," Felix said, and it was obvious Kenny was standing next to him. "He has left me to come up with a solution. I think I have one."

I hung up and told Sam what he had said.

"He's not going to settle shit," Sam growled. "His father is pissed off about getting his drug business fucked over and the old man doesn't give a shit about what happens to our business, or us, now."

We organized our guys—eight of them in three cars—in the lot, behind us and out of sight of the driveway Felix would use. Within five minutes, a little after midnight, Felix and Kenny drove up in one car. Sam and I were standing outside of my car off to the side, just behind the building. They drove up, and got out of their car.

Two of us, two of them started walking toward each other and stopped with ten feet between us. Before anybody could say a word, Kenny pulled a gun from under his jacket.

Immediately, our guys turned on their headlights and startled them. A shot was fired from behind us and Kenny was hit in the shoulder. He dropped his gun and Sam ran into the shadows to pick up the five-gallon gas can we brought with us. He sprinted toward Kenny and after smacking him in the head with the heavy can, doused him with all the gasoline he had. Sam continued to beat him almost unconscious while our guys held Felix at bay.

Finally, Sam stopped. Out of breath and reaching into his pocket, Sam turned to Felix and handed him a book of matches.

"Finish him," Sam ordered.

"No, I can't," answered Felix, shaking.

"Finish the fuckin' job!"

"No. Please, no," Felix said, again and again.

It was very important to Sam that he make Felix do what he wanted him to do.

"I said finish the job! Do it *now!*"

But Felix looked to the ground and shook from head to toe.

With my gun in hand, I leaned in close to Felix and told him, "My friend, you have to finish him off because if you don't, you are going to die."

We stared at each other. He didn't say a word. Sam was seething. Things were getting more tense. Kenny made a low groan but didn't move.

"He's a rat!" I yelled in Felix's face. "He is going to rat us out and take you down, too, just to save his sorry ass. He's talked too much already. O'Brien told the Feds Kenny is their best bet, the weakest link."

"Do it!" Sam shouted, shoving the matches in his fist into Felix's gut. Felix doubled over.

I stepped between them and tried again. "Don't be stupid, Felix. Kenny is gonna die tonight anyway. You don't have to. Just do the right thing."

Sam shoved the matches at him again.

This time Felix took them and with shaking hands, struck one and lit the whole book. Turning half away, he threw it at Kenny. He fell to his knees when Kenny screamed as flames wrapped him in torture.

I looked at Felix, who was puking. I saw the chilling look on Sam's face as he watched Kenny flop around, on fire. He was enjoying this. It was all enough. It was too much. So I turned around and with one shot, put Kenny out of his misery. That had to be done.

Sam and I left our guys to drive Felix back to his house in his own car and take care of the cleanup. All the way back to his place, Sam yelled and cursed at me.

"When the hell did you, big shot Mr. Mike the Match here, go so fuckin' soft?" he shouted. "He deserved to suffer. It was a statement!"

Sam was furious with me the whole next day and stayed annoyed over it for a long time after. It was our only major conflict in the two decades we knew each other. He took it very personally.

A week later, Felix, trying to make up some of the money he had lost with the bust, made another drug deal. He got popped and went to jail. His father Fernando left the country. At the same time, the Agulars were having problems at home. Nick's South American pal, Enrique Barrella, was consolidating his hold on Latin drug cartels and made a strong move to take control of the Agular enterprise. Barrella won, with Agular promising to play by his new boss's rules. Among other things, it meant paying the D'Angelo family a larger tax from Agular coffers and reining in Felix.

On our own home front, the FBI started asking a lot of questions, poking into our business even more. Earlier that same year, an undercover FBI plan, Operation Greylord, investigated corruption in the courtroom. Nearly one hundred people, including thirteen judges and fifty-one attorneys, were convicted of a variety of corruption charges. A lot of the Family's defenses were destroyed.

We kept business going as usual but used extra caution. We avoided making new contacts in case there were undercover guys sneaking around, and kept a tighter rein on some of the wilder guys in the ranks who could bring attention to us by being too aggressive while collecting taxes or planning big heists. More than ever, we watched our backs at every level, at every turn. The heat was on.

23

THERE'S NO GOING BACK

When my phone rang in my office, I was just getting ready to head over to my parents' house. Paulie had been given a one-day furlough so he could see his sick father who had taken a turn for the worse. Paulie had already seen my Uncle Mario and was visiting with my dad. I wanted to get home to spend a little time with Paulie and see how he was holding up. I missed him. But I didn't walk away and leave the phone to ring. I had to answer.

"Yeah, hello," I barked, annoyed by the delay.

"Michael, it's me. I need to talk to you. Can we get together? Please?"

Angela didn't have to announce herself. I knew the voice, but I was so surprised to hear from her, I didn't respond immediately.

"Michael? I'm sorry, did I catch you at a bad time?" she said, sounding disappointed.

"No, no, it's okay," I finally answered her. "I was just finishing up some work and heading out the door. What's up?"

Geez, I wasn't so sure that was the thing to say. Her babies had both died two months earlier. One during the heart operation and the other before they could do the surgery. I was in New York at the time and didn't go to the funeral, but I sent flowers and condolences. Now I wondered if I should say something about that, or if I'd only be bringing up something painful. I decided not to say too much about anything. Let her talk.

"Michael, I'm having some trouble. I need to see you. It's really important to me."

I wanted to say no, I'm busy, go away, I'd rather see Paulie. But she caught me unawares. So instead, I said, "Where do you want to meet?"

"Mario's? For lunch in an hour?" It was one of our old hangouts, during our first year together.

"No, I don't think so." I nixed that memory-filled place.

We quickly agreed to meet at a coffee shop off the parkway, halfway between my place in Addison and hers in Bloomingdale. I didn't want anything the least bit romantic, or that held memories. I really started thinking that I shouldn't even go, but how could I say no? She sounded like she was in trouble and needed me. If she had a problem I could fix, I would. But I promised myself I wouldn't take a step toward her. No matter what I felt.

I got to the coffee shop before her and sat in a booth by the window. When she pulled up, I watched her cross the parking lot, pulling her long wool coat closed around her. There was a scowl on her face, and when she sat down I really saw how tired and fragile she looked. The sparkle was missing from her eyes. She was beautiful, but the strain showed on her face, in the way she carried herself, and in her voice.

"Thank you, Michael," she started. "I feel kind of foolish. Maybe I shouldn't be here."

"Don't be silly," I told her. "Whatever your problem is, if I can do anything, I will. You know that."

"I need somebody to understand," she rambled. "Nobody else does. I know you will. You always knew me best. Maybe you still do."

The waitress took our order. Just two coffees.

"When my babies died," her voice cracked, "I wanted to die, too. One died, and I told myself I had to hang on for his baby brother. Then he—," fighting tears choked down her words.

She stirred feelings inside me. I moved over to her side of the booth and put my arm around her. She rested her head on my shoulder, and I tried to soothe her without words, just holding her and smoothing the hair from her face.

"I have no one to talk to, Michael," she sniffled. "My dad is always busy, my mother is so religious she thinks everything is to be 'offered up to God,' and Will went into his own shell."

This was not the kind of problem I could solve. What could I do? I took her hand in mine, rubbed it softly, and searched for the magic words that would take her pain away. I couldn't find any, and my heart broke for her. We had talked about children when we were together. She wanted so much to be a mother. I would have cut off my arm if that would fix things. I wanted to tell her she would have more kids some day, but that didn't seem right to say. I had no words. I knew she could feel the love I had for her and I hoped she found some comfort in that.

"What's the matter with me, Michael?" she asked, starting to compose herself. "Why are the people I love so much taken away from me? My babies, you."

She paused and hit me with, "Why did you push me away? What did I do? Our life could have been beautiful."

Maybe I was wrong, but I felt like she had set me up for a sneak attack. I felt awful for her, but now I wondered if this was the real reason she wanted to see me. I had let my guard down. I couldn't keep it down.

"I just did what I had to do," I said, trying to draw up my defenses. "It was the best thing I could do for you. Let you go. Really."

She wanted answers. I had none, and I didn't need questions. I kept my arm around her, but pulled back my heart. Angela wanted too much from me again. If I gave her a little, she would want more. If I gave her everything, I'd be lost. Without meaning to, she would get in my way. I would resent her. I would hate her. It was better to feel nothing for her. So I forced myself to pull back. I took my arm from around her and shifted a bit away.

"You did nothing," I told her. "You want one kind of life and I want another. It could be no other way."

Angela looked up at me with those eyes and I felt a sudden, but passing twinge, a surge of . . . what? Guilt, pain, longing? I patted her hand and moved the conversation away from us.

"What are you going to do now?" I ventured. "Maybe get pregnant?"

"No!" she snapped. "My babies are dead. I don't want Will to touch me. I hate him. I hate my life. I hate that God took my babies."

And she cried again.

I wanted to run outta there. I couldn't bear this. But I waited and she settled down.

"I'm sorry things are so bad for you right now," I said. "Give it some time. Will is dying inside right now, too. You two can work things out."

"I want to be with you, Michael, not with him."

"You are married to the man," I reminded her. "You are his wife."

"But I never loved him like I loved you," she said. "Like I still love you."

"I'm sorry you're not happy with him, Angela. But either you work things out with him, or you don't. That's between you and him. You and him, hear me?"

I wanted to tell her I loved her more than any other woman ever, that if only things were different I would make her my wife. But that was out of the question. I had made my decision on the evening of my initiation and there was no turning back now.

"You said you would be there for me," she prodded.

"Yeah, if you need a situation fixed. If you need money. If you need a friend, sometime to talk to, maybe. If you need a husband, you got one, go home to him." I stood my ground.

The waitress refilled our cups and asked if we needed anything more. I put a ten down and told her we were fine, as Angela pulled herself together and stared blankly out the window.

Quietly, she still looked for a shred of hope. "Michael, will our time ever come?"

"Angela, it came and went." I told her the truth. "You gotta live your life the way you want, but without me."

I put my hand under her chin and lifted her face. She looked so sad. I felt like running out of there. I gave her a peck on the cheek.

"I gotta go, hon," I said and meant it more than she understood. As I got up to leave, I said, "Call me if there's really something I can do for you. C'm'on, I'll walk you to your car."

"No, let me stay here for a while," she said. "You go on. I love you."

"I love you, too," I said. I had nothing more to give her.

By the time I got to my parents' house, Paulie had already been escorted back to prison. I felt twice as lonely and sad. But I had no idea just how dramatically my choice to see Angela rather than hurry home that afternoon to be with Paulie and my dad might've changed the future not only for me but my whole family.

24

THE BEGINNING OF THE FALL

For a few months, we heard talk of some heat coming down, but when nothing happened, we forgot about it. Then, one night when I walked out the front door of The Playground, I had a bad feeling in my stomach; the hair on my arms felt prickly. Something was up. I could sense a presence, eyes on me. It was eerie, and I should've immediately gone back into the club, but I kept going to the car. I had a date; it was already well after nine. I just wanted to get into my car and drive away. I raised the key to the car lock.

Wham! A half-dozen bodies slammed into me. Several officers grabbed my hands, my legs. My instincts told me to fight back, but I was totally overpowered and cuffed in no time. Still, one bad-ass Chicago state cop, Melvin Jackson, kept coming at me, while no less than fifty other law enforcement people surrounded me. Jackson rammed his knee into my back, twisted my arms as the handcuffs cut into my wrists. I couldn't do anything to protect myself, so I spat in his face. Then he really went crazy, punching my ribs, my face, my back. It took several other cops to pull him off me. By that time, I was in bad shape. They had to take me to Resurrection Hospital.

At the hospital, the doctors and nurses were all very professional and treated me well, even though I was in handcuffs and the whole place was suddenly packed full of agents with walkie-talkies, arguing over who would have the final right to haul me off. There were about two dozen of them, and none of them were going to leave.

As I was wheeled to the X-ray department, several agents came along. They declined to take off my handcuffs, even when the technician insisted. It was nearly impossible to move around the X-ray table with my hands locked together. And it would interfere with the X-ray pictures, too. The agents kept refusing. I got into position as best I could and the technician was ready to shoot some images. She told them to leave the room. They wouldn't. At last, she said, "I hope you two have children because I'm back here behind the lead shield and you're not."

That did it. Finally, they stepped just outside the door. After they left, she asked me what I had done. I said, "I didn't do nothing."

"Stick with that story," she said.

She was cool. So were the doctors who wanted to keep me there in the hospital for a day or two. However, the agents wanted me to be fixed up good enough so they could take me out of there right away.

I had a spinal injury, a couple of broken ribs, my face was bruised and swollen, and my hand and arm were fucked up. That Jackson really had beat the living shit out of me. Eventually, he got what was coming to him. Jackson came across as a supercop, but he was actually kicking back drugs from police raids to dealers in downtown Chicago. Just as soon as I could, I put word on the street that set the wheels in motion. A few of my crew members got chatty with low-level gang members who would rat out Jackson to his police pals to cover their own butts when they were next busted. And rat they did. Jackson was investigated, demoted, then finally thrown off the force. Soon after that, the gang leaders who he could no longer supply and protect took care of his demise.

As for me, I was in bad pain and had to spend seven days in jail before my bond hearing. It felt like an eternity in Hell and, at the time, I didn't have the satisfaction of knowing Jackson would get his. I only hoped.

At the hearing, I found out about the long list of charges brought against me. There was something for everyone: the FBI, Secret Service, DEA, state police, ATF, and local Cook County police. Someone from every agency wanted to be there when I was picked up. Every one of them wanted to have me. Finally, the FBI got me. My charges included bookmaking, running a house of prostitution, counterfeiting, money laundering, bid-rigging, interstate wire fraud, possession of guns, extortion, running a chop shop, drug trafficking and tax evasion. In total, there were twenty-three counts of racketeering, and I was looking at some very serious time.

The Secret Service was there because of the counterfeit money I got from the Colombians. When I was peddling it, a car dealership owner introduced me to someone who wanted to buy some counterfeit bills in denominations of ten and twenty. The guy seemed to have good references, but a kid who knew my business got arrested for drugs and told the agents I had paper. When I went to the guy, who turned out to be an undercover agent, I gave him a sample. A week later he called and said he wanted a hundred grand. I sold it to him. The federal government doesn't arrest anyone on the day they get the goods on you. They wait and build a stronger case. The drug trafficking charges were bogus. A bar owner stashed his own drugs inside the poker machines my vending company rented to him. It was my machine, so I got popped.

The state will often offer plea bargains; Feds don't. But everybody offers something. Any time I was arrested, prosecutors reminded me that I could make things easier on myself by making a deal. If I gave them some information on someone else, they could reduce my sentence, or—depending upon the value of the information—even put me into WITSEC, the Federal Witness Security program. Take a couple of years in prison, or rat out my family and issue my own death warrant. What kind of a deal is that? I felt it was always better to stand strong, take the punishment and do the time. It's better to suffer for a while than to spend the rest of my life looking over my shoulder. Everybody in the Family knows someone could rat on them, but not doing that earns respect.

I was only the first of many to be arrested. The day I was popped, ten others were, too. The following day, my dad and several others were picked up. My dad's lawyers had already alerted him. The police came with an arrest warrant and knocked on his door. They didn't have their guns drawn or use any physical force because my dad was a boss. They knew what to expect from him and treated him with dignity. On the other hand, I was a wild one. They didn't know what to expect, so I got rough treatment when they came for me.

My bond hearing took longer than the others because of the number of charges involved. My dad was out on bond in twenty-four hours. During that late summer, the FBI, IRS, and Cook County State's Attorney investigators executed fourteen search warrants as part of what they called Operation Safebet. It targeted mob-controlled prostitution throughout the Chicago metro area. Before they were finished, they claimed the indictment and conviction of more than thirty individuals.

From the beginning, my mother never questioned or ever doubted me, or anything I did. I could yell, scream, swear, and a million other things and she never took offense with me even though I put her through so much misery and heartache. Until that day, I don't think she had any clue about the extent of my involvement with Family business. When they read off the list of charges at the hearing, I think reality crashed in on her. I remember seeing her take a sudden deep breath. She was shocked.

I've always been able to confide in my mom about a lot of things, but when it came to business, we protected women—mothers, sisters, wives—from a lot of things. They knew our business was not always up-and-up, but the extent of things and any details were left unsaid. My mom knew when I was having a hard time with something without me saying anything. She knew that if it was about business, I wouldn't tell her any more than my dad would've. I had many ghosts, more and more over the years, and she somehow understood. Without me saying or explaining, she consoled me, never scolded me. That's love.

My bond was set for a half-million dollars. At this point in my life, money was not a problem. I paid the bond and I was out of jail, at least for a while. My lawyer drove me to his office where my mom and dad were waiting for me. I was so happy to see them.

When we got home, my mom made me a big bowl of pasta and meatballs. All she said was, "I love you. Everything will work out." Mom was always my best friend.

After we had dinner together, my dad took me aside and said he had to talk to me. I could see by the look in his eyes that he was very upset. This talk was going to be something very serious. I saw an expression I had never seen before. When his anger was directed at me, he looked disillusioned, like I had let him down. That was not the expression on Dad's face. This look was of rage and something else. Maybe hurt, or a hint that he was going to say something that would disappoint me. I couldn't read his emotions clearly and for the first time ever, looking at his face, I felt scared as we went downstairs to the office.

The office was a special room that was totally soundproof. It was where we counted our personal take from the business. It was where we could talk about crime family matters and feel secure. Dad and I walked in, he closed the door and locked it. He was silent, almost brooding as he poured us each a shot of Sambuca. We tossed back the drinks and sat down. Dad began.

"The FBI has someone inside our organization," he said, his voice low and pained. "This person is involved in a lot of our business; what he's not involved in, he knows about. He knows everyone and everything."

Dad paused and took a breath.

"This is a person especially close to me, and you, Michael. You and I trusted and respected him. We loved him," he said, his voice starting to tremble in anger and hurt.

"This fucking rat is about to destroy our lives in exchange for his freedom," he spat, and paused.

Then his words slammed me.

"It's Paulie Boy."

At that moment, my blood rushed through me and I leaped to my feet. I could feel the arteries in the sides of my neck pulsing as if they were about to burst. My whole body was shaking with fury, pain, disbelief.

"No! No! Not Paulie!" I heard myself scream. "There's gotta be a mistake. He's our blood! Like my brother!"

I collapsed back into the chair, trying to catch my breath, clear my thoughts. I couldn't believe what I was hearing about my friend, my cousin, one of my dad's best producers, his nephew. I was beyond words; mad sounds rose from my throat. The hurt went so deep. I could never have imagined a betrayal so bitter, so foul. Then I slowly calmed myself and the pain became a dull but lingering ache. I think I was in shock, and I felt cold from head to toe.

"Paulie Boy." The words whispered repeatedly in my head. "Paulie Boy. Paulie. A rat. Paulie Boy. How could you do this to us?!"

We sat in silence a few minutes. I still thought there could be some mistake. I thought I really knew Paulie well. I found out I knew nothing. But I was learning my first hard lesson in betrayal.

My dad explained. The wheels had started moving even before Paulie turned on us. He was the last straw, the final blow that gave the Feds the most information and strongest ammunition against us. But it had started about six months earlier with the two Jewish guys who owned National Credit Service, the credit-card processing company that handled card receipts from our nightclubs. One of the guy's sons got caught with a half kilo of cocaine. To help his son out, he told the FBI that if they let his son go, he'd tell them all about cleaning money for the mob. So they let the kid go. Then the Jewish guys told us that they were retiring and introduced us to their cousins. We continued doing business with them until it turned out these cousins were actually undercover FBI men who secretly tape-recorded our conversations with them.

This happened just before Paulie got popped for tax evasion. Paulie got a three-year sentence in a minimum security federal prison for white-collar offenders. That's no fucking big deal, but he couldn't take it. He couldn't do any time. The big baby was in the joint for six months, and he was crawling the walls. He had everything in the world, then nothing; he went from a high-rise penthouse to a cell. The Feds saw what prison was doing to him and turned up the heat, saying they had enough on him to keep him in jail for twenty years. They knew how to turn him against us. Paulie was sweating after two months; he didn't think he could make it through three years. The thought of being locked up for twenty years was too much for him. So Paulie made a deal. The Feds already had a lot on us and were ready to file an indictment. They used Paulie to put the final nail in the coffin.

The Feds told Paulie what they needed and that if he got the information for them they would get him into the federal witness protection program. When he agreed, they got him out of prison on a one-day furlough under the pretense of visiting his dad Mario, who was legitimately very ill. That was the day I went to see Angela at the coffee shop. After Paulie spent an hour with his dad, he spent most of the afternoon with my dad. Paulie was wired, got my dad drunk, got him talking, tape-recorded him and had everything. *Ev-ery-thing.* A month later, all the arrests came down.

Everyone learned what had happened. Paulie had turned his back on his blood family, the Cosa Nostra, his friends, our way of life. Paulie was a rat. As soon as it became known that Paulie was the one who betrayed us all, word came down. My dad was the one who got the paper because Paulie was his nephew and did a lot of damage to the entire Family by betraying my dad, getting the information from him. If a man can't take care of his own family, his own crew, he loses respect and trust. He needed to clean house. That's what it came down to. Because my dad was already very sick, it was expected that he would pass the job to me.

But Paulie had disappeared into WITSEC, so it was impossible to get to him. There was nothing we could do. It would take time to find him and during that time, Paulie would start to feel more comfortable and believe he got away with betraying his family. It's always easier when the prey gets fat and lazy. Then, eventually, the information, the right time and place all come together.

25

ADVENTURES IN OHIO

My guts were torn apart, and my head was reeling. Paulie's betrayal was killing me. The frustration of not being able to carry out my promise to take care of him ate at me. Still, after a few weeks, I knew I had to get back into things. There were a lot of people relying on me, and I couldn't let them down. I had a lot of people working for me, a lot of people I had to feed. In any other business, if a company shuts down, everyone loses a paycheck. In my world, it's up to the boss to keep things together, pay everyone's bills. My guys had homes, wives, kids, tuition. I had to maintain my income, and theirs. Besides, the last thing I wanted to do was sit and dwell on what had happened to me. I had enough of that while I was in custody. I kept thinking about the trial I had to face, the possibility of prison. I was miserable, depressed, really questioning my life. I kept thinking about Paulie and what that fuckin' cocksucker did to us, and I kept thinking about what I was going to do to him someday. I was up and down with this guy. If I hadn't loved him so much I wouldn't have been able to hate him as much. I was confused; my head went through twenty different things about him. He was my blood, this guy who turned on me. I wanted to scream in his face, "How can you betray me like that? How can you be such a fuckin' weak man to not be able to do the fuckin' time?"

Then Sam DiNapoli looked at me one day and said, "Kid, you gotta fuckin' let that shit go! You gotta be a man. You gotta do what you gotta do to make money. You don't worry about what's gonna happen to you down the road; you take care of today."

Unfortunately, I wouldn't be able to do my usual work because the Feds were still keeping tabs on me. The heat was on and it was hard to feel free even outside jail when I couldn't move around, go places, do things without someone watching. I couldn't go to the clubs, do bookmaking, do anything at all because every morning the Feds were outside my house and followed me everywhere. Every night, they saw me to my home. So nobody wanted to be near me. They'd see me coming and know I would be bringing the Feds right on my tail. Word spread.

This put a real crimp in my plans. I had all kinds of activities going on and I was the only one who could really keep them going. I was in control and I had to keep serious money tied up and I had to keep it coming in. Some of the bosses and my father got together and figured out a plan to keep my business going. I could go to Cincinnati, Ohio, and take control of all the labor union trade papers.

But first, I had to shake off the Feds. Lucky for me, although the FBI is a huge operation, they had their separate task forces, local offices, and even individual Family squads for the D'Angelo and every other Family. Like any big organization there was plenty of politics and power struggles between them. And every one of the smaller groups had a number of different things to do, so in the long run, they really didn't have the manpower to watch over me when I wanted to lose them.

We put word on the street that I was going south, like somewhere in Florida or New Orleans. Then we got a number of cars set up at different places on the highways going out of Chicago. It was like playing a shell game: Which car am I in? After a few switches, they didn't know and they didn't have the men and money to follow every car they suspected I was in. We drove day and night after switching cars two or three times. Then when we got near Cincinnati, we switched a few more times to make sure we were clean. It was fun to fuck with them that way. It bought us time before they knew where we were, and then, it would take them more time to get their local office to get the orders requisitioned. It always came down to manpower, and a different local office that didn't want to pick up another squad's problem.

MOST OF THE IMPORTANT UNIONS like those for labor, building trades, and coal mines, had headquarters in the Cincinnati and Cleveland areas. We had control over the unions' trade newspapers. A huge, bulldog-tough woman, Penny Metzger, was our front person, the one who appeared to own the publications, and she was the hard-core union editor of all of them. They weren't anything big, just monthly bulletins of eight to ten pages congratulating the union members on whatever good job they were doing any particular month. It gave us some editorial say with the unions and built a good foundation with them. The newspapers gave us a bit of power, but there was no money coming from them. My dad was not happy about that, so I was sent with some other crews to figure something out. We were a tough bunch, mean and ready to take care of business any way we had to do it. Joey Diamonds, Dino Rizzo, Louie Velman, and me. Sam DiNapoli was also involved.

The first Monday morning we were there, we all drove out to the complex of about a dozen offices in Middleton, Ohio, about a half-hour drive from Cincinnati. The five of us walked into Penny's office and told her, "We're here now. You're out. From now on, we're running the papers. Good-bye." She had no choice. Penny had to leave her office immediately, and so did all the people who worked for her. We used her a little bit. Had meetings with her, and continued to use her connections, but she was not active in the business. Hell, she'd been skimming off the top for a couple of years.

Later that night, over dinner, I figured out what to do with these papers now that we were going to run them. I came up with a new advertising campaign that would boost revenues overnight. In the morning we started visiting every single company that had union workers. We strongly suggested that, since it was nearing the holiday season, they should each take out a full- or half-page ad wishing their union employees a Merry Christmas. Some ads, for big companies like Red Wing Shoes and Coca-Cola, cost twenty-five thousand dollars. A half-page was fifteen thousand dollars and a quarter page, ten thousand.

Some of the company executives were a little reluctant at first but I'd say, "You don't want to pay that much for your ad? That's all right. Oh, by the way, did ya' know there's gonna be a strike at noon today? Your union workers are gonna walk off the assembly line."

"You can't do that in my plant," he might say, trying to stand his ground.

"Maybe you're right," I'd counter. "But I don't think the trucks you need to haul your product are gonna be on the road this afternoon. I hear there are some serious problems with their engines. You get the point? Buy the fucking ad and save yourself a lot of problems."

We got the job done. We made more than five times the usual

income from those trade papers. One of them was steadily making over one hundred thousand dollars a month. And for every month, there would be something to celebrate: Labor Day, Halloween, Valentine's Day, even if we had to make something up like Union Solidarity Day. There were enough big companies that we didn't have to hit up the same ones every time. It was a good plan.

WHILE IN OHIO, Sam had to make a large collection from some guy who had an office near where we were doing our union business. Sam asked me to go along and be his backup, just sit in the car while he went inside and handled the guy. So we drove over to the guy's office just after dark, about six o'clock. Sam went in the back door and I waited outside in the alley in the car. After about fifteen minutes, Sam came out with a corpse. Something went very wrong and now we had a cleanup on our hands.

He struggled with the body and ordered, "Open the trunk! Open the trunk!"

So I popped it and got out of the car to help him shove the body in the trunk. It was a Lincoln Town Car so there was plenty of room back there. We got the body in and I asked him, "What the fuck happened?"

Sam was pretty tense and not about to explain as he hurried to the passenger seat while telling me, "Go! Just fucking drive!"

"Son of a bitch, Sam, we got to find a place to get rid of this. And we don't know this town," I said, really annoyed.

"Just drive," he kept repeating.

We drove about ten miles down the highway and then the car broke down, just stalled and came to a total stop. We were on the side of the road in the middle of nowhere.

"Do you fuckin' believe this?" I said at the same moment Sam said the same thing. It was too unreal.

We called a tow truck from my cell phone and waited about

twenty minutes for it to show up, all the while trying to figure out where we could dump the body that was going to start stinking up the trunk. Finally, the tow truck got to us and the guy, a total country bumpkin, was chatty, asking what was wrong with the car, where were we from, where were we going.

Sam and me were not interested in chit-chat and told him, "Just tow the fucking car!"

So Bumpkin shut his mouth, but started to hum a tune to himself, and started to hook up the car to pull up the truck. I was already in the truck cab and Sam was about to get in when for no apparent reason the Town Car's trunk popped open. The Bumpkin just stood there looking into the trunk at the dead man staring back at him.

Sam ran to the rear of the car with his gun out, grabbed the guy who was still dazed, and told him, "Just slam the fuckin' trunk closed and get into the truck and drive. Move your ass!"

The tow truck guy was shaking like crazy with Sam's gun in his side but he managed to drive and he got mouthy again. "I don't care what you did. I'm just a tow truck driver."

"Shut the fuck up!" I yelled while I was thinking: I was only going to cover for Sam for a few minutes in a back alley. Now I was driving down a highway in a tow truck, with a broken-down car in the back, with a dead body in its trunk, and now Sam was going to whack this poor guy whose only mistake was bad luck. We were being driven down the road, by who knows who, to who knows where. This was not good. But we had to act like we were in charge.

"Just keep driving," I said, sounding like Sam, and then I asked him, "You got any ideas where we can get rid of the body?"

Now this pathetic Bumpkin started to cry and blubbered, "Yeah. I think so." He started to cry and whimper even harder and I was wondering if he was going to drive right off the road.

"Get a grip on yourself! Be a man!" Sam yelled and poked him in the ribs with the end of his gun. "Just help us get rid of this body. Make it good."

So Bumpkin drove in silence with tears streaming down his face for another ten minutes and turned off the highway for about a mile. He brought us to a great location, a new-looking little cemetery in the woods with only about a half-dozen headstones.

Sam liked it, too. "Hey, no sweat. We'll do some digging and stick the body in a casket with another stiff. They can keep each other company," he laughed.

Bumpkin was still shaking and crying when Sam just about shoved him out of the truck. Then the guy told us where there were shovels, and with Sam following right on his heels, he got three of them. We started digging, and Bumpkin stopped crying.

Finally, we got a casket and opened it up. It was empty.

"What the fuck is this?" Sam wanted to know and looked at Bumpkin, who looked like he was going to faint at any time. When he didn't answer fast enough, Sam jammed the shovel into his stomach.

Bending over in pain, the guy groaned with whatever breath he had left, "We do insurance scams."

Sam and I were both surprised by that answer.

We just looked at him as he sputtered more information. "People claim relatives have died, but they just move away and wait for their cut. We have the funeral and burial."

"Should I fucking whack this son of a bitch right now?" Sam, fighting a smile, asked. "Or should I give him a pass?"

"Give him a pass?" I asked, like that would be ridiculous.

"I dunno," Sam muttered under his breath and shoved Bumpkin toward the road.

We got the body from the car and dumped it into the casket and filled in the grave. Bumpkin shoveled fast, afraid he would end up under the dirt if he didn't. When the shoveling was finished, Sam took out a cigarette and took a deep drag. He looked at the guy who didn't say a word. He was too tired and scared to shake, cry, or piss his pants. Sam just stared at him, debating what to do.

Finally, only after he finished his cigarette, he said, "I know a little bit about you now and you know a little about me. I'm going to give you a pass because you're kinda like one of us. But if I hear anything even vaguely like what happened tonight, I will put you on top of that motherfucker and you can spend eternity in each other's arms."

We all got back into the tow truck, and Bumpkin drove to an auto shop where we left the Lincoln to be repaired the next day. Then we called someone to pick us up.

HOW DID WE GET AWAY with doing all this stuff? There's always a way. Being in Ohio, we were off our usual turf, exposed, and sooner or later, the Feds would be on us. So we needed some local political protection. My dad had me meet with a high-ranking state official who was happy to become my man for a cool ten thousand dollars cash every month. Dad made the call, then I got a call from one of the official's most trusted aides. The aide would set up the meeting. It was always a very social thing. I would meet Mr. Powerful in a restaurant, usually Johnny Q's Steakhouse or Sans Souci, and we would enjoy a gourmet meal while making small talk. The conversation always got more interesting after I passed him his envelope full of cash. After he started doing business with us, he was trapped. He took the money and became ours. I liked being able to buy people like that. It was a high for me.

Mr. Powerful would tell me about what was going on, who was being investigated, not only in Ohio, but lots of places. This man had Washington connections and knew something about just about everything going on in New York, Philadelphia, and Chicago, so he kept me informed about those places and it served me well. He also introduced me to the sheriff and police chiefs of the local counties. Basically, he handed us free rein over Cleveland and Cincinnati. And he told me about the misappropriation of contracts to people in New York and Philadelphia construction companies. He knew a lot about construction job bids and upcoming projects. I got the inside track on who was bidding for what big highway or major civic building job and how much they bid. He told me who to contact about the last bid, and what it would take, usually a nice bribe, to lock in a good bid.

Government contracts always paid top dollar. Even if the job was only to put in all the windows, we were talking a couple of million dollars. This kind of information put some money in my pockets at a time when my usual business was curtailed by the situation I was in with the Feds. Making the bid contact, finding out and using information on written bids and passing it on to the right boss or crew member involved with a concrete, glass, or paving business brought me some easy kickbacks and revived my income. If they landed a one-hundred-thousand-dollar job, I'd get five to ten thousand kicked back to me. Not bad for a couple of phone calls.

Mr. Powerful was also willing to tell me who was being investigated. He knew because all major FBI investigations come out of Washington, D.C. That office gives the final approval and then the local office in Chicago, New York—wherever—gets the go-ahead. Mr. Powerful knew what was happening before there was any word on the street; he knew before the local FBI office knew what was going on. That would give me and the rest of the Family time to move an operation or disappear for a while. That's how it worked. That's how Mr. Powerful earned his money, and how I got mine.

After about eight months, we got word that the Feds were on to some of our action in Ohio. We thought it was all because of the newspaper ads, a little extortion. Mr. Powerful got the word, passed it on to us and made sure we left safely in time.

We went to New York, but it was hot there, too. I was out of Ohio but I couldn't do much in New York, and nothing in Chicago. So I just hung out with my buddies. About two weeks later, we heard what happened to Louie, who chose to stay behind in Cincinnati. While we were running the newspapers, Louie started some action of his own that we didn't know about until after it fell apart. Louie wasn't a made man; just an associate. But we brought him into a lot of our projects because he was not only a nice, seventy-year-old man who everyone liked right away, he was also one tough gangster. Under his charm, there was a stone-cold killer.

Well, Louie discovered what was to become the drug of the century. Ecstasy. On his own, he put some of his guys together in a team, set up a lab and made the stuff. He brought Penny and her son Eddie in to distribute the product because they had contacts in the area, and Penny needed the income. But the lab got raided, Louie lost several hundred thousand dollars worth of Ecstasy and was busted. Only a few of us knew it was his side business that nearly caused us heat in Ohio. Every one of us who could get away with it because we had earned the unofficial right occasionally had a little private business. We didn't say anything and anybody who might've heard about it back in Chicago, didn't get upset even though his business had to do with making drugs. It was unusual that Louie didn't get any reprimand from the bosses for that. But he was always a good earner, and he was getting old, so they looked the other way.

Through all this, the idea of Paulie free as a bird never stopped nagging at me. The more I dwelled on it, the more it made me meaner, angrier. I produced more because I took all this energy and turned it into making more money. All in all, Ohio was a good place to have been. I got sent there to keep a low profile and what happened? I did a great job, made plenty of contacts, and made big money. Old timers, everybody, noticed that no one could keep me down. I was good. I earned more respect.

And I had my first affair with a really wild woman, a woman who was not interested in any kind of relationship, just sex. She'd call me up and we'd arrange to meet at some hotel. She'd show up dressed like a hooker. Or she'd come up with all kinds of games to play in the Jacuzzi. It would be a few hours of sex here and there, and that was it. I loved it; she loved it. She didn't even want flowers, nothing. Hey, you know what they say about all work and no play.

26

REVENGE IS BITTERSWEET

After the confrontation with the Colombians, Sam was busy in Ohio with us. Once we got back to Chicago, he did lots of shakedowns and plenty of hits for several bosses. He was always a busy man.

Sam liked to party, too, but only after taking care of business. He was very dapper, very classy. He loved his customized Corvette, with its bulletproof Teflon top. The windows were bulletproof, too. The inside was all custom and had two little monitors that allowed you to see better than you could through the side and back mirrors without turning your head. He got the same kind of respect as Nick, but Nick was an international player and Sam was strictly Family. A real good guy. Everybody loved him, but around this time, even though Sam was only in his late sixties, his mind changed.

My father was already sick with cancer and had started to lose some of his influence. Sam, like Nick, didn't answer to a specific boss. Sam didn't like Joe Figorelli for the simple reason that Joe was pushing too strong for control in Chicago and was disrespecting my father. Because of that, there was a lot of undercurrent animosity between them. But it was a personal beef that got Joe and Sam going after each other. It was something stupid over a card game; but because they were both powerful people, problems escalated.

Sam was now dangerous because he had gotten to the point where he wouldn't think twice about taking Joe out. Personally, I think Sam was ill but didn't tell anybody. His mood swings were abrupt. He became violent very quickly, and then he wouldn't remember what he did. Get a man like that mad and he could blow your brains out in a heartbeat. When Sam got popped for a simple bookmaking charge, Joe made a nasty move. He went into Sam's house, knocked holes in the walls, and stole his cash. Joe knew this would infuriate Sam, who would suspect Joe did it.

Of course, Joe denied it. Sam's anger, threats, and unpredictable moods gave Joe reason to get permission to take Sam out. Of course, even while Sam was in jail, he realized Joe was going to try to get him, so he figured he would definitely have to whack Joe first. It was tough for me because I was in the middle of this.

The situation resolved itself when Joe himself was diagnosed with cancer and backed off from his political maneuvering and from Sam, too. Likewise, Sam just turned his back on Joe.

When Sam was sent down to Florida to do a job, I had a feeling he wasn't quite himself. He wasn't right. He asked me to go with him but I told him I couldn't. It was true because I had things to take care of at home in Chicago and New York. It was also true because I had to watch my own back. People knew how close we were and some wondered if I had taken his side in the Family politics. These things were always complicated.

Sam was down there about ten days. Nobody had heard from him, but sometimes that's how he worked. I've always admired men who are lone wolves, the ones who stand apart from the rest. My father stood alone even though he worked within the group. Both Nick and Sam often worked alone, too. They were feared because of their own reputations, and not just because of their group. I thought that singular respect was the ultimate power.

Sam was the kind of guy who would analyze everything and never jump into anything without planning, unless he had to. And he was cool and calm. The most dangerous men are always that way. Very self-contained. He took me to places and whacked somebody while I just hung around outside waiting for him to come back out. When he did return, it was like he had just stopped to make a phone call or use the john. Never was he the least bit flustered. So I wasn't worried about him going to Florida alone. If something was really wrong with him in any way and he couldn't handle the job alone, I believed he would've told me.

It was a humid Chicago summer afternoon, and I was visiting my mom. My parents lived next door to me and I was out on their backyard deck, overlooking the pool, when the mail came. I collected Mom's and mine and came back inside. As I came through her front door, I was in the foyer when I looked more closely at a little box among all the bills, letters, and junk mail. I realized it hadn't been mailed, just put into my mailbox. That was weird. It just had my name on it. I put the other mail down on a nearby table.

I ripped off the brown bag paper wrapping and lifted the lid off what looked like a jewelry box. What I saw made my blood run cold.

A human finger was inside the box.

"Oh God! Oh God!" I wailed in barely a whisper. My breath was knocked out of me. I fell against the mirrored wall and let it hold me up.

My mom ran from the kitchen, asking, "What's wrong?! What happened?!"

Words didn't come. I felt myself flush, the veins in my neck pumped blood so hard I thought they'd burst. I held out the box for her to see.

"How awful!" she recoiled, not fully comprehending. She looked confused. Blood, gore, and body parts had never got this reaction from me before.

"The ring, Mom," I choked and tried to pull myself together.

"Wha . . . ?"

I cut her short. "It's Sam's ring. It's Sam's finger. Sam is dead, Mom! The fuckin' Colombians killed him!"

Now the shock hit her, hit her hard, and I reached to hold her up, hardly able to stand up myself. I was blind with rage, shaking, and heartbroken. We both cried and consoled each other, the mirrored walls multiplying our grief around us.

As I caught my breath and calmed down a bit, my shock and grief turned to sheer anger. I made sure my mom was okay, and I left. Alone in the office behind my game room, I sat in silence, plotting what I had to do. It would take time, but I would avenge my friend's death.

There was no doubt that the Colombians killed him. A lot of people within the Family could have whacked Sam, but the problem with Joe had blown over when he got sick, and if anyone in the Family had whacked him, they would've said so. And anyway, the Colombians were bragging about it. The finger was a "fuck you" message to me. It became a situation I had to avenge. Anytime somebody outside the Family whacked one of us, they were whacked. Someone in the Family would avenge the death. It's the law. After Sam was killed, even the people who wanted him dead stood up and said, "They don't have the right to whack one of us. We don't ask outsiders to clean up. Now they have a problem with us."

A few months later, I would make things right. Nick came back from a business meeting in Lima and asked for my help with some gambling prospects in Florida. I went down and we took care of the business in half a day. From Miami, Nick went on to New York. I stayed in Florida when I found out that the Colombian guys I wanted were there. I called for a meeting about the money laundering and things came together. I had to get the person who actually killed Sam. To do that, I had to break the person who gave the orders. I knew I could do that with ease, and even some pleasure.

I had had a confrontation with Felix long before the parking lot incident over Kenny. We had been in my office and gotten into an argument over what he thought was a discrepancy in the amount of money laundered and due. I called him a damned liar. He was high on coke and pulled a gun on me. We went one on one. I could intimidate without a gun.

"Just don't miss," I taunted Felix as I walked right into the pistol. I felt invincible and I looked him in the eye the whole time. I saw his surprise. He was thrown off balance and he realized that he was dealing with the devil. It became a staring contest until he finally put the gun back into his waistband and walked away. After that, he knew he couldn't intimidate me ever again because I knew he didn't have the balls to back up his threats.

IN MIAMI, I ARRANGED TO MEET Felix at a Cuban restaurant. Our history didn't matter. He couldn't jeopardize his business with the Family by not meeting with me. At first he was wary, but after a few drinks and chummy conversation, he let his guard down. After dinner, I suggested we go find some women. He drove with me. I gave him some bullshit about an underground party in a warehouse district. He bought it.

When we pulled into an area of crowded buildings, I slammed on the brakes and knocked him out with one punch to the head. I had made arrangements at a wholesale meat packing plant. I cuffed Felix and dragged him inside. There, I laid him naked on a stainless steel meat cutting table that had a grate for blood and crap to fall through and be easily washed away. I laid Felix out and with handcuffs on his wrists and ankles secured him to the table, and put duct tape across his mouth. I slapped him awake and started working on him. Fear and adrenaline kept him alive. Felix knew that as soon as he told me the name of the trigger man who whacked Sam, I would kill him.

One by one, I called out the names of people who worked for Felix.

"Julio?"

Felix shook his head back and forth.

"Philippe?"

Again, he shook a negative reply. I slapped him several times.

"Are you telling me the truth?"

He nodded yes, with eyes wide.

"Luis?" I continued the litany.

No, he shook his head, tears streaming. Guttural noises rose from his throat in protest and fear.

"Julio?" I asked again, just to antagonize him.

The list of names was repeated over and over again for a half hour, even though I suspected who the assassin had been and withheld the name.

Finally, when I knew he wanted to be put out of his misery, I asked, "Eduardo?" Eduardo was one of his cousins.

For an instant, he froze, then gave a low moan and nodded, yes.

I finished Felix and found Eduardo the same night and brought him to the meat packing plant, too. He paid for what he did to Sam. For more than two hours, he begged to die. Eventually, he did, but not because I was merciful; his heart gave out.

After the trouble they had in Chicago, the Agulars were not supposed to be in the U.S., but they took their risks. Florida was the safest place for them to be, with the fastest exit. The Agulars were getting forty-five thousand dollars per kilo of cocaine. In their own country they were among the highest ranking guys second only to Enrique Barrella, who had won control over them. In the States, the Agulars sauntered around in their Miami Vice wardrobe with open buttons on their silk shirts, and drove fancy cars. Most of them weren't prepared for the violence of the business. They were on my ground. If they fucked my people over, I served justice.

Barrella wanted to make peace, erase the mistakes of the Agulars, and continue to do business with us. When he found out that Felix had killed one of our important men over a nobody like Kenny, Enrique expected repercussions. He used the situation to his advantage. He looked the other way when I took care of Felix and Eduardo.

And because Enrique wanted to send a strong message that he could clean his own house and rid himself of Agular's incompetence, he took care of Fernando himself. At his jungle compound, Enrique had Fernando tied, an arm and a leg each, behind two strong horses. He was slowly stretched in a standing spread-eagle as Enrique's men tortured him with knives. Finally, Enrique stepped close and offered Fernando a bullet to his head to put him out of his misery. Fernando begged for the blessing of the bullet. Enrique stepped back and pulled the trigger. The bullet went high into the air, the shot intentionally startled the horses as their handlers let go of their halters, and Fernando was torn limb from limb.

27

WELCOME TO PRISON LIFE

After many months, I finally had my sentencing. I was given four years in state penitentiary.

Even though several federal and state agencies had wanted a piece of me and fought to take me into their jurisdiction, the Feds finally gave me up to state authority. According to federal guidelines, I would have gotten only probation. But the state charges brought a tougher sentence and the Feds were happy to see me in any prison serving a longer time.

From the courtroom, my first stop in the system was Division Six of the Cook County lockdown for serious offenders. There were two dozen cells in a two-level tier inside the unit, with a common area twenty by thirty feet. In that section there were metal picnic benches welded to the floor and a TV; lunch was brought to us in our cells, where we were locked down.

I never slept. It was so noisy, with everybody screaming, yelling and talking from one cell to the next all night long. Besides that, there was only a steel bed, without a sheet or pillow. There was a toilet in the cell, but it was close quarters, and shared with another guy. You could shower all you wanted, but there were no towels and the shower, a small room with two spigots, was filthy. There were no windows and no outside yard. That's where I stayed for three weeks after my sentencing and before they transferred me.

Finally, someone somewhere decided exactly which penitentiary was going to take me and I became part of a group headed for Joliet State Penitentiary. My hands were cuffed, my feet were shackled, and I was chained to another guy. Nobody could walk in all that heavy metal. You took the tiniest steps, or kinda hopped. There was just no way anyone was gonna try to run away. It was impossible. Somewhere during the bus ride, the reality of what was happening started to dawn. And when I got to the penitentiary, it hit me in the face.

Joliet, one of the oldest prisons still in use, was built in 1860 and looks like an old limestone castle. Very mysterious and Gothic, with thick walls that go thirty feet into the ground and thirty feet high. They're topped with barbed wire and there are gun turrets all along the top.

My first day there was horrifying. We were led like cattle into a huge processing room. There I got my initial checkup. While I paraded around stark naked with fifty other guys, technicians drew my blood. I swear, I thought, Do they actually change the needles? Sure they did, I hoped, but the attitude and atmosphere made me wonder. The doctors seemed like either quacks or gumps—they looked like they enjoyed giving the rectal exam and groping everyone's personal equipment.

Then we had to be deloused. They've changed the procedure

since, but at the time, they stuck us one by one into a booth. I held my breath and a fine powder spray hit me from every direction. After that, I was herded to another line and was handed a towel, blanket, sheets, a cup, toothbrush and a piece of lye soap. Anything else I wanted I would have to buy from the commissary or through other inmates. Everybody is supposed to get new shirts, a new pair of pants, a pair of shoes, and underwear but none of the stuff they gave me was new. I would not touch old underwear with stains on them. I told them what they could do with those.

From the Annex, I went into Joliet's West House. My crazy cousin Bruno was back in prison, this prison, and he had people he knew inside, so I figured he had eased the way for me. I'd immediately have contacts for everything I needed. People knew I was coming. Things were supposed to be good for me. Sure, like anything was going right for me.

Somehow, some way, I got listed as maximum security. They took me straight over to the regular Joliet units in the other building. Hard core, hard time. There were more deaths inside that place than in the neighborhood around it. An average of one death per week, so it was no surprise to me that it had its own graveyard in the back.

My cell was six feet by eight feet, and was on the third tier. In the summertime it was hot, with no ventilation to speak of. One of the air-conditioning tricks inmates used was to find a good-size rock in the yard, bring it back to the cell and use it to break the window. At least there'd be a breeze. There was a downside to that. Nobody in charge ever fixed the window and it would be fuckin' freezing in the winter.

There was no shower in the cell. No shower in the entire building. I had to be escorted every three days with everybody else to an outside setup. Again, it was like herding cattle the way they took us out there, maybe fifty men at a time, and had us stand underneath a long pipe with spigots coming from it every two feet. We all stripped naked and, elbow to elbow, front to back, when the water came on, we tried to shower as completely and quickly as we could. It was one of the most demeaning procedures to go through.

On my first day in West House, I went to lunchtime chow with everybody else. We had to go outside and into another building to eat. So I went, sort of noticing that there were all these guys walking in a group, getting ahead of me. Other inmates were stopping and letting them go by. Somebody, a biker type, said to me, "Hey man, they're the Latin Kings, and they eat first."

He told me how it all broke down. The largest gangs went first. Then the next powerful gang, and down the line. So here, it was the Latin Kings, then the Black Disciples, the Vice Lords, and a few other gangs. Just about everybody belonged to a gang, and if not, at least found some support in their color group.

Eventually, I was moved into the appropriate white bunch and walked along to the dining hall. There, I took only a glass of juice from the counter because I had no appetite, and went to a table; but I recognized everything had its rules and structure, so I hesitated. I didn't know where to sit. Finally, some guy yelled, "You got to sit over here." So I did.

All of a sudden, as I sat down, two guys a few feet from me started fighting. The familiar biker then tackled me, threw me to the ground and before I could slug him, *bam! bam!* there were shotgun blasts. Of course, the biker had helped me out; I had no friggin' idea there'd be bullets served with lunch. As I was lying down faceup I saw the ceiling was filled with holes. Whenever a fight breaks out, the guards shoot two warning shots into the ceiling. That time it didn't break up the fight.

One of the fighting guys had a shank, a homemade knife, and stabbed the other inmate. As I turned, I heard *bam! bam!* two more shots, and bodies fell on top of me. The guards shot the guys who were fighting. Good shots. Simple solution. In a few seconds, everything quieted down. Everybody but the two dead guys got up and went back to eat. A few minutes went by and guards picked up the bodies and hauled them off. Nobody said a word about it.

So I sat there with my juice, wondering how often things like that were going to happen. While everybody was chowing down, I tried to make conversation. The guy across from me had long hair and looked like Jesus.

"So what are you in for?" I asked.

He only lifted his Charlie Manson kind of eyes from his plate. "Never ask anybody why they're here," he growled. "And never ask how much time anybody is doing. It's none of your goddamn business."

What could I say to that but, "I'm very sorry. I'm just fuckin' curious."

After he stared at me a second, he told me he was in there doing two life sentences without parole. "I raped a couple of nuns and then killed them. God told me to sacrifice them," he offered through dripping mouthfuls of beans.

That was my first dining experience in Joliet State Pen. There were other occasional mealtime disruptions, but nothing that bad again while I was there.

Everybody got forty-five minutes of yard time. That's when you could just hang out, go to the pile and work out with weights or use the telephone. I wanted to call my family. Like so many other things, the telephones were segregated. There was a phone for the whites, the blacks, the Latinos. The line for the white phone was a mile long. I looked at that line and figured it was useless to wait, free time would be over before I got to the phone. So I was just hanging around when an older Spanish guy, Doc, with a crown tattooed on his shoulder, came over and stood in front of me. He ran all the Latin Kings.

"Some people told me to look out for Mike the Match," he said.

"What people?" I asked, not sure what to expect next.

"Your people. Your Family," he explained, adding, "We know who you are. Bruno got word over here. So, what can I do for you?"

"I need to use the phone," was the first thing I said.

There were forty Latino guys waiting for their phone. Doc went up to the guy still talking on the phone, took the receiver out of his hand and hung it up as he waved me over.

"You got a phone," he muttered, walked away and I made my calls.

It was no surprise that in prison the social atmosphere was structured by color. Everybody bonded close with their own. If you walked into a prison and talked to a black guy you became a nigger lover, a nigger's bitch. Whites excluded you and you got treated badly by the blacks. Spanish stuck with their own. Indians had their own little culture and stuck together, too. They were maybe the most religious, with their rituals, sweat lodges, and shamans. In each group there were the shot callers, the head guy. The Disciples liked to call their shot caller, The Prince. Whatever. I became the shot caller for the whites. It was a position that was either given, or taken. I didn't have to take it. You become a shot caller when you can do things for people, solve problems and have people follow you. People wanted to follow me because not only could I get pizza brought in because I had the finance to manipulate the guards, but also because I didn't take shit from anybody and knew how to handle certain situations. There are followers and there are leaders. My reputation as a leader preceded me. Money and power. That's what it's about.

It's the shot caller's job to settle things. If there's a problem between a Latin and a white for example, instead of the Latinos and the whites all going to war, the shot callers of both groups put their heads together and worked out some kind of a solution. We figured out who started the problem and why, who had the beef, and how to settle it. If a guy needed to be disciplined, it was handled by his own group according to what the shot callers decided. Usually the guy had to take a beating.

In prison, the inmates, not the officials, make the rules that really count. Long before I got to Joliet, gang leaders and shot callers had developed the rules of conduct for how gangs related to other gangs or groups. Some of the laws: no rip-offs between gang members; each gang stays out of other gangs' affairs; in a dispute between members of two gangs, members of any other gang stand clear; no gang will muscle in on a dealer already paying off another gang protection; gang leaders will discipline their own members in the offended party's presence; and, the gangs cannot claim to protect non-members as friends.

Gay guys were in a class of their own, and usually somebody's bitch. Sometimes straight guys became gumps in prison. I don't believe a guy can get it in the ass or give it to a guy in the ass and still think of himself as straight because it was just recreational. He's a gump. With women, that's a different story. Two women together, that's like artwork. In the joint, you can call a guy a lot of things, an asshole, a prick, but if you call him a bitch, you got throw-down time. Time to fight. If someone walked by you and called you a bitch and you let him get away with it, you *were* a bitch. You were fucked; you lost everybody's respect. You were better off if you let your ass get kicked. At least people respected you because you went down with a fight. You let anybody call you a bitch and you walk away, you might as well put a big bull's-eye on your ass.

Child molesters or rapists are always going to have the hardest time in any jail. Child molesters were called "Short Eyes" because they have their eye out for short people, kids. They're considered worse than criminal. They're sick predators and are going to get hurt. Informants are also going to get cut. You can't trust someone if he's a rat. You get rid of him because there is too much shit going on for him to talk about. Other inmates, like drug dealers, murderers, bank robbers, thieves, and forgers are just mainstream guys.

There were some very sad cases. There was an old man, about sixty-five, who was in for manslaughter because a burglar broke into his home and he killed him. But because the intruder fell outside the house as he was dying, self-defense became manslaughter and they gave this man three years even though he had a lot of health problems, like asthma and a heart condition. Yet they treated him like he was a twenty-year-old gangbanger. He got no special treatment. It was hard time for a man who just defended himself. I read his court transcripts and really think he was innocent. The system failed him.

There was another guy who was very slow. He probably had an IQ of eighty. He got led down the wrong path selling drugs, and I really think he didn't know better. A guy like that shouldn't have been in jail. He needed some kind of help.

And there was Marty, who was a pretty decent country kid. Marty was very depressed and came to my cell every day to talk. I was like his counselor or something. I got him a job in the kitchen, in the bakery department. He was serving a seven-to-ten-year sentence for manslaughter. Marty had a terrible temper and when his girlfriend's baby didn't stop crying, he shook it. The baby's neck snapped, and she died. A moment of blind rage ended one life and changed Marty's life, and the baby's mother's life. They had to live with that heartbreak. In my opinion, it really was an accident. A horrible and stupid thing he did, but not intentional. Doing time wasn't killing Marty, what he did to that baby was killing him every day, and would forever, even after he got out of prison.

There was probably one escape every month, but the guy was usually caught. There weren't too many attempts because those country boys liked to shoot. In some states, among the inmates, there's an average of one death a week, sometimes more. Nobody cares. Nobody talks about the beatings, stabbings, and shootings in prison.

The prison system does not rehabilitate. Worse, even if a man has the potential for straightening out his life, it works against him. He's more apt to come out of prison harder, colder, and meaner than he went inside. It's a matter of survival. If a guy isn't tough, he'll be chewed up and spat out. He'll be turned into somebody's bitch. And everyone comes out a better criminal. There's no better place to learn something new than in prison. All the experts in every field are there and, once they accept you, they're willing to tell you all about what they did and how they did it. You can learn from their mistakes.

The logic of sending someone to prison is strange. The judge tells you, "I'm giving you ten years so you can think about what you did. Rehabilitate yourself and come out a better man." Sure. Tell me how I can be made a better man when, from the moment I arrive, I'm stripped of my clothes, my dignity, and my basic rights? It's only human nature to rebel against that, to get tougher, to get better at what I did before so I don't get caught again. Prison doesn't make you a better person, and it's really not even supposed to. It only punishes.

Like so many other things, prison is all about money. It's a profit-making industry. You want to eat good food? You will have to find a way of getting it because the three meals a day they give you is the worst fuckin' food you will ever eat in your entire life. There's mystery meat and pigeon they pass off as chicken. Some of the food that comes in says right on the box "not suitable for human consumption." It's always the lowest grade. More like dog food than human food.

Welcome to prison life.

28

FROM RIOT TO HOLE

Expecting bullets to start flying at any time is a tough way to live. I swear, it wasn't as bad on the outside. But sometimes it was even worse than that. There was no warning, no strained atmosphere, nothing before the riot broke out. It just happened one day when I was coming back to my cell from the yard. A fight broke out on an upper tier. Sirens started blasting, inmates went crazy.

The first thing the inmates did was set rolls of toilet paper on fire and throw them out, over the tiers. Next, burning mattresses came flying out. It was a concrete building, so nothing else was going to burn, but the smoke was terrible as it rose up through the place. It was indoors, a huge area with cells several stories high. The narrow catwalks that ran along the cells were open mesh-like metal; a narrow handrail ran along it on the outside above the twenty- and thirty-foot drop. Anybody who fell off that had a problem. Through the smoke, the noise and chaos, the momentum built.

The warden had been making his tour, doing a cell check when the riot broke out. Some inmates picked him up and tossed him off the tier. He was killed. Other guards were thrown off and broke bones; one guy had a broken back. A couple of inmates were killed, too.

If there was any animosity between guys or groups, that was the time to get it out. It was every man for himself, a free-for-all. Blacks and whites were going after each other. Guys didn't know who they were hitting, or even care. If you were smart and close to your cell, you could duck in and wait for the bedlam to settle down. Me, I tried that, but I was nosey, too, so I leaned half out of my cell to watch the action.

All of a sudden, this guy ran at me from down the catwalk, ready to tackle me. He barreled down on me and I could see he wanted to slam me. I saw he was carrying a shank. He wasn't somebody I had known. He was a stranger, only he had a somewhat familiar face. We had no beef, but he just wanted to whack somebody. I wasn't going to let him pen me in my cell, so I stepped out, onto the catwalk, and faced him. I tackled him at the knees and pushed him up and over my back. He landed on the catwalk behind me. He also landed on the shank he had made. Stabbed himself in the chest and died. Two guards on the catwalk saw him collapse.

Outside assistance wasn't called because the inmates didn't take control of the prison. That's the only time they would call for help.

After things were brought back under control three hours later, the place was on lockdown for months. Nothing got issued. No toilet paper. No replacement mattresses. And I was charged with murder.

If an inmate gets convicted of the murder of another inmate, he gets two or three years for it. It's not a big deal, as if the life of a prisoner were worth less than the life of a civilian. The body generally ends up in the cemetery in the back of the prison. Unless there's a big riot and a civilian is hurt or killed, the death of prisoners doesn't even make outside news. It could affect federal funding.

I was found guilty of inmate manslaughter, and while waiting for official disciplinary action, I was taken to the Tombs and thrown into the hole, which is hell. It's deep in the bowels of the prison. As they took me down the narrow stone stairs, I could smell the urine everywhere. The stench got worse when I was left in a tiny, empty cell without any light. There were shit stains on the damp limestone walls. The solid steel door closed. No window, no light. There was a narrow dip under the door where I would get a plate of food passed through. And, eventually, some toilet paper. I was kept in there for almost a month.

I was alone in the hole. No distractions, no one to talk to, no other inmates to watch, no phone calls, no contact with anybody. All kinds of thoughts started crashing inside my mind. I began to think about the life I had gotten myself into, the Honored Society I had willingly joined. My whole life I had thought this life was the greatest, but I started realizing it was not. All I could do was think and feel more deeply than ever before. So many emotions started flowing through me that it was overwhelming. The conflict inside me tore me apart day and night.

I thought a lot about my first heist and the guy who tried to steal everything from us. I remembered how he was brought to me when he was caught. His fate was in my hands. It was the first time I had the power of life and death over someone. What I had really felt at that moment, back then, was scared. And powerful. And I felt a brief fraction of a second of sadness for that guy. But there was the overwhelming sense of some kind of justice, too. He fucked me; I fucked him back. Bottom line: I had the power, and he didn't. He got what was coming to him. By that time, at only seventeen, I had already learned that my emotions had no place in business. They were there inside me someplace and every now and then I'd take a look at them, but I couldn't carry them around. I had to put them away, turn my emotions on and off only when I wanted them. That's not easy to do. It takes conditioning. It's complicated, and it's dangerous.

A man who is emotional cannot make clear decisions and cannot control a Family because if you can't control yourself, how can you control others and have them respect you? You can't. In this world, people must fear you to respect you. And a man who respects you doesn't always fear you. Think about that. If you walk into a room and a guy is nervous because of you, he's going to pay you respect. He doesn't know what you're going to do. He's off balance, and you've got the upper hand. If a guy only respects you, yeah, he's a good guy, good people, but you won't make him nervous. That means he's got the upper hand. He's not on guard with you, not off balance. You are on guard. The way to take control of people in a room is to make them fucking fear you. Let them think you are nuts, let them think you are always plotting. Keep the enemy suspicious and keep him close so you always know what he is doing. This isn't only my thinking process. It is the thinking process of most gangsters.

I thought about so many things. My whole family has always been powerful, and corrupt. I mean, we have owned many legitimate businesses and projects but all the serious money came from crime. It was dirty money coming—directly or indirectly—from prostitution, gaming, drugs, liquor, you-name-it. I've come from quite a family. It's a very powerful feeling. My grandfather Carmine was a major boss, Grandpa Vince, a dangerous hit man. My father was an important man in the organization. Those things gave me status, defined who I was. With my heritage I didn't have people telling me, "You shouldn't do this; you shouldn't do that."

There was constant approval, so it was easy to continue the Family tradition.

My father was different from my grandfather. All in all, I would have to say that I think my father was the much better man. He had a bigger heart. He was always more willing to give to those who didn't have. I'm proud of my father for that. And I wanted to believe I was more like him.

While I was in that dark, slimy hole, I thought. Maybe too much. My ghosts came back to torture me in my dreams. My waking hours were filled with the kind of introspection I had avoided at all cost before. Surrounded by scum and slime for twenty-four hours a day, what else was there to do but think about my life? I realized that the deeper I had gone into Family life, the more I became a colder person, capable of doing violent and horrendous things. As much as I knew it was wrong, I could not allow myself to think about what I was doing at the time I did it. I had learned to be calm in the darkest parts of my business. I was good at that, and that ability to keep my emotions in check helped to make me successful. At the same time, it destroyed me as an individual. It destroyed my love life and other close relationships. This life that seems so glamorous does devastating damage.

When you see a guy walking down the street and he's supposedly somebody, well maybe he is, but how did he get there? What kind of ghosts are inside his soul? We've all got a soul. If somebody says any different, they're fucking full of shit. One person might be willing to sell his soul, another won't. Me, I had made a deal with the devil.

And I knew I couldn't buy it back. Not yet. When I thought of Paulie, I put all emotions but anger behind me. It overshadowed everything. I would become so full of rage, I'd start to shake as I did when my dad first told me that it was Paulie who betrayed us. I knew I had to make that motherfucker pay for what he did to us. This was a guy who was so close to me that I would have died for him, gone to prison for him, anything. Still, he turned on me. He was the guy who was going to have to pay. That backstabber would suffer someday. No matter what else I was thinking and feeling about the life I had led, what I felt about Paulie burned inside of me.

Eventually, the disciplinary committee reviewed my file and declared what happened during the riot was justifiable self-defense and dismissed the charges. But I still got the Diesel Tour.

29

MASTERING PRISON SURVIVAL

The Diesel Tour was another way to fuck a prisoner. They threw me on it just to try to teach me another lesson. I was sent by bus to a different prison every few weeks. Because that made me a newcomer at each prison, I never got mail because it didn't have time to catch up with me; I was kept in solitary confinement because I was a temporary; I had no visitors because it takes four weeks to get a visitor list approved; and so I never had much contact with anybody. They did this to me for three months, moving me to Stateville just five miles away, Hill Correctional Center in Galesburg, Menard, Vienna, East Moline, Pontiac, and finally Vandalia. No doubt about it, I was doing hard time.

I finished my remaining solid time in Vandalia, a medium maximum prison with mostly lockdown facilities. I became the head cook, which was a good job.

Every morning, I got up at four and walked to the main gate of my tier. From there, guards would escort all the workers to the kitchen in another building. Once there, I was free to do my work. I had an ID card that allowed me to check out a knife for the day, but if I needed to get into a cooler I would have to ask the guard to open it. Commodities, like bricks of cheese, were like gold and kept under lock and key. After a while on my shift, when the guards got to know me, they left the coolers unlocked so I didn't have to ask twenty times to get into them. Not all the cooks and kitchen help got that kind of waiver but in exchange, I'd cook something a little better for those guards. If we had plain old meatloaf, I'd make them extra-thick bacon cheeseburgers.

If another guard came in and caught me making a half-dozen specials, and asked, "What are you doing? These aren't on the menu for today."

I answered, "I'm cooking them for you."

That's when he'd say, "Oh, could you put extra bacon on mine?" and not hassle me again.

I'd be in the kitchen until almost noon cooking breakfast and lunch. Then the rest of the day was mine. I'd walk the tier, read, write letters. We had yard time daily from five to six. After dinner until ten, we did things like shower, play cards, and have little parties. I always had something good cooking.

There was a slaughterhouse about four miles away, and guys that had really light sentences got to go out there to the farm and kill steers. So some of us had fresh meat, nice steaks, coming in every day. They were for the warden and civilians, but I made sure I always got myself a few. One time I stuffed some wrapped chopped meat down inside my underwear and I got patted down before I got back to my cell. The guard grabbed my crotch. He was taken aback. I just said, "Hey! I'm a very manly man," and he just growled, "Hit the road!" and passed me through, back to the prison building.

Some prisons let you have a hot plate, or at least a hot pot, but others don't. You could sometimes make a stinger, which was what you use to warm up a cup of something when you didn't have a hot pot. It was usually a spoon you hook up with some wire to conduct electricity from an outlet. You put it into a cup of water and it would heat up. Getting caught with that got you a week in the hole. Knowing how to make one of those was very useful. When I was two weeks here and a week there, my stuff stayed packed up, so I had to improvise.

When they finally kept me in one place, I always smuggled stuff back into my cell. I got a lot of write-ups because at night I would cook inside my cell with a tiny hot pot. I'd bring back little pieces of meat all diced up and cook it with garlic and oil. I'd make spaghetti sauce. Over time, I had every seasoning imaginable in individual little baggies and little cans of tomato paste. I like to cook and sometimes, with three or four hot pots going, I made enough to share. I'd have a little party in my cell because even though it was lockdown, with the main door of the tier locked, we could walk from cell to cell until ten o'clock at night. Everybody who could, brought something. If a guy worked in the bakery, he'd get his hands on some flour, sugar, or bread. The guy who handled the cheese for the day would bring back some cheese. The vegetable guy, he would bring vegetables. We had our own little co-op.

Once in a great while, a guard would come by and take a little taste. In the federal system, guards are very distant but in the state pens you get close to them. By inmate standards, a great guard comes in every day, punches the clock, and just does his twelve-dollar-an-hour job. He doesn't fuck with nobody and he has no big statement to make, has no personal cause. He looks the other way more often than not.

A guard, nicknamed Maddog, brought me liquor, gym shoes,

food, anything I wanted. For a price. Occasionally, there was a guard who didn't want much more than a simple favor here and there. There was an ex-Marine, Robinson, who was the guard in charge of the kitchen. We bonded a little bit because he didn't really know much about the food business and I helped him. By helping him, he was willing to do things for me. While everyone else was having grits, I was eating the sausage he brought for me with some eggs. If I wanted to take something back to my cell with me, he'd shrug, "I ain't gonna look."

When he decided to take a vacation in Las Vegas, I told him I owned a piece of a restaurant and he should check it out. I gave him the telephone number of my partner in that place, Cousin Gino—Marcello's brother—and told my mom to give Gino a call, too, so they could set up accommodations as well. Robinson and his girlfriend ran up a two-hundred-dollar tab for dinner. No problem, it was on the house. I also got him a nice hotel room, so I saved him like a good five hundred dollars that week. When he came back to work, there was nothing I couldn't have.

He would sneak in pizza for me or, sometimes when he was on graveyard shift, take me out to town to get some good food. One or two of the other guards knew, but they kept their mouths shut. Robinson was pretty well liked by his buddies.

Of course, there are the other kind of guards, maybe forty percent, who are the inmate haters. They constantly shook down your cell or wrote you up for not having your shirt tucked in. They liked to take away your privileges, bust your balls.

For example, if you ran out of toilet paper on Wednesday, they told you, "You'll get some on Friday. Just squeeze your cheeks and hold it."

Or if you were sick with a fever, they said, "That's too fuckin' bad because the nurse doesn't come in until next week. You can talk to her then. What the fuck do you want me to do about it? You shouldn't have committed the crime."

Most of the abuse was simply making sure you got as little to make you comfortable as possible. It was very rare for guards to beat up on an inmate like you see in movies. But it's not like it never happened at all. When it did happen, it was usually because the guards were involved in some kind of drug distribution. If someone didn't pay, they'd do their own justice. They weren't being guards at that moment, they were drug dealers with a badge.

Most guards were between the two extremes. Just human beings with good and bad days. A guard nicknamed Thump, a little butterball guy, got on my nerves one day. He was usually pretty good, but he must have had a bad time at home and so was taking his frustrations out on us, just busting our balls. There was a delivery of meats and other groceries, and while I was trying to get lunch ready for hundreds of inmates, he started ordering me around, wanting me to help haul the meats into the freezer. Then he wanted a special lunch, some spicy meatball soup, so I gave him some with plenty of red hot chili pepper, cayenne, Tabasco sauce, and even some Chinese mustard in it. He was hungry and slurped up three or four spoonfuls before he came up for air. By that time there was fire coming out of his ears.

"Sonovabitch!" he sputtered with about twenty inmates watching. "You're trying to kill me!"

"You said you like it hot, I made it hot for you. Sorry if you don't like it," I said in a calm voice. Everyone else got a laugh out of it.

Thump used it as an excuse not to work for the rest of the day. He tried to get back at me the next day, but I was the head cook and Carbo, who was the guard in charge of the kitchen, wouldn't let him touch me because he couldn't afford to lose me. I did my job well, and I also made special dishes with great pasta sauce.

Carbo told him, "D'Angelo is here to cook, and I don't care what happened. Unless he shot or stabbed you, you'll live."

None of the guards sat in on our card games, though. They had their own. My game was poker; I owned and organized that game.

We took old cards and cut them up to use like betting chips. Instead of cash, a guy would buy in with twenty-dollars worth of commissary goods, bars of soap, candy bars, whatever it was, and I gave him the value in chips to play. Some of the guys were more serious, one-hundred-dollar bettors. They would pay, or get paid, from the outside. Sometimes I'd have money, maybe seven, eight hundred, put into my prison bank account through their friends and families and mine. The account was the same no matter which prison I was sent to.

But it took time for mail to catch up with me. When letters I hadn't received while doing the Diesel Tour finally got to me, there were a couple from Angela. God, it was awful and wonderful. Sometimes, I read her letters and thought about what could have been. I let such a good person go. It had been another sacrifice that I had had to make in my life. I thought I was trading something good for something better. It wasn't better. I made a bad choice and had to live with it. I read Angela's letters; there were three. And she had sent a photo. She looked so good, so happy, so beautiful. I kept her letters a long time and reread her words, "I'll always love you . . . always want to be with you," and they ripped my heart. After a while, I threw them away. They made me sad. I kept her picture though, put it on the wall, but not where I would see it night and day, but where I'd see it when I wanted to look at an honest smile.

Visitors came once a week with different groups, Saturday or Sunday. My mom had to drive four hundred miles and get searched just to visit me for one hour a week. She was the only person who visited me. My dad couldn't come because felons are not allowed. No friends, cousins, or lovers ever came. That surprised me at first, and then I just got bitter. It made me realize you walked in those doors by yourself.

The one person who did more hard time than my father and I put together is my mom. She did the longest time anyone could imagine. She suffered the most from all the horrible things we did, but she still smiles and always has positive thoughts and words for me. She even came to the state pen when she had to be strip searched, harassed and demeaned so she could see me.

It didn't matter if it was raining or snowing or steaming hot, she visited me. She is a tiny woman and traveling alone was not an easy thing for anyone, so she bought a German shepherd, Champ, who came with her in the car. He stayed in the motel room with her, too. I'd see him in the car from the window; I'd wave and he'd bark.

Every once in a great while, someone would shoot me some cash, put a little money on the books for me, but that was rare. The only way an inmate got money was when his family sent it. Otherwise, you had nothing except what you got paid if you had a job inside. Like, I got paid about twelve bucks a month for being a cook. That wasn't much when you had to buy soap at two bucks a bar. At least it was better than the state-issued bar of lye. Shampoo was about five bucks for eight ounces. You had to pay for shaving stuff, and underwear, socks and shoes if you didn't like what they gave you. My prison bank book always had thousands in it. Believe me, there was nothing sorrier than an inmate without money. Often, they were the ones who were state-raised, in and out of the joint since they were ten years old. Most couldn't read, had no vocabulary, and didn't know the difference between a salad fork and a knife. Some of the gangs tried to help their own. They had a "poor box" system. One guy was assigned to collect cigarettes or some other stuff from his members and kept them for those who didn't have anything. When a member made a good score, he was expected to share. Inmates, one step above the state-raised guys, often tried some jailhouse romance. Through friends on the outside, they put ads in the personal, lonely-hearts columns of newspapers. It was funny how many women wrote to prisoners and thought they were really girlfriends. Inmates who did that were maybe a little lonely, but mostly, it was just a con to get money, postage stamps, telephone calling cards, and anything else they could get.

If you wanted to help somebody out with some cash, or pay off a guard for a favor, it was done on the outside. Someone would put money on another inmate's books, or a friend on the outside would meet a guard at a local bar and give him cash. For example, if I wanted a pair of good gym shoes, the guard would bring them to me after first collecting the price of the shoes plus a hundred bucks from my friend outside. Just about every one of the guards had their price. They would also bring heroin and syringes, cocaine, uppers, downers, and booze. Guards would sell stuff for ten times its street value. You could get a gun if you had enough money. Visitors also sneaked stuff in with balloons filled with heroin, cocaine, and pot. Most of the time a visitor was not strip searched, so they stashed the balloon in their privates and would transfer it to an inmate who would stash it in his privates.

Inmates sell stuff, too. Pot is called a cap; a small, toothpick-size joint would cost ten dollars. Some guys got heavy into drugs while locked up, and when they couldn't pay their source, they'd get whacked. The guards ignored most inmates on drugs unless they were causing problems. Out of maybe eighty men in a cell block, I'd say maybe fifty used some kind of drug as regularly as they could afford. There was no rehabilitation, just incarceration.

Booze was harder to get because it's bulkier than drugs and doesn't go as far. So those who wanted it usually made it themselves. It just took some sugar, bread for the yeast (because regular yeast is hard to score), and juice or fruit chopped up in small pieces put into a garbage bag. Leave it to ferment in the toilet bowl in your cell for about a week and you made some pruno, homemade liquor.

There's one thing about a long-term inmate's cell. He'd keep his toilet bowl sparkling clean. It wasn't only where he shit, it was where he stored things, like if the water is cold, he'd put a small carton of milk in there, or even wash his clothes in the bowl. If a guy gave money to a launderer, he still might lose his clothes. A good pair of pants, a shirt, or socks would always disappear. So it was always better to buy laundry detergent at the commissary and do it yourself. If a guy could afford it, he bought a bucket and washed stuff in that.

While I was making pruno, smuggling food out of the kitchen so I could eat halfway decent and showering with the gumps, Paulie was living a rather normal life in regular society while in the witness protection program. And even when Paulie had been in prison, it was a soft federal joint where he could play ping-pong, bocce ball, tennis, and golf. Even that was too hard for him, the fuckin' rat. I did all my time like a man. It never crossed my mind to sell out someone else to get myself off the hook.

Paulie had everybody's support all the time, no matter what, but he still turned around and ruined everybody's life. Paulie played everybody for a fool to get himself clear. He got his freedom by betraying everybody the day he got a furlough pass and came to my sick dad's house, all wired up. Paulie destroyed his own relatives because he couldn't take three years of country-club living. Geez, he probably would've been out in less than twenty-two months. He could've come out and been a boss after doing some time. Every day I spent in prison, I hated him a little bit more.

30

THE ULTIMATE BETRAYAL

Through some friends of mine, and a lot of effort on my dad's part, the governor shortened my sentence. My dad had dealings with a guy who owned a major car dealership in Chicago, and a senator was getting a new car from him. This senator was vulnerable because of some gambling debts, and he was also close to the governor. With some passing of cash-filled envelopes, the senator spoke to the governor, and other envelopes were passed along to influential people around the governor. Pretty soon, the governor was inclined to do my family a favor and took care of my prison time.

After serving two years of my four-year sentence I was put on a sort of semi-parole. I was sent to a work release center where I was supposed to work all day, for eight hours, and come back at night. Guess what? I worked twenty-three hours a day and showed up for an hour a day after sleeping at home. My dad bought a new truck from the car dealer with the political contacts, and came with a handful of paperwork showing that we had set up a couple of businesses that I ran legitimately. That was my work release, working for a restaurant, and setting up a wholesale furniture sales joint. I had an office, and ran all my old vending companies from it while I did my time. Football season was coming up, so I started bookmaking again. We were thinking about taking over more adult bookstores. I went right back into my action again. My parole officer came to dinner every Sunday and picked up two hundred dollars. I was officially paroled about three months later. From start to finish during this prison term, I served three years, some hard time, some less hard, never easy. I was so happy to be back out.

But I had a lot of thoughts and mixed feelings about changing my life. There were times I wanted to leave the business. Even though there were generations of mobsters in my bloodlines, while I was in prison, I thought I wanted to be the one who was different. But it's not so easy. I would miss the high, the addiction to money, and the incredible power. When I got out, it was all there, waiting for me. My blood family, my friends, the people I did business with on a daily basis were not going away. They were all I had, and they were deep into the criminal environment. My dad's health was failing rapidly and I was the gangster's only son with responsibilities to him and others.

I WAS BACK WITH MY FAMILY and had to deal with all the changes that had taken place while I was in prison. I still blamed Paulie for most of it; he helped put a lot of us behind bars. Yet, because I was free again, some of my anger had quieted down. There was a small part of me, deep down that hoped I wouldn't have to do the job I promised my dad I would do. I already had enough on my mind because a lot had changed while I had been gone.

During the two years I was in the pen, my dad had deteriorated quite a bit. He was terribly bloated because of the medicine he was taking; the cancer had spread throughout his entire body. He was often in pain, and his mind was not as it used to be. It was heart-breaking to try to have a conversation with him, a man who I used to admire was now so pitiful, so weak. It hurt to see him that way. It angered me that the younger guys coming up didn't see him for what he had been. He had lost his business status and was losing his personal dignity. It hurt.

So many things were out of balance. My father's bodyguard, Big Mike, had been stealing from him for years. I found that out when I looked into some things. That betrayal caused my family a lot of pain. Handling the problem was one of the last things my dad ordered to be done.

Also, because of his failing health, my dad's businesses got passed on to other people. They were Family businesses, and when he started to decline, it became harder for him to conduct things properly. Other bosses passed on the running of the operations to other guys. Since I was in jail, that was their decision. It was understood that I would take the places back when I got out, but that was not always how it worked. New guys thought that because they had the key to a building, they controlled it. Lots of the older guys had gone to prison and I didn't have much respect for most of the new regime.

I came back hard because the new guys had to be put in their places. I took back my territory and reminded them that they worked for me, they paid me taxes.

"Eh, fuck you!" I got from some of them.

"Fuck me? We are going to go to fuckin' war!" I told them, and meant it.

The next day, I had the cops and fire marshals at the clubs and closed everything. I fired some people in other businesses. I had to let everybody know I was boss. I did that very quickly by having a license pulled, and closing a couple of strip clubs and bars. Everybody knew I still had the fuckin' juice and the game was not going to be played without me. Soon I got calls. Everybody wanted to play ball. End of problems.

About six months after I was off parole, Paulie's father, my Uncle Mario, died. He had had cancer for a number of years, but it was the heartbreak of what his son had done that crushed the man's will to live. About three hundred people came to the funeral home for the viewing that lasted three days. Paulie had destroyed his father and his family; it caused a lot of turmoil and hard feelings for everybody. But Mario himself had been loved and well respected. What Paulie did broke his heart, but Mario held his head high even through his illness, and Paulie's mom, Teresa, was well liked. Everybody felt bad for them.

At the funeral parlor, people came and went all day and into the evening. At a quiet moment, I offered my aunt Teresa my condolences. As I embraced her and offered kind words, I knew she would be losing her son sometime soon, too. Again. Paulie had turned his back on everyone and left them all behind when he ratted and entered the witness protection program. He was already dead to them. This poor woman had been through so much. I felt for her, but she was a strong woman, an old-fashioned woman who had learned how to cope with loss. What Paulie had done to her family was devastating.

The night before the funeral, a parish priest led the rosary for the family and friends. The room was full, almost suffocating with the number of people sitting in rows of folding chairs, and floral arrangements of all sizes along all four walls. The scent of death and flowers was unmistakable. I stood at the back.

Seeing Uncle Mario's waxy face in the coffin and being around people I hadn't seen since I was a kid brought back too many memories, too much bullshit melancholy. Mario and Paulie looked a lot a like. I wondered what Paulie looked like now. Had his hair turned gray?

Thoughts about Paulie flooded over me. I was so furious with him but, maybe because a wake isn't the place for anger, I found myself thinking of the Paulie I loved before everything changed, before our lives went different ways. He was there for me when the first dead body I ever saw scared the shit out of me. He got me out of trouble in grade school. It was Paulie who listened when I talked about how I felt inside. The other guys didn't want to know I had a broken heart over Angela, and they never talked about the horror of what they did. They never admitted they had ghosts; maybe they didn't. Maybe they had no conscience at all, no soul left, not a scrap. Paulie had ghosts that haunted him worse than mine did. They made him weak and got in the way. Was that his soul fighting back? In spite of everything would he be the one to get into heaven, if there is such a place? Damn. I shook away those thoughts. He ratted. That hurt in so many ways. I realized his betrayal had hurt so deeply because I had loved him so much.

But I wasn't even there to pray. There was business. I had gotten a phone message from Nick that afternoon. He said to meet him after the service, but I didn't see him in the room. Standing in the back, I got some fresh air from the door and periodically stepped outside. About halfway through the service, Nick walked in and stood beside me. He leaned over to me.

"When this is done, come with me to my car," was all he said.

We stayed until the priest finished the prayers and said a few kind words about Mario. As most of the roomful of mourners got up to leave, Nick and I turned to go. At the door, a parlor host was handing a holy card to everyone who exited. I took what he gave me and put it in my pocket.

Nick and I made small talk as we walked to the street at the far end of the overflowing parking lot and got into his Lincoln. As he settled behind the wheel, I waited.

"We got word from inside WITSEC," he said. "Paulie's coming to the cemetery tomorrow. Capelli knows. He wanted to be sure you know."

Immediately, my blood started pumping hard at the sound of his name. Tomorrow. I knew what this would mean.

"But how's it they're gonna let him come to the funeral?" I asked, shocked and disbelieving.

"They're not *letting* him, he's on his own," Nick explained. "They told him about his father's death, and he started making noises about how bad he felt about not seeing him before he died. He wanted to come to the funeral."

"He's crazy!" I blurted, almost feeling protective. But revenge soon rose like bile inside me.

"He's not allowed to do that," Nick acknowledged with a nod. "But they suspected Paulie would try to sneak out on them, and they let him. He disappeared from his location twelve hours ago after telling someone he figured for a friend that he was coming here. He's not stupid enough to come to the funeral, but he told this guy he wants to be there before they bury the coffin."

"Why didn't his program agent yank his chain? Come after him?" I asked, still stunned by this turn of events.

"Think about it," he said while watching the stream of cars leave the lot. "Inside WITSEC not everybody knows he's AWOL, and the one or two who do, don't care."

"They're letting us have him!" I realized.

"You got it," Nick said with an ironic grin. "They don't need him anymore. They sucked every piece of information they could outta him. Now he's useless and taking up time on their roster. They don't care about his rat ass."

Blood was pumping inside me like crazy. I had to get out and move, work off some steam and get focused.

"I gotta go," I told Nick and started to leave.

"If you need me for anything, call," Nick said as I slammed the passenger door behind me.

I don't remember getting into my own car and getting home. My mind was filled with vengeful thoughts. I had to make a plan. I had to sort out some of the things I was feeling. Some of these emotions and memories of the Paulie I knew as a kid had no place in my heart now, would only cloud my thinking. I willed them out of existence and focused only on revenge and the commitment ahead of me.

As I undressed, I reached into the pocket of my suit jacket and pulled out the memorial holy card and looked at it for the first time. It had a picture of the thorn-wrapped bleeding sacred heart of Christ on it. Not St. Christopher like the one used in my initiation ceremony. Still, it was reminder enough.

The next morning, my parents were driven in one of the limousines, but I drove alone. I joined about twenty cars and limos for the procession to the cemetery for the internment. Like most burials, it was a solemn occasion. Among the mourners, about four of us knew there was important business yet to be done that day. Capelli wasn't there, but he had sent his right-hand man, Georgio, as a sign of respect for Mario. The ceremony went as expected. Solemn faces everywhere, lots of tears from the women, muffled words here and there. Behind my sunglasses, my eyes scanned the cemetery. It wasn't likely Paulie would come this close, this soon, but I kept a lookout.

As mourners filed one by one past the casket suspended over the grave and threw flowers, I made my pass and kissed Aunt Teresa's cheek. She held my arm and gave it a squeeze. "Thank you," was all she said. For coming she meant, I'm sure. Teresa couldn't have known, but if she had, I know she would have understood the inevitable.

I got into my car and drove around to another section of the cemetery and waited. From a distance I could see Mario's family and friends getting into vehicles and leaving by the exit closest to the plot. Before the last people disappeared, I got out and walked back to the area and took a waiting position behind a group of mausoleums that faced Mario's grave. It was an overcast late fall day, but I was warm in my suit and overcoat.

In the shadows, as I leaned against the crypt, my mind was totally focused on the job at hand. This had to be done. No more feelings to distract me. I needed to be numb. I was. Not everybody knew that the Feds had a leak who told us about Paulie. It would appear that the job got done in spite of the federal program that was supposed to protect him. Pulling one over on a government agency felt good. I held that thought and let it feed me.

While my emotions were in check, I still couldn't help thinking about Paulie. I never understood what he'd been thinking when he ratted on everyone. He must've been deluded not to realize there would be consequences. What did he think? That he could talk, and we would all forget? I don't know. I'm sure that after living the high life, anything he had or could do in witness protection was only a little bit better than being in the joint. Maybe he couldn't go through life that way anymore. He was a thug, a street guy. He must have known what was going to happen to him. Going to the cemetery was suicide. He knew what could happen. He probably even realized who they would send to do the job.

You keep your friends close, and your enemies closer. You don't expect your closest friends or family to take you out. But that's how these things are usually set up. You can be sitting with your friends, relaxed, and get whacked. That's it. It's very rare that it comes from a stranger.

Mario's casket had been lowered, but the grave hadn't been filled in. Almost two hours later, I saw a small dark car enter from the direction of the main gate. It moved slowly and made a pass. It returned in a few minutes from the opposite direction and stopped close to Mario's gravesite. The lone driver didn't get out right away. I took a monocular from my pocket and raised it to my eye. I could see it was a man with both his hands on the steering wheel, motionless.

Was it Paulie? Why was he waiting? Before I could start to form answers to my own questions, he opened the door, got out and stood straight. It was Paulie. Leaner, somehow smaller than I remembered, he looked around and walked to the grave. He picked up something small from one of the chairs at the site and while looking at it turned toward the grave. I pocketed the spyglass and from the other pocket retrieved another cylinder, took the gun from my shoulder holster and attached the silencer. I scanned the area again before I stepped from behind the mausoleums with my gun held under my coat.

Paulie stood about fifty feet in front of me at the grave, looking down at the casket, his back to me. He seemed to be praying for his father, or maybe quietly asking his forgiveness. I walked with stone-cold determination between the headstones. There was nothing in front of me but a target. With each step, my adrenaline surged. When I was a few feet behind Paulie, time went to slow motion. Paulie turned as he felt my presence. He looked at me.

There was no surprise; no words. The briefest glimmer of a smile quickly turned to a sad, penitent expression and clouded his face. Paulie dropped his chin and lowered his eyes in acceptance. If my heart lurched, I don't remember. It might have in the slow second I raised my gun, fired, and stepped over the blood-speckled holy card that fell from his hands and hit the ground before he did.

I took easy, measured strides to my car and drove away.

Paulie was found, at his father's grave, with a bullet in his head.

The Honored Society. Loyalty. Devotion. Betrayal. It's a way of life, and death.

EPILOGUE

After I left the cemetery, I went home and made one phone call.

My dad answered on the first ring, "Hello."

"It's done," was all I reported, and I heard him exhale. Maybe he couldn't find the words. Nothing more needed to be said. We hung up.

I turned off my phones, took a hot shower and made myself a tall Absolut before I sat down in my armchair. Listening to Bach, I wanted to drift off somewhere I didn't have to think. Music soothed me. This time it also threw me into an unexpected melancholy.

Paulie.

I didn't want to think about him. He no longer existed. He

didn't exist from the moment he turned rat. With remote in hand, I turned up the stereo volume.

Paulie.

I slugged down my drink and as I made another, I felt the warm haze of alcohol blanket me and muffle my mind. I kicked back the recliner and waited to drift away.

Paulie.

I felt a weight resting on my chest, over my heart. I heard an uncontrollable moan rise through me. The sound surprised me. I took another slug. The music played. The booze made my limbs heavy. I closed my eyes and started to drift.

Paulie!

Then I recognized it. It wasn't the voice that goaded me to break up with Angela. Not the one that urged me through so many jobs over the years. Not the one that made me angry enough to survive near death and prison.

Paulie! Paulie! Paulie!

It was the voice of the six-year-old kid who saw a bloody, mutilated body for the first time in his life. It was the kid who needed someone to take him by the hand and lead him away. He didn't cry out then. He never cried out after. Paulie had always been there, without being called. Until he ratted.

Paulie.

"Shut up!" I screamed and in near stupor, downed the rest of my drink. I wanted to get up and run. Run anywhere. But my body was too heavy to move and my head spun. But the voice seemed to obey.

Paulie.

It was barely a whisper.

Suddenly, my sobs were not. They were loud, angry, choking. A tidal wave of despair rolled over me, slammed me and was pulling me drowning back out to an endless ocean of darkness.

Through the sobs, I heard myself make a noise close to a laugh.

I didn't care if I died. I welcomed the black hole where I was certain my soul would disappear forever.

"Damn you, Paulie!" I muttered through another lunatic laugh. "You always did touch my soul." I didn't realize how deeply until that moment.

Womanizer. Screw-up. Rat. He was the one man who was my emotional lifeline. I hadn't recognized that before. I loved and hated him so intensely, killing him had been like blowing a nine-millimeter hole into my own gut.

Through my pain I saw all my old ghosts. Their horrified faces staring at me, mouthing soundless pleas for the mercy they never got from me. In the darkness of my dream—it was a dream, wasn't it?—I was back in the hole at Joliet, alone, at rock bottom. What was I doing there?

What was I doing here, with my life? I never had a choice. I was the gangster's son. I was born into this life. I was bound by blood in heritage and initiation. I had made the best of it. Wanted the best. Did the best. But at rare moments like these, I didn't remember the best of times. The good times, no matter how good, didn't have the same impact.

My dad was dying. Things were changing, and people were looking to me to keep things on track. Take care of the Family business. Could I do that and never make another hit, take another life? In a strange way, for a fleeting moment, I thought I understood a shred of what Paulie felt every time he tried to dodge the paper.

Don't go there!

It was that other voice, the one without a soul.

Paulie!

No. I couldn't fight this battle. Not now. The music stopped. The empty glass fell from my hand. I, thankfully, passed out.

The gangster's son still had a lot to learn.

ACKNOWLEDGMENTS

Joel Gotler, thank you very much for giving me the opportunity for a new life and career. You taught me so much, and every time I talk to you I learn something new. You are the world's best agent for a writer, and more importantly, you are a great man with deep passions and beliefs. You are a special friend. Joel, you are truly my long-lost brother Number One.

Noah Lukeman, thank you for all of your support and input. You are the one who cared about me primarily as a person. I am blessed that God brought you into my life. I look forward to our new journeys together. You are a great friend, and Noah, you are my long-lost brother Number Two.

Russell Lyster, my friend. Thank you for believing in me and helping me change my life. May our friendship never end. May God always bless you.

George Lucas, my editor and now my friend. I want to thank you especially for believing in me and the project, and for giving me the opportunity to share my stories. I look forward to many more projects, and our journey, wherever it may take us. You are a true gentleman.

Lorraine Zenka, How ya' doin'?! Thank you for believing in me and this project. I'm certain that a Higher Power brought you into my life, and I am so grateful for this. You are so talented. Thank you for sharing the secrets of your writing world. It's a wonderful place and I look forward to many more projects together. Not only are you a great friend, but I consider you a member of my family. You have been there for me in every way from the very start and have never let me down. I thank you from the bottom of my heart. May God always bless you; you are always in my prayers.

And to editorial assistant Shari Warren, a big thanks for all your hard work. Working with you is a pleasure, and a barrel of laughs. I also appreciate the efforts of Jeny Baina and Melanie Evangelista for your editorial and research assistance.

I thank John and Tina Spitale for being great friends.

Justin Manask and Karen Hwang, I thank you both for your support. You've been absolute pleasures to work with and I look forward to seeing you through future projects.

Thank you to all the wonderful people at Pocket Books: Judith Curr, Tracy Behar, Lisa Keim, Karen Mender, Kara Welsh, Liate Stehlik, Craig Herman, Lynn Grady, Barry Porter, Rick Richter, Seale Ballenger, Laura Mullen, and Chris Lynch. Also, Wendy Walker, Bernadette Bosky, Arthur D. Hlavaty, Paolo Pepe, and Tony Greco.

Special thanks, too, to Michel Legrou and Frederique Abramovici for making me look so good.

And to Meshell. I thank you, especially, for all of your love and support. You are my love. I look forward to a long future with you. Love, Michael.

And finally, I've read that with enough time and patience, anything can be accomplished. Even a mountain can be moved if enough time, attention, and care are given. I'd like to thank you, the reader, for helping me move my mountain.

—MICHAEL GAMBINO